Bardo

EMILY GALLO

The author may be reached at ecegallo@gmail.com

www.emilygallo.com
http://emilygallo.blogspot.com/

Also by Emily Gallo:

Venice Beach
The Columbarium
Kate & Ruby
Roads Not Taken
Murder at the Columbarium
The Last Resort
DREAMer

"Ms. Gallo has expertly intertwined social issues and current topics of the day through the story like a skilled weaver, creating a masterpiece that is filled with emotion, suspense, empathy, and love for others."

-InD'tale Magazine

"Gallo's writing style is intoxicating, she draws the reader in to a calm, peaceful life where we are introduced to incredibly complex and likable characters who make us feel at home in their world."

-Amazon Review

"Emily Gallo transports the reader into her book. Filled with well defined characters and an intriguing storyline, the book is hard to put down."

-Amazon Review

"You'll love the personalities and stay for the mystery as Gallo uses her great characters to tell an interesting story that weaves the past and the present together beautifully."

-Amazon Review

"Emily Gallo is a master at laying well-placed breadcrumbs to keep the plot twisting, the suspect list growing and the "who done it" moment a surprise until the very end."

-Goodreads Review

"The contrast between tone and content is a characteristic talent of only a few authors. Gallo pays as much attention to her sentences as she does her plots, shifting or consolidating meaning with the use of a single word. Her writing is impeccably honed, full of juxtapositions and qualifications that help to create an authentic and emotional atmosphere throughout."

-Goodreads Review

Bardo is the space between past and future, having and losing, knowing and not knowing.

"The best way out is always through."
-Robert Frost

Chapter 1

STORM AFTER STORM BORE DOWN ON THE EMERALD TRIANGLE, WASHING AWAY RECENT MEMORIES OF SMOKY, SMOLDERING SUMMERS. The California counties of Humboldt, Trinity and Mendocino are rugged but loosely piled---held together by forests regularly stripped for lumber and largely illegal grow sites. Cities famous for rain, such as Seattle, pale in comparison to Garberville's average of sixty-seven inches of rain a year. Locals are used to the Eel River rising quickly and even flooding. It's a tradition, so to speak, to be isolated by mud and high water---one much older than fire.

Winter was once the busy time of year for emergency responders, but that was before Garberville became the largest cannabis-producing region in America and the center of the illegal pot growing industry. The legalization of recreational marijuana in 2016 affected these operations very little, as the illegal trade was deeply entrenched and fees and taxes applied to legal trade were sky high. Growers continued to do as they had done highly successfully for decades. There are as many trimmers as tourists in the summer and fall, but come winter the harvest is over and the workers move on, leaving the region to a very few soggy tourists and locals holding up a skeletal local economy until next season. The spats and gunfire fade into the patter of raindrops, and the sheriff settles into his chair to finish end of year reports. Dispatch fields the usual calls of fences down and wayward cows, of people tired of the isolation and wanting to be rescued, and cars skidding off slick roads. The latter usually doesn't cause as much alarm as loose cattle or being out of milk, but when a driver spun out and came face to face with a skeletal hand sticking out of a muddy embankment, the deputy got a little excited.

Unsurprisingly, the driver was long gone when the deputies arrived on the scene. He was yet another person with something to hide, petty or otherwise. Only plastic shards of a headlight littered the churned up ground beside the road---and that hand, almost as if it was waving down a ride. The hand dangled from arm bones---much more than had been reported, as if the mud was giving birth. The deputies stepped back and studied the scene. What they presumed was a buried full skeleton was outside the fence line above, but since the earth was obviously on the move there was no telling where it originated.

"Ya know who owns this land?"

"Dutch Bogart, I think."

"Good," huffed the senior deputy. "He's less of an asshole than most. Still, you better back me up."

"And leave this unattended?"

"Like we have a choice?"

The other deputy studied the scene for a moment. "I guess it doesn't show unless you know what you're looking for. Better make this quick."

They drove about a quarter mile up the road to a driveway blocked by a gate with a code entry. "Call dispatch and get Bogart's number."

They called the number given to them and reached Dutch Bogart quickly and easily. Dutch gave them the code and they found themselves going up a long drive-way, past lush forests and gardens, to reach a beautiful, Frank Lloyd Wright-style house.

A man with a long gray ponytail and a friendly smile opened the front door. He was a familiar face from the sixties music scene. "So what's up, officer?"

"The remains of a body were found on the land just outside your farm. We need to ask you some questions."

"Okay." Dutch did not seem nervous or shocked.

"Were you aware of this?"

"No."

"Any thoughts as to how it got there?"

"No."

"Do you live here alone?"

"No." Dutch was apparently a man of few words.

"Uh, can we speak to the others who live here?"

"Okay. I'll be right back." Dutch came back with a motley crew of characters: three women and three men. Two of the men, one Black and one White, were quite old, maybe in their late eighties. The other man was Black and looked to be about forty. The three women all looked like they were in their twenties or thirties. "Do you want to talk to them privately?" Dutch asked.

"We can interview them together. Did you explain why we're here?"

"Nope."

One of the deputies began to explain. "A body was found just outside this farm. Anyone know anything about it?" There were noticeable glances among them, but they all shook their heads. The old White man was trembling while one of the young women stepped next to him and took his hand. "Why you shaking old man? You know something?"

"You---" the young woman bit her tongue. "He has Parkinson's!"

"Hey girl---"

"My name's Juniper, not girl!"

"Whatever! I wasn't accusing anyone of anything." Juniper snorted. "Okay," the deputy sighed, taking out a pad of paper. "Juniper's your name. How about the rest of you?"

"This here," Juniper announced, lifting the old man's hand, "is Mr. Shaker."

"Cool it, Juniper," Dutch said and then turned to the deputies. "I can give you a list of their names. They all live here with me." Dutch left and returned with a pen and piece of paper. He jotted down the names and handed the paper to the deputy who hadn't spoken.

The bossy one, however, snatched it from the other deputy and read the names aloud. "Which one is Tasha?" One of the women raised her hand. "So you're Scarlett, I assume?" he said, turning towards the other young woman.

"Yes," Scarlett murmured.

"Homer's the man with Parkinson's," Dutch added. "Buster's the older gentleman and Luther's the younger one."

"How long have all these people been living here?" the vocal deputy asked.

"Juniper and Homer for several years," Dutch answered. "The others for a year or so."

"Anybody got any idea at all who that body might belong to?" the other deputy finally spoke up. They all shook their heads again.

"How about you, Luther?" the more obnoxious deputy asked with a smirk.

Luther took a deep breath. He knew what was going through that deputy's mind. There were very few Blacks in Garberville and Buster, at eighty-something, didn't fit the profile. "No idea, officer," Luther finally asserted.

"Where you from, Luther?"

Luther looked at Dutch who nodded to him. "Um, Bay Area."

"Whatcha doing here? Don't you boys stay in the city?"

"He works for me," Dutch interjected.

The deputy looked down at the paper. "Luther Banks? That's your whole name? No aliases?"

Luther sighed. "Yes that's my only name."

"We'll be back after we get the medical examiner's report."

"I'll see you out," Dutch said as he led the deputies to the door.

"Don't go anywhere, Luther," the quieter deputy said.

The group went en masse to the kitchen table and sat down. They said nothing while Juniper prepared a vape pipe for Homer. He was shaking uncontrollably until he took a few tokes from the pipe. "You okay now, Homer?" Buster asked.

"Yeah . . . I'm okay."

"You did a good job keeping cool, Luther," Dutch said as he entered the room.

"Yeah, I wanted to punch that asshole!" Buster said.

Luther snickered. "Probably wouldn't have been a good idea."

Dutch looked around the table. "We all have a pretty good idea who the body is, but it seems Luther is the one they're focusing on."

Juniper jumped in, "That's good for Tasha, but not so much for Luther!"

"Let's not get into it," Dutch replied.

They were all quiet, glancing furtively at each other. Finally Buster spoke. "Dutch, couldn't you go to the cops and tell them the truth?"

Dutch looked into Buster's eyes. "You know I can't, not without implicating people I need to stay on the right side of."

Buster nodded and looked away. Juniper stood up, slapping her hand on the table. "Not even for Luther's sake?"

"Luther, come with me." Dutch got up from the table and Luther followed him out the door.

They got to the music room and even before they sat down Luther said, "It's okay, Dutch, I get it."

"Do you?"

"Yes. You'd be in a great deal of jeopardy."

"I'm surprised Juniper demanded it. She knows better than anyone what would happen if I let on."

"She's just trying to help me. She isn't thinking of the big picture."

"It will all die down soon enough. But maybe, it would be a good idea for you to go somewhere for a while."

"I know. I agree. Especially once they figure out that I had been in prison for murder."

"Does it still show up on your record even though you've been exonerated?"

"You have to sift through the court records to see it, but yes. I'm a Black ex-convict. That's a lot of strikes against me."

Dutch sighed. "Where will you go?"

"I don't know. Jed?"

"Maybe it's best if we don't know," Dutch answered. "I need to talk to the others first, before anybody does something without thinking."

"Juniper wouldn't, but Tasha might. You know, to try to ease her guilt."

"None of it was Tasha's fault."

"We know that," Luther said. "But if she and Leo hadn't come here––"

"Do what you think is right," Dutch interrupted as he went to a closet door. He put in a key code, opened the door and stepped inside. He came out with an envelope and handed it to Luther.

Luther opened it and looked inside. "You don't have to do this––"

"It's an advance on your salary," Dutch interrupted.

Luther chuckled. "What salary?"

Dutch smiled. "Just take it. And don't hesitate to ask for more if you need it."

Luther smiled back, shook his head, and pocketed the envelope. "Thanks."

Dutch nodded and watched Luther leave.

Chapter 2

JED AND MONICA WERE JUST FALLING ASLEEP WHEN JED'S CELL PHONE RANG. Monica covered her head with her pillow. "Who's calling at this hour?" she groaned.

Jed took his phone off the night table and looked at the screen. "Luther?" he said, getting up and plodding out the door.

"Did I wake you? I'm so sorry."

"It's alright. What's up?"

"I need to leave. Can I come there and I'll tell you when I see you?"

"Of course. Now?'

"I'll get there at a more reasonable hour."

"Well, we might be at work——"

"I'll come straight to the columbarium. Still start at nine?"

"I'll be there by eight-thirty getting ready to open."

"Okay. I'll see you in the morning. Thanks, Jed. I really appreciate it."

They hung up and Jed went back to bed. "What did he want?" Monica asked.

"He's coming here tomorrow morning and he'll tell us when he gets here."

"Is something wrong?"

"Seems like it."

"Hm. I wonder if something happened between him and Juniper."

"Well, he was in prison for twenty years and he was awfully young when he went in. Maybe he needs to sow some oats."

Monica sighed and turned over. "Let's try to get sleep. We'll find out soon enough."

Jed tried, but couldn't keep his mind from overflowing with thoughts and worry. What could be wrong? He finally stopped tossing and turning and got out of bed. By the time Monica joined him in the kitchen, he was on his third cup of coffee. "I'll make you a fresh pot," Jed said, standing up quickly.

"How long have you been up?"

"Too long. It's okay. I'll survive."

Monica chuckled. "Maybe you can curl up in one of the niches and take a catnap."

"Sure," he winked. "Sam and Sadie have a double size and they don't take up much room." He kissed her and left to take a shower and get dressed.

Luther arrived at the columbarium just after nine and found Jed setting up chairs for a memorial service. Jed had started working at the columbarium as a handyman. He now called himself the caretaker/historian, telling the stories of the people whose ashes were in the glass-doored niches to the many visitors to the incredible copper-domed building. "Can I help?" Luther said as he entered the large atrium.

Jed hugged him tightly. "I'm almost done. Why don't you go say hello to your mother and I'll be upstairs shortly. The service isn't until eleven."

Luther climbed the stairs to his mother's niche. He had wanted to add some things to her apartment, the word Jed used to describe the recesses in the wall that held the ashes of a few thousand people. Unfortunately, he hadn't been back to San Francisco since leaving for the farm, less than a week after being exonerated. He stood in front of his mother's picture that was placed next to the urn and let the tears flow. Jed watched from the stairs until he saw Luther wipe his eyes and turn towards him. "I keep meaning to decorate her apartment with some stuff that would show people what an incredible woman she was."

Jed put his arm around him. "Maybe the time is now."

"I don't think I should stay here."

"Do you want to tell me what's going on?"

"It might be better if I don't. Then you could honestly say you don't know anything . . . if anyone should ask."

Jed stared at Luther for a minute, puzzled yet accepting. "Whatever you think is best. Do you want to go to the house? I'll get the key."

"No. I don't want you and Monica to be in the middle of this."

"Decide what you want to do. I'll be downstairs getting ready for the memorial service." Jed patted Luther on the back and left.

Luther stood in the back and watched the service, wiping tears even though he didn't know the person. He mourned the fact that he had not been able to go to his mother's service and the predicament he had been in then and how it led to the one he was in now. He'd had nothing to do with any murder and yet here he was, being blamed again. He watched as Jed's compassion and integrity spread over the grieving friends and relatives. He couldn't put Jed and Monica in any position of jeopardy. He couldn't think of a place he'd rather be than with them, but he wouldn't. He needed to go further away than San Francisco. The city would be where they'd look for him since that was where he was from originally . . . before prison and the farm. His mind was made up, but where would he go? "Can I give you a hand?" Luther asked Jed when the last of the mourners left the columbarium.

"Sure. You remember where the chairs go?"

"Yeah," Luther grinned. "It wasn't that long ago that I arrived here straight from San Quentin."

Jed smiled. "Seems like an eternity."

"Can you leave for lunch or should I get us some pizza . . . for old times sake?" Luther asked when they had finished cleaning up.

"Yeah, get us a pizza." Jed reached into his pocket to get his wallet out.

"I got it," Luther winked as he walked outside.

They discussed mundane things as they ate . . . the rainstorms, Homer's condition, the music festival the previous spring at the farm that had been the last time they'd seen each other. After the last piece of pizza had been eaten Jed said, "So do you want to hang out here? Go to the house? See the sights of San Francisco?" He chuckled. "I hear there's this beautiful bridge here."

Luther laughed. "Yeah, I heard that too."

"Luther, I'm not afraid of anyone coming here and asking about you. Let me know what's going on."

Luther sighed, still unsure if it was wise to tell Jed, but he needed his help. "They found a body right outside the farm. I guess the rain washed it up from where it was buried."

"So what does that have to do with you?"

"Nothing. I mean . . ." Luther exhaled loudly. "Except I'm the obvious suspect."

"Why? Because you were in prison? Because you're one of the few Blacks in Humboldt County? That's bullshit."

"Well, you and I know that but——"

"Have they come right out and accused you?"

"Pretty much. I haven't been arrested or anything . . . yet."

Jed sighed. "You think they'd look for you here?"

"Yeah. I do. After all, I did grow up here and they can find that out easily. They probably figure I still have relatives and friends here – places I could go."

"Does Dutch know you're here?"

"No. And I don't want to put him in an awkward position either."

"Dutch is quite capable of taking care of himself. I wouldn't worry about him. He's been skirting the law longer than you've been alive."

Luther looked into Jed's eyes. "This is different."

Jed hesitated before finally asking the question neither wanted him to ask. "Do you and Dutch and the others on the farm know where the body came from and who it is?"

Luther ignored the question and picked up the pizza box. "I'll throw this away on my way out."

"Hold it. Where are you going to go?"

Luther shrugged. "I'll figure something out."

"Luther! Wait!" Luther was startled. He'd never heard Jed shout. "You can't just wander the streets. It's not like you have the FBI after you with all its resources. It's a couple of cops from a small town. I think it was smart to leave Garberville, but I doubt they will look all over the country for you. They don't have the manpower or the experience."

Luther sighed. "I'm just so scared of going back to prison. And being here in San Francisco is just a little too close to San Quentin."

"I get that. But California's a big state. There are other places to go."

Luther was silent for a couple of minutes. "Like where?"

"I know people in Los Angeles. My friend Finn's daughter, Kate, lives there, as do Malcolm and Savali. I was in your position once, remember? And I had my fingerprints on the victim."

"But didn't they find out you hadn't done it?"

"Yes, but not before I left Venice Beach. I, too, was on the run, so to speak. And they didn't really look for me here."

"So you think if I went to Los Angeles I'd be okay?" Luther asked.

"Yes. Or anyplace really. Do you want to go to LA?"

"Not really." Luther grinned. "I'm kind of digging the country life."

"There's plenty of country life in California other than Garberville," Jed smiled back. "Why not come home with me tonight and we'll talk about it. Maybe Monica has some good ideas. After all, she's the one who thought of Dutch's as a good place for you to go."

"Are you sure?"

Jed shook his head. "Please stop worrying about us. Yes. I'm sure. Now, do you want to hang around here with me the rest of the day or take a key and go to the house?"

"I guess I'll stay with you."

"Do you remember where the utility closet is?" Jed winked.

"Sure. I remember." Luther winked back. "I can earn my keep!"

"How about cleaning the glass doors on the niches on the top floor to start. You can work your way downstairs and do as much as you have time for."

Luther actually enjoyed wiping down the doors. It took his mind off his immediate problem. He put in his earbuds to listen to music and didn't even notice when Jed approached him a couple of hours later. Jed had to tap him on the shoulder to get his attention. "Oh, sorry," Luther said as he turned off the music.

"You've done plenty. Come on downstairs." Luther put his supplies away and met up with Jed in the main foyer. "Monica is going to be a little late tonight, so she asked if I wanted to pick up some dinner. Got any requests?"

"Anything is fine."

"Do you like sushi?"

"Huh? What's that?"

Jed laughed. "I guess there are no Japanese restaurants in Garberville."

"I wouldn't know. It's not like we go out to eat when we're at the farm."

"Are you up for trying it?"

Luther shrugged. "Whatever you want is fine with me. I guess it's good to try new things."

"Would you rather do Chinese?"

"At least I've had Chinese food before. You know. Before I went to prison."

"There's a restaurant over on Clement. It's just a few blocks."

"That's cool," Luther nodded. "I'll buy."

"No. You don't have to do that."

"Dutch gave me some money before I left."

"You may need that, Luther. You hang on to it."

"He can send me more." Luther smiled. "It's not like he pays me a salary, you know. I just look at it as back wages."

Jed smiled. "I guess he has plenty and doesn't spend much."

They locked up the building and the outside gate and started walking. "Do you like living in the city, Jed?" Luther asked as they strode up towards Geary.

"I don't know. I don't care where I am that much. I've lived in a lot of places, Luther. Done a lot of traveling around the country. I'm happy with my job and my wife and my house. And I guess that's all that matters."

"I'm happy with my life on the farm, too. But everyone keeps telling me that after losing twenty years of my life, I should want to experience a lot of places and things."

"You do whatever you want, Luther. You know you don't have to listen to anyone else. And anyway, when you don't know what to do, it's better to do nothing at all. The right thing will show up and you'll know."

Luther nodded and they walked the rest of the way in silence.

Chapter 3

THEY PICKED UP DINNER AND ARRIVED HOME JUST AS MONICA PULLED INTO THE DRIVEWAY. After the hugs and warm greetings, they set the table and sat down to eat. "I told Luther that he's welcome to stay as long as he needs," Jed said.

"Of course!" she answered. "Jed could use help at the columbarium anyway. Tony's away for a month, right? He usually stops by once or twice a week to help."

"But he shouldn't feel obligated one way or the other." Jed winked at Luther, hoping he remembered their earlier conversation.

"I'm kind of in limbo," Luther said, smiling at Jed.

"Well, sometimes that's the best way to be," Monica replied.

"That's what I told him. And she's smarter than me, so you better heed her advice." Jed smiled back at Luther.

"Well, since I seem to be the wise one around here," Monica laughed, "let me also add that the best way to make decisions is to talk them through with others. You don't have to follow other people's advice, but listening to other opinions helps you make a decision."

"Thanks . . . both of you. It helps a lot to know I have you guys to count on." They finished eating and Luther added, "I didn't get much sleep last night so I think I'm going to turn in."

After Luther left the room Monica turned to Jed. "Is he okay? I can't believe the police are doing this to him again."

"And of course it's not about being Black!" Jed answered derisively.

"Now Jed," Monica admonished. "Let's keep things positive for Luther's sake. We don't need to go there."

Jed nodded. "I'm ready for bed, too."

"I'll join you in a while," she replied. "I have some work stuff to finish up."

Jed was the first one up in the morning, as usual. He made the coffee and turned on the television to the local news. The reporter was describing the flooding along the Eel River as Luther entered the room. "Damn. I hope the farm is okay."

"They're on high ground and Dutch is resourceful." Jed looked at the clock. "Oh boy, I'd better get going. You're coming to work with me, right?"

"Yeah," Luther replied. "I need to keep busy and I like it at the columbarium. It's peaceful."

"Well, I'll jump in the shower first while you have some coffee. There's some bread in the freezer, if you want toast and some eggs."

"Okay, thanks. I'll find something to eat."

They arrived at the columbarium and found several people milling around the gate. "We actually don't open until nine," Jed told them as he unlocked it.

"Yeah, we know," one of them answered. "We can wait. We have a niche to decorate. Our father died last week."

"Well, come on in if you want to get started. I just have some early morning things I need to do before we actually open."

"That's awfully nice of you. Thanks." The group followed Jed and Luther into the building. "Oh my God!" one of them exclaimed, looking around the rotunda. "I never imagined it would be this beautiful!"

"Do you know where your father's apartment is?" Jed asked.

They looked at him quizzically. "Uh, my father used to live on Potrero Hill——" one finally said.

"He meant his niche," Luther interrupted. "Jed calls them apartments."

"Oh." Soft chuckles spread over the group. "Well, then, we better finish it to his taste."

"Do you need any help?" Luther responded.

"I don't think so." The man patted the shopping bag he had in his hand. "Got all the stuff Dad chose right here."

The group started upstairs and Luther turned to Jed. "I wish I knew if my mother had chosen some stuff to put in hers." Then he shrugged. "Not that I could have done anything about it, being ostracized by my family and in prison."

Jed put his arm around Luther's shoulder. "Things you put inside don't have to be hers. You can just buy some things that would represent what she loved."

"Yeah." Luther then sighed. "The sad thing is I can't remember what she loved. I can't remember her saying anything about it. Or maybe I just wasn't listening."

"Well you can––meditate on it while you work today. You know. Don't try to recall her words, just feel her around you. Bet something will come to mind then." Jed paused as Luther let the idea sink in. "Do you want to follow me around or start right off on your own?"

Luther seemed to come out of a daze. "Is there anything I can do outside? I miss working on the farm."

"Tons. Let me finish up on the opening chores and then I'll show you what needs doing. Meanwhile, you can go upstairs and see how that group is doing."

"Sure."

When Luther approached the group, he realized the niche they were decorating was only a few doors from his mother's. He glanced inside and saw the urn with his mother's ashes sitting all alone. He vowed to make decorating it his first priority. Trying to remember what she liked and how she had lived her life was difficult, though. He had never known her as an adult, and now she seemed so far away. So far behind the grief and anger of prison life. He heard weeping and thought it was his mother in their dark apartment. It was too real.

Too close. He glanced over at the group, now standing in a circle and holding hands. Someone took a deep breath. They were now silent and their eyes were closed. He didn't know if they were praying or just lost in their own thoughts. But he decided to stand at his mother's apartment and close his own eyes to try to conjure up everything he could remember about her.

Someone tapped him on the shoulder. "Are you okay, Luther?" Jed asked.

Luther opened his eyes and noticed the group had left. He was sure he'd been standing there quite a while. He smiled at Jed and answered, "I'm just fine."

Jed nodded and turned to go down the stairs. Luther followed him outside to the tool shed. Jed unlocked it and said, "Right now you can weed and rake."

Luther spent the morning outside and realized this was his element. He may have been raised in the city, but working with plants gave him a serenity that took away most of the anxiety and fear of again being pinned for a crime he did not commit. Jed came outside and Luther asked, "Is it time for lunch?"

"It's almost one."

"Really? Wow."

"You're in your element aren't you?" Jed said with a smile.

Luther nodded. "I do like being out here with the plants."

"Have you ever been to the Botanical Garden?"

"No. Where is it?"

"It's in Golden Gate Park. Probably about a half hour walk from here. You could go this afternoon if you want."

"Oh man!" Luther exclaimed. "I'd love that."

"Why don't you go out and pick up some lunch for us and then you can meander over there. Monica works very close to there. She could pick you up on her way home. Do you have her phone number?"

Luther took out his phone. "I don't think so. Can you give it to me?"

Jed recited her number for Luther to put in his phone and then directed him to a deli just a couple of blocks away. After bringing some food back to the columbarium, Luther scarfed down his sandwich and was on his way to the San Francisco Botanical Gardens. As soon as he got to Golden Gate Park, however, he realized that he didn't need to waste his money on the entrance fee to get into the botanical garden. He was perfectly content to just roam around the park. Golden Gate Park is huge and there are plenty of places to meander and hide.

He started to walk towards the ocean and found himself in a grove of redwoods. This felt like home to him. He could stay among the trees for hours at the farm. He found a stump to sit on and contemplated his predicament. Among the trees, he realized that his wasn't such a hopeless situation at all. There was a peace and serenity to be found in any nature setting. It just reinforced what he already knew. City life was not for him. If he couldn't go back to the farm, he could still find a situation that would meet his needs. Maybe he could go to school and learn about botany like Tasha did. It felt so good to brush off the anxiety he'd been living with for the last several days. He closed his eyes and actually fell asleep.

Chapter 4

LUTHER'S PHONE RANG A SHORT TIME LATER AND STARTLED HIM AWAKE. He glanced at the screen. "Juniper?"

"Luther! That asshole deputy won't leave us alone. He keeps demanding to know where you are and refuses to believe that we don't know. I just thought you should know."

"Thanks Juniper," Luther sighed. "I guess I won't be seeing you for a while."

"Please take care of yourself." Juniper stifled a sob. "I miss you."

"I miss you too . . . all of you."

"I hate that you're going through this."

"I've been through worse. At least I'm a free man, for now."

"Don't say that, Luther! They can't put you in jail for this."

"Juniper! They've done it before. Why not?"

They hung up and Luther checked the time. He decided to walk back to the columbarium instead of calling Monica to pick him up. He got there just as Jed was locking the front door. "Hey Luther," Jed called out to him when he saw him walk through the gate. "What happened? I thought you were calling Monica to pick you up."

"I didn't go to the Botanical Garden. I just enjoyed being in the park. But I got a call from Juniper. That damn deputy is being a real pain in the ass at the farm. I'm really glad I didn't tell them where I was going. But I did tell the deputy that I was from the Bay Area. Do you think he'd look for me here?"

Jed shrugged. "He might contact the SFPD, but they have much better things to do than look for you. Anyway, they wouldn't look here. They may contact your relatives."

Luther scoffed. "Yeah. And my relatives don't have a clue where I've been . . . or care."

Jed put his arm around Luther's shoulders. "You can stay and help me here til things die down."

"I don't know, Jed. Maybe I should go further away."

"I could contact Malcolm in Los Angeles. You two would really like each other."

"I don't know, Jed. Maybe I should leave the state."

"Are you serious?"

"Well..." Luther hedged. "I dunno. California just doesn't feel big enough right now."

Jed grabbed him by the shoulders. "You trust me?"

"Yeah, of course."

"I'm going to make a call, and I trust you'll follow through. Don't let me down."

"Now you're scaring me."

"All I mean is I'm asking a favor of a friend for you, okay?"

Luther nodded. "Okay. Thanks, man."

Jed took out his phone and walked back inside the columbarium. Luther sat on the step and waited. "Okay," Jed said as he swung open the door. "There's a flight leaving in two hours, so you need to get to the airport now."

"A flight? Where am I going?"

"New York."

"What?" Luther laughed. "I've never been anywhere other than that trip to Phoenix with Dutch and Buster. I've never been on an airplane either."

"Well, there's got to be a first time and I guess this is it."

"But what am I going to do when I get there?"

"My friend, Finn, will meet you at the airport. You'll stay with him. I called Monica and she got you a ticket and printed out the boarding pass. She'll take you to the airport. You just need identification. Do you have a driver's license?"

"Yeah."

"Do you have any money?"

"Yeah, what Dutch gave me."

"Do you need more?"

"Not yet."

"Okay. Now, you'd better get out there and wait for Monica."

"Jed . . ." Luther's voice cracked.

"Call me when you get there and you're with Finn." Jed hugged him tightly. "Now scoot. I've got to finish closing up."

Luther went outside and waited for Monica to come. She arrived a few minutes later. "Did Jed tell you how he and Finn got to be friends?" she asked as they turned off Loraine Court onto Anza Street.

"No."

"They met when Jed lived in Venice Beach. Finn is a renowned author and wrote a book about Jed's experiences in Jonestown."

"Jonestown . . ." Luther thought aloud. "You mean that Kool-Aid cult in Africa back in the 1970s?"

"It was in Guyana in South America," Monica corrected. "But yeah, that one. You didn't know that Jed escaped from Jonestown as a child? Or that he was homeless, living on the Venice Beach boardwalk?"

"Jeez! No, I knew he had been homeless at one point in his life, but that's all."

Monica smiled. "Well, now you know."

"So Finn's a famous guy? And so is Jed I guess, since he had a book written about him."

"Jed's not famous. He isn't even mentioned by name in the book. Finn wrote a couple of bestsellers, but I don't think he's written anything recently. He's not a young man." She laughed. "Of course neither are we, but Finn's even older. He's in his eighties."

"Well, I'm used to living with old men. Buster and Homer are not exactly my age."

"That's true, but they're a lot nicer," Monica smiled. "Did Jed tell you that Finn could be a real curmudgeon?"

"A what?"

"A mean old fart. Just don't take anything personally. It's just the way he is."

Luther bit his lip as a wave of misgivings flooded over him. They were silent a few minutes before Monica spoke again. "But you'll like Finn. He's probably Jed's best friend, even though they hardly ever see each other anymore."

Luther brightened up a little. "Well, maybe you and Jed could come to New York while I'm there and visit."

"You know, Luther, that's a great idea. I'll see if I can get the time off and if Jed can get Tony to handle the columbarium for a few days."

They arrived at the terminal. "Here you are, Luther. Take care of yourself." She hugged him. "Here's your boarding pass."

"Monica——"

"No need to thank us," she interjected.

"It's not that. I, uh . . . I've never been on a plane before."

"Are you scared?"

"No. It's just . . . what do I do?"

"Oh. You just have that backpack so you don't need to check baggage. Just look at the monitor by the ticket counter and see what gate your flight is leaving from.

The flight number is on your boarding pass. Then you'll go through security . . . you don't have a knife or any of Dutch's favorite weed or anything?"

"No. Just some clothes."

"Okay. Then you'll give the person at the security line your boarding pass and your driver's license, put your backpack in one of the bins along with your jacket and your shoes––"

"My shoes?"

"Many years ago somebody tried to blow up a plane with a bomb or something in his shoes. Now we all have to take off our shoes to board a plane."

Luther laughed. "That's crazy."

"Lots of craziness in this world. Just watch what others are doing. You'll be fine."

"Okay. See you in New York." He opened the door and winked as he got out.

Chapter 5

LUTHER'S FIRST-EVER FLIGHT WAS SMOOTH AND ON TIME. He got off the plane and looked around for an old man at the gate, but soon realized that nobody was waiting there to meet anyone. He followed the crowd and found himself in the baggage area, even though he had not checked any bags. He glanced around and felt a tap on his shoulder. He turned around and was looking at a scowling old man, small in stature, with a full head of white hair. "You Luther?" the man said.

"Finn?"

"You got a bag checked?"

"Uh, no. Just this backpack."

"Then let's go." Finn turned and started to walk away. Luther scampered after him.

"Thanks for meeting me at such an early hour," Luther said breathlessly as he caught up with Finn.

"Yeah, well, I don't sleep much so it doesn't really matter."

Luther found himself almost jogging, trying to keep up with this man in his eighties. "You sure walk fast."

"All New Yorkers walk fast. You never heard of a New York minute?"

"No."

"Hah! If you don't do things fast you'll never get anywhere in New York. Hurry up. We need to get on the Airtrain to get to the subway station. Then we get on the E train. It'll probably take an hour or an hour and a half now. Everybody's going to work."

"Not gonna get there in a New York minute I guess," Luther grinned, but his joke didn't go over. Finn pushed him onto the crowded tram and they rode in silence until they finally reached the Jamaica subway station.

"Let's go," Finn said as he pulled Luther's arm. They practically ran to the stairs down to the subway station and Finn shouted over his shoulder, "I bought you a ticket good for a few rides." He held the card over his shoulder and Luther took it.

"Where do I put it?" Luther asked as they approached the turnstile.

"Just watch how I do it." They got through the gate and rushed to a platform where a train was approaching. "Ah, perfect timing. Here's the E train." The doors opened to an already crowded car and Finn pushed his way through the crowd. Luther hesitated and watched as the doors started to close. "Get in here!" Finn yelled as he put his hand on the door to open it again. Luther scurried in, embarrassed to be pushing all the people out of his way, but realizing that New York was going to be quite a new and different experience.

Luther spent most of the train ride trying to keep his balance. After living on the farm in rural Humboldt County, the throng of people standing throughout the subway car was unnerving. Nobody made eye contact; in fact most of the people sat or had a strap or pole to hang onto and had their eyes closed. The others, like him and Finn, were focused on not falling into the people crowded around them. Legs were splayed, arms were held close to the body, and most of the women had their handbags clutched tightly to their chests. Even prison yards and cafeterias never produced a scenario of such tight-knit quarters.

Keeping Finn in sight wasn't too difficult because he, the White male, was very much in the minority. Luther had never seen such diversity in color and class. As more people entered the car at each stop, he found himself getting pushed further and further away from Finn. He didn't have any idea at what stop they were getting off. He managed to push through the crowd enough to yell, "Hey, Finn, where do we get off?"

"Washington Square," Finn answered. "I'll let you know when we're close."

"But——" Luther was interrupted by a sudden jolt of the train coming to a stop and more people getting on, pushing him further away from Finn. He sighed and decided to just watch the signs and get off at Washington Square. At the station he should be able to find Finn so he settled in to people-watch. Although he had slept on the plane, he felt his eyes close as the rhythmic swaying of the train took over. He might even have fallen asleep for a few minutes until it got louder while the train sped through the tunnel under the East River.

It didn't take long before Luther noticed a wall sign saying West 4th Street and in smaller letters, Washington Square. He looked for Finn in the sea of people, but Finn was rather short and had disappeared into the milling crowd. Luther pushed his way through the throng and got off, just as the doors were about to close. Finn was standing on the platform, grinning at Luther. Finn chuckled. "The city got you gob smacked?"

"Well, kinda. I grew up in San Francisco, but this place is nothing like that."

"Nope, there's no place like New York. Come on up these stairs and you'll really see this city."

Luther followed Finn like a little puppy, looking all around, but still keeping close to Finn. He was afraid of getting lost because he didn't even have Finn's phone number, let alone his address. They seemed to be surrounded by young people and then Luther noticed a sign saying New York University. Ah, college kids. Next Finn turned down a street and the Washington Square Arch loomed ahead of them. "You live near here?" Luther asked, again breathless trying to keep up with this man who was twice his age.

"Not far. You hungry? I don't have much food in the apartment. Maybe we should pick up something."

"Yeah, I am hungry."

"Let's just get some lunch. We can worry about groceries later."

"There's a hamburger place," Luther pointed across the street.

Finn stopped and stared at him. "You don't come to New York City for hamburgers. You gotta have pizza."

"Pizza's good," Luther replied. "Whatever you want."

"It's not what I want, but you haven't eaten pizza until you've had New York pizza."

"Okay." They walked a few more blocks and Finn led the way inside a pizza parlor where he ordered two huge slices. "You don't have to pay for everything for me, you know," Luther said as Finn scoffed at him for taking out his wallet.

"We'll work it all out later. Let's just sit down and eat." They took a couple of bites. "That's not how you eat pizza in New York. Watch me." Finn folded his large pizza slice lengthwise. "Got it?" Luther nodded and copied Finn. They finished their slices and then Finn asked, "So what's the trouble you're in?"

"Jed didn't tell you?"

"Nope, just that you needed to get away for a while."

"Well, the short version is that a dead body was found near the farm where I live and they think I did it."

"Who thinks you did it?"

"The county sheriff and deputies."

"Why would they think that?"

"There aren't many Blacks living in Humboldt County and, uh, I was in prison for twenty years."

Luther watched Finn closely to see how that last statement registered with him, but saw nothing resembling fear or surprise on his face. "I've been exonerated, but it still shows up on my record."

Finn nodded and said, "How long do you think you'll want to stay?"

"I don't know. If it's inconvenient, I can get a hotel room."

"First of all," Finn answered, "if it was inconvenient, you wouldn't be here. Secondly, you haven't any idea what a hotel room in New York costs. Even a fleabag SRO is gonna cost you a pretty penny. Doesn't matter . . . I was just wondering. Let's go," Finn said, standing up and bringing his paper plate to the trash bin. They arrived at a brownstone and Finn took out his key to unlock the front door. "Guess I better make you a set of your own keys."

"You live here? In this whole building by yourself?"

"Hah! Hardly. I got a one bedroom on the third floor. You'll be on the couch."

They climbed the stairs and Finn opened the only door on the third floor. "You climb all those steps every day?" Luther asked, still marveling at how spry and agile this old man was.

"Yeah, instead of going to the gym!" Finn laughed. "There's your bed," he said pointing to the sofa. "I didn't have time to clean up."

Luther looked around the living room at the piles of books and papers scattered on the floor and the sofa.

"I'll do it. It's the least I can do. But where should I put everything?"

"That's the problem with living in New York. No place to put things. We'll figure it out. I'm going for a nap. I don't sleep much at night so I take short snoozes. See you in twenty." Finn went into the bedroom and shut the door. Luther, meanwhile, cleared off the sofa, piling things up on the floor, and lay down himself. Before he had a chance to think about all that had happened in the last twenty-four hours, he was fast asleep.

Chapter 6

LUTHER OPENED HIS EYES AND LOOKED AT HIS PHONE. He was shocked to see he had slept for three hours and sat up abruptly. He looked around the apartment for Finn. The bedroom door was open so he peeked inside. It was empty. He was in the bathroom when he heard the front door open. Finn was putting groceries away when Luther entered the kitchen. "Didn't sleep much on the plane, I gather," Finn said as he closed the refrigerator door.

"It's been a long and tiring last couple of days."

"Yeah, probably so. Didn't know what to buy, but we can always go again tomorrow if you're a picky sort."

Luther laughed. "After twenty years in prison you can't be too picky about what you eat."

"Well, this is New York. Best place in the world to be picky about food since there's nothing you can't find here."

"You seem to really love your city."

"Nah. Most New Yorkers have a love-hate relationship with it. Hey, I lived in California for a pretty long spell too. Not to mention the first eighteen years of my life in Ireland. Do you drink?"

Luther looked at him warily before answering. "Uh, yeah. What do you mean?"

"I don't mean anything. Just asking. It's almost cocktail hour."

"What time is cocktail hour?"

"Let me clarify. It's almost my cocktail hour which changes depending on my mood."

"Okay, so what you're really asking is if I want a drink?"

"It was just a simple question," Finn scoffed.

Luther now understood Monica's description of Finn. He certainly was curmudgeonly. Luther took a deep breath and then answered, "I'll have whatever you're having whenever you're having it."

Finn snickered. "Aren't you the picture of bonhomie."

"I don't know what that means."

"It means you're amenable, affable, congenial . . . uh friendly and flexible."

Luther wasn't sure if Finn was teasing him or not, but he decided to drop it and change the subject. "Do you have a copy of the book you wrote about Jed? I'd like to read it."

Finn went into the living room and brought out a copy of *Those Who Forget the Past are Condemned to Repeat It* and handed it to Luther. "You ever heard that saying before?"

"I don't think so. Where's it from?"

"Guy named George Santayana. He was a philosopher. It was on a sign posted at Jonestown. You know Jonestown? The Kool-Aid and all that?"

"Not much more than that except that Monica said Jed had escaped from there."

"Then read the book and you'll find out."

"Thanks. I will." Luther took the book into the living room and sat down on the couch to start reading.

Finn entered a few minutes later with two glasses of amber colored liquid over a couple of cubes of ice. He set the drinks down on the coffee table, took a copy of the New York Times and sat down at the other end of the sofa. He turned to the crossword puzzle and said, "Would you hand me that pen over there?"

Luther found the pen on the side table next to him and gave it to Finn, and then took a sip. "Whoa! That's some strong stuff."

"Irish whiskey is not for the faint-hearted."

"I guess not."

"I've got some beer if you'd prefer."

"I'll drink this." Luther smiled. "I don't want you to think I'm not a man of my word."

Finn smiled. "Wouldn't expect anything less." He turned to his crossword puzzle and started filling it out. They sat in silence, sipping their drinks, while Luther read and Finn filled out the crossword puzzle.

"You're a good writer," Luther said as he downed the rest of his drink.

"Better be. I was an English teacher for a lot of years."

"And the whiskey's not bad when you get used to it."

"Well don't get liking it too much," Finn replied. "Wouldn't want you to wind up like me." Luther wasn't sure what Finn meant, but he knew better than to ask. "Do you want another?"

"I don't know. Maybe a beer would be better. I can get it." Luther got up and took his glass into the kitchen. He took out his phone to call Juniper and noticed an old text from Jed, asking if he had arrived safely. It must have come while he was sleeping. He started to text back, but then decided to call when he got back to the living room so Finn could talk to him too. But he was too late. When he got to the living room, Finn was on the phone.

"Here he is, Jed. You can talk to him yourself." Finn handed his phone to Luther.

"Hey Jed. Sorry. I just saw your text."

"No problem," Jed answered. "Just checking that you made it okay."

"Have you talked to Dutch?"

"No, but no news is good news. Right?"

"I was going to call Juniper——"

"Remember, it's better if they don't know where you are," Jed broke in. "You don't want to put her in an awkward position if she's questioned by the cops. I know you miss her and I know she's worried."

"I do miss her and the rest of them."

"So what are you planning to do in New York while you're there?" Jed tried to sound upbeat.

"Hadn't thought about it. I guess look for a place to stay." Luther glanced at Finn, but couldn't read his reaction. He wasn't sure if he was supposed to stay with him indefinitely.

"Well, you just got there. Settle in and enjoy the city. It'll be quite a change of pace from Garberville."

"For sure. Thanks again, Jed, as always." Luther handed the phone back to Finn.

"For Christ's sake, Jed," Finn said. "He can stay here as long as he needs to." Finn glanced over at Luther who smiled at him. Finn, however, didn't smile back, but Luther already figured out that Finn didn't smile much. "You a good cook?" Finn asked after hanging up with Jed.

"Not really. Actually, I don't know how to make much of anything. You don't get to cook in prison and I didn't do much in the kitchen at the farm except eat and wash dishes."

"I guess that means I'm making dinner."

"I'd like to learn, though."

"Well, take your beer and follow me. I'm not anything like a gourmet chef, but I can teach you the basics." Finn opened the refrigerator and took out a beer. "And I'll tamp down my drinking in your honor."

Luther wasn't sure what that meant, but it didn't matter. Finn was an interesting character, kind of like Buster up at the farm. Old and cranky, but lively and lovable at the same time. Good people, both of them. People you can count on and turn to. He saw how Finn and Jed could be best friends, even though they were as different as night and day. "You don't need to tamp down your drinking for me."

"That was a joke. I drink what and how much I want. You're not one of those California vegetarian, granola types are you?"

"Nope. I'll eat anything."

"Good. I bought steak and potatoes."

"That'll be a real treat for me. We didn't eat that at the farm."

"Easiest meal on earth. I'll even boil some cabbage so you can have the whole Irish experience." Finn laughed, surprising Luther, but he joined in, even though he wasn't sure what he was laughing at.

Luther watched Finn wash the potatoes, poke them with a fork, and put them in the oven at 450 degrees. He admired Finn's way of cutting the cabbage in four quick strokes and then throwing them in a pot with some water. "That's it?" Luther asked.

"Yep. I'll broil the steaks when the potatoes are done. Can't bake and broil at the same time." Finn looked at Luther warily. "You never watched your mother cook or anything? You really know this little about it?"

"Well, she didn't cook that kind of food, I guess. And I didn't really pay attention."

Finn shook his head. "The potatoes take an hour, so let's go back to the living room."

Luther noticed a record collection in the bookcase and got up to see what Finn's music taste was. "You got any of Dutch or Buster's records?"

"Who's Buster McCracken? I know Dutch owns the farm."

"Buster lives there. You know that Dutch was a rock and roll musician in the sixties and Buster's an old blues man."

"I don't have their records but go ahead and take a look at what I have. I doubt you'll find something to your liking, though."

"That's okay. I was just curious." Luther sat down and sipped on his beer.

"So . . . what's your story before you went to prison?" Finn asked.

"Grew up in San Francisco, just my mom and me. She died while I was in prison." Luther gazed into Finn's eyes. "I was a good kid. I wasn't into gangs or anything like that. I was supposed to go to college til they pinned that murder on me."

"Why'd they think you did it?"

"I was playing basketball with a bunch of guys I didn't know. They robbed a store and killed the clerk there. I was sitting in the car and when I ran in to see what happened——"

"And you were the one standing there when the cops came," Finn interrupted.

"Exactly."

"Bad break. Why'd it take twenty years to get you out?"

"I didn't find out about the Innocence Project for a long time."

"Well, you're out now. And you've still got a lot of life left to live."

"I hope so."

"Just stay under the radar for awhile and those yokels up in Humboldt County will have bigger fish to fry soon enough. But you might not want to go back there for awhile."

"That's what Jed and I think too. But it's hard not to be really angry. You can't imagine what it's like to be accused of a crime you didn't commit . . . twice."

"I can imagine." Luther looked at Finn, perplexed. "Happened to me too. And Jed."

Luther waited for Finn to explain, but he didn't. "Well, maybe you can tell me that story sometime," Luther finally said.

"Yeah." Finn got up. "Gonna turn on the cabbage and check the potatoes." Luther watched him leave the room, not sure if he should follow. When Finn didn't return in a few minutes, Luther picked up his book and continued reading. Maybe there'd be an explanation of what Finn meant in there.

They had more than a couple of beers before dinner so by the time they finished eating, Luther could hardly keep his eyes open. He wasn't used to drinking this much, but felt the need to keep up with Finn until he realized that was an impossible task. They had talked mostly about Jed and Jonestown, not touching on their own personal stories. "I need to go to sleep," Luther finally admitted as he got up from the table and picked up his and Finn's plates.

"Go to bed, lightweight," Finn chuckled. "The dishes can wait."

"Thanks," Luther replied as he put the dishes in the sink and scurried off to the bathroom. Finn cleared the rest of the table and went to his bedroom.

Chapter 7

FINN OPENED HIS EYES AND BLINKED AT THE CLOCK. He had slept all through the night, a whole six hours. That hadn't happened in a long time. Maybe having someone else in the house was a bit of a comfort to him, although he'd been alone for a couple of years now. He had lived with his daughter, Kate, in Venice Beach after his wife died, but after a series of only somewhat satisfactory living arrangements on the West Coast, he decided to come back to New York. He still wasn't sure it had been the wisest decision.

"Hey, Finn?" Luther asked through the bedroom door. "Is it okay if I take a shower or do you want to use the bathroom first?"

"Yeah, let me take a whiz."

"No hurry." Luther went back to the living room and started folding his sheet and blanket.

Finn passed through the living room on his way to the kitchen and muttered, "Haven't slept this late in many a moon."

Luther looked at his phone. "It's seven, not that late."

"Hah. That's late."

By the time Luther finished his shower, Finn was on his second cup of coffee and the second section of the New York Times. "Gee, I haven't seen a hard copy of a newspaper since the library at the prison!" Luther exclaimed.

"Computers are fine for writing and Googling, but I like to hold what I'm reading in my hands." Finn poured a cup of coffee and set it down in front of Luther. "So, what do you want to do your first day in New York?"

Luther shrugged. "I hadn't thought much about it."

"You don't want to see the Empire State Building and the Statue of Liberty?"

"I guess so. This was kind of spur of the moment. It's not like I looked at a tourist book or anything first."

"Hey, we don't have to go anywhere if you don't want. Or you can come with me on my rounds and you'll get a flavor of the city."

"I just hadn't given any of this much thought."

"You're forty years old and you've been basically nowhere." Finn shook his head in disbelief. "You're telling me you've never given it any thought?"

Luther was quiet. He truly hadn't. He liked his life and the people he lived with on the farm. "Well, I guess I did when I was in prison. But then when I moved in to Dutch's, I was just happy to have a place to live that I liked and felt safe in."

"I tell you what. Come with me today as I go about my business and don't worry about making any decisions about anything."

"Thanks, Finn." Luther took a sip of coffee. "What's this business you're referring to, anyway?"

Finn stared at him. "What do you think I do all day? Sit around this apartment and watch television?"

"No——I just thought you wrote all day."

"Well, I don't. I'm not a hermit like some writers."

Luther winced and tried to change the subject. "Can I make you breakfast?"

"I thought you said you didn't cook."

"Well, I can make toast or something."

"Forget it. I'll make us an omelet."

"I'd like to help somehow."

"Helping would be watching me make the omelet, so you can learn how to make a real breakfast. Then you can wash the dishes afterward."

"Okay. How many eggs do you use?"

Finn stared at him a moment. "Well, depends on whether you're making a two-egg or three-egg omelet."

Luther sighed. "I see. Do you put anything in it besides eggs?"

Finn shook his head. "If you're making a cheese omelet. You'd put cheese in it."

Luther decided to stop asking questions and just watch. When they sat down to eat, Luther decided to try again. "Where are we going today?"

"You'll see."

"Well, what time do I have to be ready?"

"One o'clock. Be ready to go in half an hour."

Luther glanced at the clock. "We need four hours to get there?"

"No. Just be ready." Finn took his last bite of breakfast and put his plate and fork in the sink. "I'm taking my shower."

Luther smiled and shook his head as Finn left the kitchen. He was definitely a character. He would follow Jed's advice about not calling the farm, but he decided he could text Juniper. She would not have to know where he was, just that he was doing fine and missed her. She answered back immediately that everyone was fine, but the police continued to hound them about his whereabouts. Luther washed the dishes and went back to the living room to wait for Finn. He opened his book to read, but he couldn't concentrate. He thought about what Finn had said about the fact that he was forty and had never really been anywhere besides San Francisco, San Quentin, and Garberville. And that the only people who cared a whit about him were Dutch and the others on the farm. And Jed and Monica. When Finn came into the living room, Luther blurted out, "Hey, I would like to see some of the sights."

"Glad to hear since that was my plan this morning. Let's go." Finn took his jacket out of the closet and started toward the door. Luther grabbed his and followed him out. "We'll check out the Village another day since I live here. I figure you need to see the obvious tourist places, just so you can say you've seen them."

"The Village?"

"You're in Greenwich Village. We can take the subway to 34th and check out the Empire State Building. Then walk up Broadway to Times Square."

"Where do we have to be at one?"

"Central Park."

"Are we meeting someone there? At the park?"

"You could say that."

They got off the subway at Penn Station and when they were up the stairs and on the street, Luther's mouth dropped. "Jeez, there are a lot of people!"

"Welcome to Manhattan."

"San Francisco can get a little crowded downtown, but nothing like this."

"There's no place like New York. Not London, not Paris, and certainly not San Francisco. You don't have to like the city, but there's no arguing that it's one of a kind."

They walked past Macy's and started up Broadway to Times Square. Finn led him past the Museum of Modern Art, the Plaza Hotel and they arrived at the Central Park Zoo around noon. Luther spotted a hot dog cart. "Hey man, how about a hot dog. I bet they're better than the ones we had in prison."

"Yeah. Sure. We can have hot dogs, but we have to go over to Nathan's sometime to have a real New York hot dog." They ate their hot dogs watching the seals in the sea lion pond, and then walked past the carousel and stopped to enjoy the sights and sounds of the joyful children. They reached their destination right at one. "Here we are," Finn nodded toward a building with a sign out front saying Chess and Checkers House.

Luther gazed doubtfully at the many stone tables with checkerboards etched on them. "Are we going to play?"

"I sometimes play a little after I teach," Finn answered.

"Teach? You teach chess? Because I'm gonna need some help."

Finn stared at Luther and grinned. "No. I teach writing."

"Here? They come here to write instead of play chess?"

"Both, either, or neither," Finn sighed as he entered the building.

Luther followed Finn reluctantly until he reached a couple of tables with a motley crew of about twenty around them. They varied in age from teenagers to grey-haired, and were all genders and ethnicities. The one thing they all seemed to have in common was their disheveled appearance. Along the walls of the building were some shopping carts filled with a potpourri of items: stuffed black plastic garbage bags, sleeping bags and backpacks, and a few dogs lying quietly. Finn sat down and motioned Luther to follow suit. Luther looked over at the Black teenage boy on his right and nodded.

"Hey man," said the boy.

"Hey," Luther answered.

"Your first time?"

"Yeah."

"You can get a pen and one of those books over there." The boy pointed to a small table next to where Finn was standing, with a cup of pens and a pile of old-fashioned, black and white patterned composition books. Luther went over and took a pen and book and returned to his seat. "I'm Theo."

"Nice meeting you, Theo. I'm Luther."

"Cool. That's Rocco sitting next to you." Luther turned around to greet the middle-aged man, but his head was on the table and he was snoring softly. "He's kinda crazy. I look out for him." Theo flashed a big smile. "Kinda like a bodyguard."

"Uh, that's nice of you."

"Oh, he pays me."

"I see." Luther wondered why he wasn't in school or working or even if he had a family, but didn't ask any questions.

"Let's get started," Finn said and the conversations around the table trailed off. "Who has a prompt for our quick write today?"

Luther watched as the group glanced around the room, wondering what a prompt was and looking to see if anyone offered one. "We start every meeting writing for ten minutes without stopping or anything," Theo whispered.

"Yes, Celeste?" Finn said, calling on an older woman.

Luther watched the woman rise slowly, leaning on a cane. "Describe an experience that changed the direction of your life."

The nodding of heads was widespread so Finn replied, "Looks like the majority likes it, so let's get to work." A few people started writing immediately, but most had their pens either tapping the table or their hand, or in their mouth as they thought about what to write.

Luther sat frozen. He knew exactly what he wanted to write about, but didn't want to share it with this group. He leaned over and whispered to Theo, "Do we have to read what we write aloud?"

"Nah, only if you want to." Fortified with that, Luther started to write and was amazed how quickly and effortlessly the words flowed. In fact, he was so engrossed that he found himself sorry when Finn announced that it was time to stop. "Wow, you wrote a lot and fast!" Theo exclaimed.

Luther smiled shyly. "Oh, I'm sure everyone here can relate to that prompt." He looked over at Rocco to see if he was awake and writing and saw that his head was off the table and there were, in fact, a few words on the page.

"Who'd like to read theirs?" Finn asked. Several hands went up and Luther listened to the tales of job loss, drug and alcohol abuse, veterans with PTSD, broken families, and the other common causes of homelessness. "How about you, Luther?" Finn said. Luther shook his head vehemently.

"I'll read mine," Rocco said, standing up and pounding the table with his fist.

Finn walked over to Luther's table. "Go ahead, Rocco."

Rocco cleared his throat and looked dramatically around the room. He raised his notebook from the table and read, " It was all my fault." He paused, looked at Finn and nodded, and then sat back down.

"Can you explain what you mean? What was all your fault?" Finn asked as the others in the room glanced at each other and shrugged their shoulders. Rocco put his head back down on the table and said nothing. Finn nodded and strode back to the front of the room. "Okay. Let's divide up into our critique groups and share the writing you did since we last met." Everyone moved around the room into groups of five or six. Luther looked at Finn for guidance about what he should do. "Come here, Luther," Finn said.

"What do you want me to do now?" Luther asked, approaching Finn.

"Just pick a group and listen to their stories. Give advice if you have something constructive to say." Luther started to walk away. "Or write your own story. Up to you."

Luther hadn't written much of anything since high school other than a few letters, but that sounded more appealing than listening to strangers' stories. He found a seat at one of the tables that was removed from the critique groups and continued writing about that fateful day more than twenty years ago that changed his life forever.

Chapter 8

AT FOUR O'CLOCK FINN ANNOUNCED THAT IT WAS TIME TO CLEAN UP. Luther watched the men and women fold up the tables and chairs and gather their things from the wall. He noticed that they put their notebooks in their bags and backpacks, so he followed suit and hung on to his. He waited for Finn to finish talking to several people and finally the room emptied. "Let's go," Finn said, motioning to Luther.

Luther zipped up his jacket and put his collar up against the dropping temperature, but it didn't help much. He wished he had a warmer jacket and some gloves. He studied Finn as they walked through the park, but Finn seemed oblivious. He hadn't even zipped up his coat. "You're not cold?" Luther asked as they descended the steps to the subway at 59th Street.

"I'm used to it. You Californians are wimps."

"Maybe so."

"You'll need to get yourself a metro card. You got a credit card?" Finn asked as they approached the turnstile to get into the subway station.

"No. Just cash."

"You can use cash in the machine," Finn said and pointed to the row of them. Luther went to the machine and tried to read the directions, but found the whole thing way too complicated for someone who barely knew how to use a computer and smart phone. He was embarrassed to ask Finn, so he tried to figure it out. "What's wrong?" Finn said impatiently as he approached Luther at the machine.

"I'm not sure how to do this."

Finn showed him how and Luther felt one step closer to living in this technology-fueled world. He watched people swipe their cards and was relieved that he didn't have to ask Finn how to do that too, although it took him a few tries before he got it right. "Hurry up, now," Finn said, grabbing Luther's sleeve. "Let's catch that train." Finn fairly dragged him towards the open door of a subway car that didn't look like another person could possibly fit inside. Luther jogged to the door and squeezed in after Finn just as the door was closing.

"This is a crazy way to live," Luther said breathlessly.

"I know. I usually try to skip rush hour for getting around, but can't change the time of my writing group. The soup kitchens serve dinner pretty early."

"Where do we get off? In case we get separated. Washington Square again?"

"No. We're on the west side now. Get off at Sheridan Square/Christopher Street."

"That's the closest subway to your apartment on the west side?"

"Yep. Are you starting to get the hang of it?"

"No. I'm just trying not to get lost."

Finn laughed. "Good idea. But we're not going home just yet."

"Where are we going now? It's damn cold out there."

"You'll get warmed up soon enough."

Luther gave up. He watched the station signs, as well as kept his eye on Finn, and it wasn't long before they were exiting the station onto Christopher Street. "Which way?" Luther asked.

"Up there to Bleecker Street and take a right. It's a just a few blocks to 11th Street, then a block to Hudson."

"So what's on Hudson?" Finn gave him a sideways glance, but didn't answer. A couple of cops were standing outside smoking in front of the NYPD precinct building. Luther quickened his pace.

They got to Hudson and turned left. "Here we are," Finn said as they stopped in front of the White Horse Tavern. "One of the oldest bars in New York." They went inside and Luther marveled at the woodwork. "It's not what it used to be," Finn said, taking a stool at the bar. "Used to be a haunt for writers, artists and musicians in the fifties and sixties. Now it's tourists and wannabes. But it's close to my apartment and they do serve a good drink." He chuckled. "Just ask Dylan Thomas."

"Who?"

Finn stared at Luther, incredulous. "Seriously? You never heard of Dylan Thomas?"

"Oh maybe," Luther lied. "Is he a poet or something?"

Finn shook his head. "Yeah, or something. You got a lot of learning to do, young man."

"Well," Luther smirked. "I guess you have your work cut out for you."

Finn sighed and called to the bartender, "Couple of Bushmills, neat." He then turned to Luther. "Bushmills is about the smoothest whiskey there is, easiest one to get down for you lightweights."

Luther laughed. "You're trying to turn me into an alcoholic?"

"No," Finn scoffed. "Trying to show you some of the finer things in life."

The bartender set their drinks down in front of them. Luther watched as Finn downed his in one gulp. "Do I have to drink the whole thing like you?"

"Drink it however you want." Finn gave him a look of disdain, but then slapped him playfully on the back and smiled.

Luther smiled back and took a sip. "I'm starting to understand you, Finn. You just pretend to be a grouch and a curmudgeon. You're actually a pretty nice guy."

"Got me pegged, do ya."

Luther grinned, knowing Finn would never admit it, but he knew he was right. The bartender automatically poured a second round. "So, what do you make of Rocco's statement?" Luther asked.

"It might be the first time he shared," Finn replied. "And maybe the first time he wrote anything. He usually uses our three hour writing class to sleep off his latest binge."

"You've never talked to him?"

"Nope. It's usually the same people who share and talk to me before or after class."

"How about Theo? The kid who was sitting next to me?"

"Yeah, he's a chatty one."

"Did you know that Rocco pays him to take care of him?"

Finn was quiet for a moment. "No. I didn't know that."

"Do you know Theo's story?"

"Hasn't written much about his life. He's a typical teenager, writing mostly horror shit."

The bartender approached. "Having another pair, Finn?"

"I'm good," Luther replied.

"Just put it on my tab." Finn said, rising from his stool.

"Are we leaving?" Luther asked, checking the time on his phone.

"Why? You have a hot date?" Finn grinned.

"No, but I snuck a peek at the menu. I'd like to buy you dinner."

"You're going to buy me dinner? I'm not a cheap date, you know."

"I've got money." Finn looked at him warily. "Don't worry. I'm being careful. Dutch gave me a nice . . . uh, advance."

Finn nodded. "I see. Well, okay. That'd be nice. Let's grab a table and make it a real meal." He walked over to the hostess and they were soon sitting at a table with menus in hand.

"Man, I haven't had chicken wings since I was a kid!" Luther sighed. "And I didn't know sweet potato fries were a thing." Luther closed the menu.

"Are you ready to order?" the waitress said, approaching the table.

Luther looked at Finn. "Go ahead and order," Finn said.

"Chicken wings, sweet potato fries and a cheeseburger, medium," Luther ordered, sneaking a peek at Finn to see if he was laughing at him.

"I'll have the same but make my burger well done. And I'll have a Guinness."

"And a drink for you, sir?" the waitress asked Luther.

"Uh," Luther paused. "A Budweiser, please." Finn scoffed and the waitress grinned knowingly as she walked away. Luther crumpled his napkin and spoke sweet and low. "And no shit from you, Finn."

That was the first time Luther heard Finn genuinely laugh. So much so that he was rather breathless until the waitress came back with their beers. "So," Finn finally exhaled. "Did you write much in your notebook today?"

Luther smiled. "Yes I did. It was kind of fun. It was like being back in school."

"Did you like to write back then?"

"Didn't think much about it. I was just trying to get good enough grades to get into college."

"Did you succeed at that?"

"Yeah." Luther took a deep breath. "I was going to San Francisco State in the fall when . . ." He stopped. Sometimes he felt ashamed even though it wasn't his fault.

"I assume that's what you wrote about to answer the prompt."

Luther nodded. "Hey Finn, how'd you get involved in teaching the homeless?"

"Jed was homeless when I met him. He opened my eyes to their plight, as they say. I was a high school English teacher before I was an author and I taught writing to the residents at the senior place in Venice Beach. When I moved back to New York, I came up with this as a way to help the homeless."

"Do you like it?"

"Yeah. I do."

"How often do you teach there?"

"Twice a week at the park. I also teach writing at Covenant House."

"What's that?"

"It's for homeless youth. They offer a lot of different services."

Luther was quiet for a minute. "Does Theo know about it?"

"I'm sure he does." The waitress brought their food and they started eating. Luther with gusto and Finn with some trepidation, but the plates were clean when they finished.

"Dessert?" the waitress asked as she cleared the table.

"I'm stuffed."

"Maybe just an Irish coffee," Finn replied. "How about you, Luther?"

"Nah, I'm good. I can't keep up with you, Finn."

"Not many can."

It was after eleven when they got back to the apartment and Luther wanted nothing more than to curl up on the couch. Finn picked up on Luther's exhaustion and went to the bedroom to read. Luther slept fitfully, however, his active mind not allowing his weary body to stay asleep for more than an hour at a time. What was he going to do? Where was he going to go? How afraid should he be of being found? He thought about Rocco and Theo and how close he had been, and could still be, to being homeless himself. He finally fell into a deep sleep, but was woken by a text. He looked at his phone and saw it was Juniper, asking him if he was okay. They texted back and forth about the farm and everyone there and it made him realize how much he missed her and the farm. He tried to get back to sleep when they stopped texting, but lay awake for most of the night.

Chapter 9

FINN TIPTOED PAST THE SOFA AS HE WENT INTO THE KITCHEN FOR HIS MORNING CUP OF COFFEE. "No need to be quiet," Luther mumbled. "I'm awake."

"Good," Finn muttered, fishing a book out of his robe pocket. "Here's a book about New York. Pick out some places you want to go." Finn threw a guidebook onto the coffee table.

"Thanks." Luther picked up the book and leafed through it. He stopped at the section on Greenwich Village and read about the bohemian culture of the 1950's and 60's: Jack Kerouac and the other poets and writers, the Beat generation, the Stonewall Inn where the gay community rioted and the LGBT rights movement started, the jazz and folk movement. "Hey, Finn, they mention the White Horse Tavern and all the authors, artists and musicians who made it famous. I guess it wasn't just Dylan Thomas."

"Yeah, but Dylan Thomas made it famous by drinking himself to death there."

Luther wasn't sure how to respond to that. Maybe Finn ought to take that as a lesson to be learned, but instead he said, "I guess Bob Dylan started out here too. I think there is plenty for me to see right here in Greenwich Village."

"Check out the book some more, but we can start here in the village."

"I'd like to keep going with you to the writing classes."

"Glad to hear it. You have a good story. You should write it."

Luther sighed. "When I first got out of prison, I was hounded by the press and the Innocence Project to write a book. There were even some Hollywood types interested. But I didn't want to be exposed."

"Don't think about publishing it. Just write it for yourself. But I warn you––you may find the act of writing empowering. And hell––your story is timely, with all the focus on racism and brutality in the police force."

"Are you in the middle of writing a new book?"

"Not at the moment," Finn answered dismissively. Then he made a crooked little smile. "If you don't get going on yours, I may steal it."

"Like you did Jed's?" Luther grinned.

"Why not? I've already written mine."

"I'd like to read yours, too."

Finn got up and took a copy of *Ode to Forgiveness: A Memoir* off a bookshelf and gave it to Luther. "Have a ball."

"Do you teach today?" Luther asked.

"At Covenant House."

"In the morning or afternoon?"

"Afternoon. Same time as yesterday. At one. Do you want to come?"

"Actually I think I'd like to stay home and read your books today, if that's okay."

Finn scowled. "Do whatever the hell you want."

"Okay," Luther laughed. "Just trying to be a good houseguest."

"Yeah, well I don't like that nice shit. I'd rather you think this is your place, even if you are sleeping on the couch."

"You got it, man. I'll do my best to be a pain in the ass, like any other roommate."

"So that's life back on the farm?"

"No, of course not."

Finn rolled his eyes. "Then for crying out loud just be yourself."

"I am!"

Finn left the room without another word and Luther felt a little nervous about defending himself. Well, Finn didn't tell him to leave, so he presumed he gave him what he wanted. Some backbone. Some pride. Luther chuckled, picked up Finn's memoir and started reading.

The day went by with little interaction between them. Finn left the house mid-morning and Luther spent the day reading, napping, and snacking. He hadn't spent a day like that since he left prison. The farm always had work for him to do and since he was the youngest and the strongest male, much of it was left to him. Luther actually relished in his lazy day and was able to get halfway through both of Finn's books, but he didn't even open the NYC guidebook. He really wasn't that interested in sightseeing. There was too much on his mind.

Finn arrived home after five to find Luther asleep on the couch. He poured himself a couple of fingers of whiskey and sat down at the kitchen table. Luther appeared in the doorway, yawning and stretching. "I guess I was more tired than I realized."

"Jet lag, I suppose," Finn replied.

"How was the writing class?" Luther asked, pouring himself his own two fingers.

"You don't have to drink my whiskey if you don't like it," Finn said condescendingly.

Luther shot him a look as he sat down. "I know."

"Glad you know it. Well, class was fine, though I may need a break from dealing with teenagers."

"Can't blame you there."

"What'd you do today besides sleep?"

"Got halfway through both your books."

"And?" Finn asked.

"You're a great writer. You really pulled me in."

"I'm not looking for a critique of my writing. I'm curious about your reaction to the content."

"You mean about the very difficult lives both you and Jed have led? That I'm not the only one who's had crap happen to him?" Finn laughed. "Well?" Luther pushed.

"I do think it's good to write out your demons. Cleanse yourself or something. Nothing more specific than that, really."

"Then let's talk about something else," Luther said and then took a deep breath. "I've been thinking about what I should do now." He paused, waiting for Finn to say something, but he didn't. "Uh, I kind of wanted your opinion."

"Then out with it and I'll give it."

"Okay. I'm just not sure that I should have run away from the investigation. I don't want to spend the rest of my life being afraid." Luther tried to decipher Finn's reaction from his face, but Finn gave out no clues. "Running away isn't going to change the things that happen to me."

Finn nodded. "I think that's true. Might even have made it worse . . . running away. Doesn't look good from the standpoint of law enforcement."

Luther glanced towards the window and then looked back at Finn. "So do you agree that I should go back?"

"Let me think about it for a while and I'll get back to you." Finn slapped his knees and got up. "Let's make some dinner. Better yet, let's go out to dinner. I don't feel like cooking."

"White Horse?" Luther asked.

"Let's go down to Katz's Deli. Can't be in New York without eating pizza or Jewish food. You've already had the pizza."

Luther laughed. "They don't have Jews anywhere but New York?"

"Food's just not the same. Plenty of Jews and delis in Los Angeles and Chicago and San Francisco, but they just don't hold a candle."

"Well, Katz sounds fine with me. I'm definitely not going to get that in Garberville."

"Good. We may have to go more than once, then, to sample all of it."

"I may be a lightweight when it comes to whiskey," Luther replied, "but I can handle a lot of food pretty damn well."

"Good, because that's what they give you - a lot of food. Are you ready to go?"

"I am as long as I don't need to shave or shower."

"I don't care. Do you smell?"

"I don't think so."

Finn walked over and took a few sniffs. "You're good. Let's go."

"Will I need my subway card?"

"You mean your metro card? No. We'll walk."

"How long will it take?" Luther asked as he followed Finn down the stairs of the brownstone.

"Twenty minutes or so."

"At the speed you walk or normal people's speed?" Luther smiled.

Finn ignored the remark and pushed open the door and turned left. "Just do your best to keep up, young man."

They were seated quickly at Katz's and Finn grabbed the menu out of Luther's hands before he had a chance to open it. "Hey, what are you doing?" Luther asked.

"I'll order for you."

Luther raised his hands in mock defense. "Okay. Whatever you say."

The waiter arrived and Finn ordered a pastrami sandwich, a kosher hot dog, potato knishes, matzo ball soup, noodle kugel, chopped liver, gefilte fish and pickles. "We'll get bagels and lox to go for breakfast tomorrow. Oh and some whitefish or sturgeon. You ever had sturgeon?"

Luther laughed. "The only things I've even heard of that you ordered are hot dogs and pickles!"

"Well, you're in for a treat then. Oh, I should have ordered tongue too."

"Tongue? Seriously? I don't think so. Even chopped liver sounds a little dicey."

"Is that a pun?"

"What?"

"Never mind. I thought you said you weren't a light-weight when it came to food."

"I just meant that I could eat a lot."

Finn scoffed. "Well, that's good because we'll need to have cheesecake and rugelachs for dessert."

"Okay, Finn. Fatten me up."

"You could use a little fattening up."

The waiter brought the food and the dishes covered the whole table. "Jeez, Finn. This is really a lot of food."

"So eat as much as you want and we can bring the rest home. No big deal."

"I'll do my best."

The waiter brought two empty plates and handed them to Finn since there was no room on the table. "I figured you were sharing all this," he said as he walked away.

Luther took half the pastrami sandwich and a few knishes. He bit into the sandwich. "This is delicious."

"Thought you'd like this food," Finn said as he cut the hot dog in half. He waved at the waiter who arrived promptly. "Another soup bowl, please."

Luther ate heartily and Finn ate enough so that between them they finished it all. "I'm stuffed, but it was all really good. I don't think I have room for dessert though."

"We'll take it home along with tomorrow's breakfast."

"Thanks for the introduction to Jewish food, Finn."

"You've missed a lot of years. You've got some learning to do."

"The teacher in you is showing," Luther smiled.

"You never lose that. Now, let's order our stuff to go and get the hell out of here." Finn stood, threw some money on the table and started walking toward the deli counter. Luther followed him like a puppy dog.

They arrived home and Finn went on his computer immediately. Luther knew better than to ask him what he was doing. He picked up Finn's memoir and started reading. He wanted to understand him better, since they would be in very close quarters for the next . . . who knew how long. After an hour or so of silence Luther decided he wanted to try the cheesecake. "Do you want dessert?" he asked Finn.

"You go ahead. Maybe bring me a couple of rugelachs."

Luther opened the bag and took out one of the rugelachs. He turned it over in his hand, looking at it from every angle, and then popped it in his mouth. He smiled, took out two more and brought them to Finn. "Good stuff," he said as he set them down in front of Finn.

"Yup." Finn took a bite and went back to typing.

Luther went back to the kitchen and took out the cheesecake. He dug a fork into it and ate it. "Wow," he said. "This cheesecake is incredible!" he shouted at Finn. Finn didn't answer, but Luther didn't expect him to. He was obviously engrossed in whatever he was doing on his computer. Luther went back to the sofa and continued reading his book, sneaking glances at Finn every now and then, as well as at his phone to see what time it was. It was getting late and what was most surprising to Luther was that Finn had not had a drink tonight. He figured that was unusual. "Uh, Finn? Just curious . . . you're not drinking. Maybe that's why you're not tired?"

"You checking up on me? I'm not an alcoholic, Luther. I like my whiskey but I don't need it."

"Okay. As I said . . . just curious." Finn went to the bedroom and Luther made up the couch.

Chapter 10

LUTHER OPENED HIS EYES AND SAW FINN LOOK-ING OUT THE WINDOW OF THE LIVING ROOM. "It's snowing . . . hard," Finn said as he sipped his coffee.

"Seriously?" Luther got up and stood next to Finn. "Wow! I've never seen it snow like this."

"You've never seen snow?"

"Not this much."

"I thought it snowed in northern California."

"In the mountains, I guess."

"You've never been to the mountains, then?"

"Well, the hills around Garberville. They are really high, rugged hills. And there's a place called Murder Mountain . . ."

Finn looked over at Luther incredulously. "Murder Mountain?"

"It's what they call a place east of Garberville where there have been several unsolved murders. There's even a documentary about it. I thought maybe you'd seen it or at least heard of it."

Finn shook his head. "So why don't those deputies look there for a murder suspect?"

Luther took a breath and stared out the window. "Yeah, they should." He then turned and walked away.

"Everything you just said and did suggests there's more to the story," Finn observed dryly. Luther said nothing more and went into the bathroom.

Finn shrugged and continued to sip his coffee as he watched the blizzard getting worse. He stood up when Luther returned. "Coffee's made. I'll get the bagels, lox and sturgeon."

Luther followed Finn into the kitchen. "Can I help?"

"Can you slice bagels?" Finn asked.

"What do you mean can I? You take a knife and saw 'em in half. Is there something I need to know?"

"There's a bit of an art to it. You want to make the halves even when you slice them. There are mathematical theories on how best to do it."

"Wow," Luther observed sarcastically. "You went from art to science. Maybe you should do it so I don't screw it up."

"If you want to keep your lox and sturgeon from falling off, then yes, maybe I should. You get the stuff out of the refrigerator. I'll cut the bagels."

"Whatever you say," Luther replied as he headed to the refrigerator. "Never pegged you as a neatnik."

"You don't know a lot about me!"

"Just teasing, Finn." Luther started rummaging around. "As Buster would say, don't have a hissy fit."

Finn scoffed. "Just get the stuff out, will ya?"

Luther put the lox and sturgeon on plates and got out forks and knives. Finn put the sliced bagels on plates and brought them to the table while Luther poured himself a cup of coffee and refilled Finn's. They sat down and Luther waited to see what Finn did, but Finn sat quietly sipping his coffee and didn't touch the food. "Uh, aren't you going to eat?" Luther asked. After the slicing debacle he wasn't about to approach the meal the wrong way.

"Yeah, in a bit." Finn sat back in his chair and smiled. Luther took a half a bagel and put a piece of lox on it. "Looks like you forgot something," Finn added playfully.

"Huh? Isn't this the lox? And the white stuff's the sturgeon?"

"It needs cream cheese."

"Well, you didn't tell me that."

"Didn't think I needed to."

Luther sighed. "You enjoying yourself? Laughing at me?"

"Yes, actually." Finn went to the refrigerator and took out the cream cheese. He sat back down. "Watch me."

Finn took two halves and spread them both with cream cheese. He put lox on one and sturgeon on the other. Luther copied him and they both bit into their bagels. "Man! This is good! The sturgeon especially."

"Well don't get too enamored. It's very expensive. Ever eaten caviar?"

"What do you think, Finn? You think a Black kid growing up in the projects has ever eaten caviar?"

Luther shook his head in disgust. "You know, you sure are an enigma."

"Oh look at you. Coming out with such a big word." Luther didn't answer. "You're just easy to tease," Finn added.

"Why's that?"

"Cuz it bothers you. If you didn't care, I wouldn't do it."

"I don't believe that, Finn. I think you get a real kick out of mocking people."

They ate their breakfast in silence until Finn finally said, "I'll clean up here."

"Okay," Luther said as he stood up.

"Sorry, kid," Finn murmured as Luther left the kitchen.

Finn stayed on his computer while Luther did some more reading and soon it was close to noon. "Don't you have your writing group today?" Luther asked. "Or won't they come out in this weather?"

"They're already out in this weather. The writing group is a chance to get some shelter for a few hours."

"Hadn't thought of that."

"Are you coming with me today?" Finn asked as he opened the closet door and took out a pair of boots.

"I'd like to, but I didn't bring boots and I don't have a heavy coat."

"Well, I can't help you with the boots," Finn said looking down at Luther's feet. "But I can put some layers on you. Let's see, where's that old raincoat? Go on, put on your jacket." Finn helped him put the coat over his jacket. "There, now you look like you really belong to the group."

"I don't think I can move."

"You'll be okay. You now have more padding if you fall."

"That's so reassuring . . ."

"Yeah," Finn replied, steering him out the door. "Now just imagine you're my age."

They took the subway and this time they got off at the 72nd Street station to be closer to the park, but it was still quite a trek to the Chess and Checkers House. Luther was covered in snow and his feet were soaked, but he looked around at the group of people waiting to get in and realized that these people had to put up with this all the time. He saw Rocco and Theo and went over to sit down. "Hey man you're back!" Theo said.

"Oh shit, I forgot my notebook," Luther answered as he saw that Theo and Rocco both had theirs open. Rocco looked more awake than he had the other day.

"Finn has extras," Rocco said.

Luther looked at Rocco with surprise. He seemed much more affable and alert. "Oh, thanks. It's okay. I'll just listen to everyone else's stories."

"What about the quick write, though?" Theo asked.

Rocco tore a couple of pages out of his notebook and handed them to Luther.

"Not a problem."

"Thanks Rocco," Luther whispered as Finn asked everyone to quiet down.

"Any suggestions for a prompt for the quick write today?" Finn asked. Luther looked around the room, but no one stood or raised their hand. "My, what a deafening response." Someone laughed and everyone was looking around, but still no prompts were offered. "I guess it's up to me. 'What do you want to resolve in your life?'" His gaze settled on Luther, and then he took out his phone and scrolled. "To resolve is to seek resolution, which involves intention, decision, determination, courage and fortitude."

The room fell silent. Everyone was looking inward, especially Luther, because he knew why Finn chose this prompt. But he was stymied on what to write. He knew what he had to resolve, but he didn't know how to do it. He was still ambivalent about going back to Garberville. He'd be taking a chance and he didn't trust the legal system to be fair. Why should he after what he'd been through? Anyway, he wasn't sure Dutch wanted him back this soon. He looked over at Theo and Rocco and they were both writing. Rocco's paper already had a couple of paragraphs, a far cry from the five words he had written the last time. Luther felt someone standing over him and looked up to see Finn gazing down at him with an expression that resembled fondness.

"Just write without thinking about it," Finn said quietly. "It's the best way. You can throw it away if you don't like it, but writing from your gut, your first impression, is always the truth." Finn walked away and Luther took the pen and started scribbling whatever came to his mind and was sorry when Finn said time was up. He had written two pages about his indecision and his lack of courage, not exactly resolution.

"I need another minute or two!" someone yelled from across the room.

Finn ignored her and asked, "Who'd like to read theirs?"

Many wrote about trying to get clean and sober or getting a job or a place to live. Then Rocco stood, but he didn't read off his paper. He just said, "There is no resolution. I should be punished for the rest of my life." Then he sat down and the room was silent.

Finn and Luther didn't mention Rocco's statement on the way home, but when they got there Finn poured whiskey into a glass and offered it to Luther. "Thanks. I think I will," Luther said as he took the glass.

"So what did you write about today?" Finn asked as he sat down next to Luther on the sofa, his own glass of whiskey in hand.

Luther shrugged. "I know what needs to be resolved, but I have no answers."

"There are no right answers. You make choices and live with the consequences."

"That's hardly encouraging."

"It's life, Luther. But it doesn't mean there aren't answers."

Luther looked at him skeptically. "I don't get you, sometimes, Finn. You just said there weren't any and now you say there are?"

"I said there are no right answers, but there are solutions and actions you can take. It depends on what outcome is more amenable to you."

"Why don't you help me out and tell me what you think is the action I should take?"

"It's not my place to tell you what to do. I'm happy to be your sounding board, though."

"I'm afraid to go back because I don't think I'd get treated fairly."

"So you'd rather be on the run?"

"No. I'd rather they found out who murdered that guy and leave me out of it."

Finn took a sip of whiskey. "I think you do know who. Am I right?"

Luther took a deep breath. "I have an idea. That's all."

"So why don't you tell them your idea?"

"Because it might get some people I care about into trouble."

Finn nodded. "I see."

Luther finished his whiskey. "I'm starting to like this stuff. Think I'll pour another couple of fingers." He went and got the bottle from the kitchen.

"So, what did you think of Rocco's quick write?" Finn asked as he poured himself more than a couple of fingers worth of whiskey.

"He certainly feels guilty about something and is beating himself up over it.""Interesting word, resolution," Finn mused. "Is it a process or an outcome?"

"I always thought it was an outcome."

"Hmm. How about decision? There's the process of deciding and then there's a decision made."

"Maybe it has to do with whether it's used as a verb or a noun?" Luther asked tentatively.

Finn smiled. "That's a way of looking at it. Where does an adjective fit in, then?"

"What is the adjective for resolution?" Luther asked.

"Resolute." Luther looked perplexed. "She was resolute in her opposition," Finn added.

"It doesn't sound right."

"You're questioning a retired high school English teacher about his grammar knowledge?" Finn raised his eyebrows.

"I know." Luther was embarrassed. "I don't know what I'm talking about."

Finn laughed. "You really do need to learn how to take a joke."

Luther shook his head and sighed. "Maybe you're right. Or maybe you need to stop teasing me."

"Aw for Christ's sake, Luther. I'm in my eighties. Too late for me to make any major changes to my personality."

"It's never too late for at least a little change." Finn gave him a knowing look. "Okay. Well, what are we doing for dinner? I'm getting hungry. Aren't you?"

Finn chuckled. "Talking about change, do you care if it doesn't include the four main food groups?"

"Nope," Luther grinned. "In fact I kind of like it that way."

Finn stood and picked up the bottle to bring into the kitchen. "Let's go pig out."

Luther started handing things out of the fridge to Finn. "Hey Finn, do you like teaching the writing groups?"

Finn shrugged. "I don't know how much they really get out of my being there. It's not like they couldn't write on their own. I see it as more of a routine they have to adhere to."

"Then that's why you're important to them."

"I think you're making way too much out of my influence." He looked at the last thing Luther handed to him. "What the hell is this?"

"I dunno. It looks like it should be eaten, though."

"Or thrown out!"

"That too," Luther laughed. "Now how does the saying go? A teacher touches a life forever. I saw that on a tote bag once."

"One teacher, one book, one pen can change the world. They are our most powerful weapons." Finn grinned back. "I can quote tote bags just as well as you can."

"Touché, Finn." Just then Luther got a text. He took out his phone and said, "Oh, it's Juniper." He opened his messages and his relaxed smile turned into a frown as he narrowed his eyes. "Shit!"

"What's up?"

"Just a sec," Luther said as he typed. He put his phone away and took a deep breath. "She said the police came by today looking for me and apparently harassed Juniper in particular."

"But she doesn't know where you are, right?"

"No. I didn't tell her on purpose. But Juniper doesn't take shit from anyone. She probably threw it right back at 'em."

"So what happened?"

"I guess Dutch intervened and they left. But not before they vowed that they'd find me, and that I'm in a heap of trouble."

"That's just their way to break down witnesses" Luther made no response, but Finn could see the fear rising in his eyes. He finally asked, "So what do you want to do?"

Luther shrugged. "I guess I can't go to the farm."

"When you don't know what to do, do nothing at all."

"That's exactly what Jed told me."

"Must be the right thing to do then."

"You mean stay here?" Luther asked.

"You were looking for some kind of resolution and we already discussed that it's a process. So staying here is part of the process. You don't have to make any lifelong decision. It's just the next thing you're doing. You ever heard the term, liminality?"

"No. What is it?"

"Look it up." Finn replied as he started opening containers. "I'm hungry."

Chapter 11

LUTHER WOKE TO THE SMELL OF COFFEE, BUT FINN WAS NOWHERE TO BE FOUND. He poured himself a cup and opened the refrigerator in the hopes of finding more bagels and lox. There was none, but he did find a couple of rugelachs. They were a little stale, but still delicious. Finn walked in just as Luther sat down with his coffee and plate of cookies. "Slept in, did ya?" Finn said as he dumped a bag on the couch next to Luther.

"Is it that late?" Luther asked.

Finn shook his head. "You just can't tell when I'm teasing you. You really need to learn that, among other things."

"What's that supposed to mean?"

"Did you look up liminality?"

"Yeah, I did." Luther scrolled through his phone. "Liminality is a state of transition between one stage and the next, especially between stages in one's life or a rite of passage." He looked up at Finn, standing over him. "I'd say that's right on."

"Does it help?"

"Help what?" Luther asked.

"Help you not worry about what to do at this moment in time."

"Yes it does."

"Limen is Latin for threshold. Liminal space is a crossing over place, leaving one place behind, but not yet in a new place. Just look at this time in New York as that. You don't have to stay here, but you don't have to go back to face the music either. Anyway, is it so bad living with this old curmudgeon?"

"Most of the time, no. Look Finn, I'm so appreciative––"

"Don't get all mushy on me. Open the bag."

Luther peeked inside the bag and took out a book. *Man's Search for Meaning.* He smiled at Finn. "Thanks."

"Viktor Frankl is a good starting place."

"Starting place?" Luther asked.

"To start your journey."

"Where am I going?"

"What were we just talking about? Think about it." At that Finn went to the kitchen.

Luther skimmed through the book. "Looks interesting, but I'm more interested in finding some breakfast first," he announced, putting the book aside for later.

Finn opened the freezer and threw a package of English muffins on the counter. "You need to be more resourceful. Look around more." He took some butter and jam out of the fridge and placed them on the counter as well. "Are you used to being waited on?"

"No! Well, maybe. I was in prison, after all, and Juniper does most of the prep and cooking at the farm." Luther grinned. "I guess I am used to being waited on."

"Then it's time to change your tune. You can do the next bit of grocery shopping. You've got money, right?"

"Yes, Finn," Luther sighed.

"I'll go with you today and show you where the stores are."

"Do you teach writing today?"

Finn shook his head. "Nope. Do you have something you'd like to do?"

"Not specifically. How about you?"

"You really don't have much interest in sightseeing do you, Luther?"

"I guess I'm just not a city guy anymore."

"You like this living on a farm business, eh?" Finn asked.

"I've just grown to like open space and fewer people."

Finn shrugged. "Whatever floats your boat."

Luther opened the English muffins and put one in the toaster. "Do you want one?"

"You gonna make it for me?"

"Would I ask you if I wasn't going to make it for you?"

"You need to lighten up, kid."

"Maybe if you had the cops after you, you'd under-stand."

"I've had the cops after me so I understand."

"You want to tell me that story now?"

"Jed never told you what happened when we both lived in Venice?"

"Why would he?"

"My wife had died and she had a nurse taking care of her towards the end of her life. Turned out Jed knew the nurse in Jonestown." Finn paused. "You wanna push the lever down on the toaster so we could eat some break-fast?" Finn looked at the clock on the stove. "Or maybe it's lunch now."

"Oh, sorry." Luther pushed the lever down and looked back to Finn, eager to hear the rest of the story. He waited but Finn said nothing. The muffins popped up and Finn took out a couple of plates and handed them to Luther who put the muffins on them. "So what happened with the nurse?" he said as he sat down.

Finn joined him at the table and spread the butter and jam. He took a bite of his muffin and set it down. "She died in a motel room in Venice and we were both under suspicion."

"Why?"

"She had come to Venice to blackmail me. But Jed's fingerprints were found in her motel room, so he was the one they were more focused on."

Luther waited for him to continue, but Finn kept eating his muffin without talking. "So how did it all get worked out?" Luther finally asked.

"I don't know. I guess they decided she died from a fall. Anyway, Jed had left Venice for San Francisco by then and they lost interest in pursuing it."

"I can see them thinking Jed was involved because of his fingerprints, but why you?"

"They knew she was trying to blackmail me."

"Why was she trying to blackmail you?" Luther asked.

Finn scoffed. "She thought I killed my wife."

Luther almost choked on his muffin. "Uh, what?"

"Jesus, don't try to eat the whole thing at once. That's enough of that." Finn stood up. "I've got a couple of things to do before we go grocery shopping. You can take care of the dishes." Luther managed to swallow and stared after him.

Finn gave him a tour of the NYU campus on their way to the grocery store. "Are you trying to send me off to college?" Luther finally asked.

"Why not? Couldn't hurt."

"I had planned to go to college, you know, until those twenty years got in my way."

"'Life is what happens to you when you're busy making other plans.' John Lennon knew what he was talking about. You just gotta go with the flow."

"Wise advice, I guess."

Finn grinned. "Yeah, I'm a regular wise guy."

They shopped with both of them throwing things in the cart that they wanted, allowing their cravings to rule over their health. They laughed together as they emptied the bags and put their purchases in the re-frigerator and cabinet. "So does this mean we are pre-paring and eating our own meals?" Luther asked. "Or should we plan on one nutritious meal a day and then eat junk the rest of the time?"

"I'm not used to thinking and planning so much," Finn replied. "I've been alone the last few years and didn't have to answer to anyone."

"I-I didn't mean—-"

"Christ, Luther, Stop apologizing all the time," Finn interrupted. "I'm not complaining about it. Just making a comment." Luther opened his mouth in defense, but closed it quickly. He was beginning to realize that some-times no response was the best response. Finn took a glass and a bottle out of the cabinet. "It's never too early for cocktail hour. Care to join me?"

Luther glanced up at the clock. "Nah, three's a little early for me. I think I'll catch up on my reading. After all, I have both your books to finish and now this one about looking for meaning."

"Suit yourself." Finn swallowed the whiskey in one gulp. "I'm going to take a nap."

Luther took Finn's book about Jed and settled into the couch to start reading when his phone dinged. It was Juniper texting. "I have some bad news," it said.

Luther immediately dialed her number. "What's wrong?" he asked when she picked up.

"Homer's in the hospital. He fell."

"Will he be okay?"

"They don't know yet."

"Did he break anything?"

"They're checking." Juniper swallowed a sob. "I knew this would happen someday, but I'm still not prepared."

"Oh Juni–– some things are just . . ." Luther lamented. "I wish I was there."

"We are all taking turns sitting with him at the hospital. Buster's taking it even harder than I am."

"Are you there now?"

"No. I'm home to try to get some sleep. Buster and Dutch are with him now."

"Will you call me when you are there so I can talk to him?" Luther asked.

"Okay. I'll let you know what the doctor says as soon as we hear."

"How did he fall?"

"We don't know exactly what happened. I found him on the floor of his room last night and we rushed him to the hospital. He said his legs just gave out, trying to get to the bathroom and he couldn't move them." She started to cry.

"Is this the first time he's fallen?" Luther asked.

"No, but it's the first time he said he was hurt and he's the one that said we needed to take him to the hospital."

"I should come––!"

"No, Luther. Don't come now. Things haven't settled down here. Those damn deputies still visit us regularly."

Luther exhaled loudly. "But Homer––"

"There are five of us here. We can take care of him. Please don't do anything foolish. Dutch didn't want us to tell you because he was afraid you'd want to come."

Luther sighed and was quiet for a moment. "Okay," he finally said. "But please let me talk to him when you get back to the hospital."

"I will. I'm going to try to sleep now. Talk to you later." She hung up. Luther put his phone down and lay on the couch, having lost all interest in reading. He closed his eyes and let the tears run down his cheeks.

Chapter 12

LUTHER MANAGED TO CALM HIMSELF BEFORE FINN ENTERED THE LIVING ROOM. He wasn't even sure why he was crying, but he didn't want Finn to see him doing it. Was it for Homer? He was embarrassed and frustrated. And a little nauseous. Maybe this is what they call homesickness. Or grieving. Suddenly there was a lot to grieve and no one to hold him up through it. "Ready for cocktail hour?" Finn asked.

Luther put on a smile. "Sure. But is there anything lighter than Irish whiskey in the house?"

"There's probably a beer in the fridge, but who knows how long it's been here."

"I'll take it." Luther joined Finn in the kitchen. "Homer's in the hospital."

"The Parkinson's acting up?"

"Maybe. He fell and they're checking for broken bones."

"He used to fall at the senior residence when we lived there, but I don't think he ever hurt himself."

"I guess this was a bad one."

"Not surprising." Finn handed Luther the beer and sat down with his glass of whiskey. "He's been dealing with the disease for a long time. Bound to get worse."

"I guess, but it's still sad."

"Luther, you're a man of surprising empathy after all you've been through." Finn patted Luther's shoulder.

"No––" Luther stuttered. "No, I was just surprised." He didn't dare look up to Finn and start crying again.

"You're a lot like Jed," Finn said quietly. "Empathy is a very good thing."

"I have a lot to learn to be like Jed."

"Less than you think. His strength is in his situation. You'll find yours." Finn, as if to shake off this sudden bout of sentimentality, quickly rose and opened the refrigerator. "Crap. I don't feel like any of this. You like Chinese food?"

"Sure. Are you going to tell me that the Chinese food in New York is better here too?"

"Of course." Finn smiled. "Come on. Let's hit the streets. I know a hole in the wall with some good spare-ribs, egg rolls and wonton soup."

"Sounds good to me. Is it close by?"

"I'm twice your age, Luther. If I can walk it, so can you."

"Hey, man, I'm not complaining. I'm just asking."

Finn laughed. "That's the way to do it, Luther. Just throw it back at me."

"My mama didn't teach me to be disrespectful."

"Sometimes you have no choice. Let's go." Finn's phone rang just as they were about to leave. He looked at the number and shrugged. "I don't know who this is."

"Just let it go to voicemail and see if they leave a message," Luther responded.

They left the building and started walking. Finn's phone rang again and he looked down at it. "Same number."

"Maybe you should answer it."

"Damn 'em! Leave a voicemail and leave me alone." Then the phone rang a third time.

"Just answer it, Finn."

Finn scowled as he pushed the answer button. "What's so important?" he barked into the phone. His frown turned to concern. "Where are you now?" He nodded. "We'll be there shortly." He hung up. "That was Theo. Rocco's in trouble."

"You gave out your phone number to the writing group?"

"Why shouldn't I?"

"Not saying you shouldn't. Do you get called often?"

"Rarely. Come on. We need to get down to the mission."

"Where is it?"

"What difference does that make? Like you know where the streets are." Finn hailed a cab passing by and got in.

Luther scrambled in after him. Don't react, he thought. Don't ask questions. Then he blurted out, "What happened to Rocco?"

"Don't know. That's all Theo said. Just that he's in trouble."

"God, he's just a kid and having to take care of Rocco."

"I'm sure Theo gets something out of it too." Finn looked over at Luther. "Don't you?"

"Don't I what?"

"Get something out of taking care of people."

"I guess so. But I don't think I would have felt that way at Theo's age."

"Well then, I guess Theo's a better person than you are."

Luther sighed. "Yeah."

Finn shook his head and they rode the rest of the way in silence. When they got to the mission, Finn paid and jumped out. Luther tried to keep up with him as he rushed up to the front desk. "I'm looking for Rocco and Theo."

"We had to kick them out," the intake worker said. "Rocco was too disruptive and Theo begged me not to call the police."

"Where did they go?" Finn asked.

"I told Theo he should get Rocco to the hospital. He was very agitated. He needs professional help."

"Bellevue?"

"I don't know." Finn left quickly with Luther at his heels.

"Do you really think they went to the hospital?" Luther asked.

"No. I think they are probably around here some-where." Finn took out his phone and pressed the call back number. "Is Theo there?"

Finn's frowned. "Alright. Thanks." He put his phone back in his pocket. "It was someone else's phone. Theo must have borrowed it just to call me. This guy didn't know where they went."

"So what do we do now?"

"We walk the streets and look for them." Luther nodded and followed Finn's lead, checking alleys and shop entrances. "Maybe we should separate," Finn said. "You go up a couple of blocks in that direction and I'll go up here. Look around and we'll meet back in front of the mission."

"Okay." Luther took off, peering into doorways and around corners. As he approached an alley, he heard voices and accelerated his pace, hoping Theo and Rocco were the sources. As he turned down the alley he stopped short and gasped. Someone was getting stabbed. By the time Luther got his wits about him, the stabber had run and the victim lay bleeding on the ground. Luther ran down the alley, grabbing his phone out of his pocket as he ran. When he got to the bleeding man, he knelt down to look closely at his face, praying it wasn't Rocco or Theo. It wasn't. He started to dial

911, but the memory of that night twenty years ago stopped him. He tried talking to the man lying on the ground, but there was no response. He was about to feel for the man's pulse, but stopped himself. He didn't want to leave any fingerprints like Jed did. And he didn't want to call because his cell phone number could identify him. He peered down at the dying or already dead man and ran away.

Luther found Finn waiting for him in front of the mission. "Any luck?" Finn asked. Luther was breathing hard and leaning against the building. He slid down the wall, winding up sitting on the ground. Finn looked at him quizzically. "You okay?"

Luther blew out his breath. "I——oh Jesus!"

"What the hell's going on, Luther?"

"Can we go home?"

"Did you find Rocco and Theo?"

"No. But I can't stay here." Luther stood up. "You stay. I'll, uh, walk home. Just point me in the right direction."

"Luther! What's wrong?"

"Please Finn. I have to get out of here."

Finn reached in his pocket and took out his wallet. "Take a cab. Here's the fare."

"I just want to walk." Luther pushed the money away.

"I'll go back with you. We'll just have to wait for Theo to call again or hopefully see them both at writing group tomorrow."

Finn started to walk away and Luther followed but soon took the lead as his walk turned into a trot. "I'll wait for you a couple of blocks away," Luther called over his shoulder.

Luther was standing inside the doorway of an abandoned storefront when Finn caught up to him. Luther stepped out from under the eave. "Are you going to tell me why you're acting like this?" Finn asked.

"Not til we get home."

They walked the rest of the way in silence. This time Finn had to try to keep up with Luther. They arrived home and Luther rushed inside and fell onto the couch. Finn walked into the kitchen and came back with two glasses, handed one to Luther, and sat down next to him on the sofa. He waited a few minutes and watched with amusement as Luther downed the entire glass of whiskey in one gulp. "Shall I get you some more?" he asked.

"I don't know. Let me digest this one first." Luther turned his face towards Finn. "I saw a guy get murdered."

"What are you saying?"

"This guy was getting stabbed in an alley and I saw it happen."

"Well, did you call the cops?"

"That's just it, Finn. I didn't." Luther took a breath and exhaled loudly. "I couldn't. I was too afraid to."

Finn didn't answer right away. He grabbed Luther's glass off the coffee table and went back to the kitchen, returning with two more full glasses. He set Luther's down on the table, sat down, and took a swig of his own before speaking. "I understand why you didn't, but we need to now."

"I didn't want it traced to my phone."

"Where was the alley?" Finn asked as he took out his phone.

"I don't know." Luther put his head in his hands. "Why does this keep happening to me?"

"What? Finn asked.

"Being around murders."

Finn sighed. "It was dark and no one saw you there, so you have nothing to worry about now."

"I left a man who may or may not have been dead already. If I'd called for an ambulance, he might have been saved. What kind of shitty person does that?"

"Luther, you——"

"Stop trying to make me feel better about it," Luther interrupted. "I've done a terrible thing."

"Now you're sounding like Rocco. You had nothing to do with this random stabbing. You were the unlucky person to witness it. You had every reason to be scared of reporting it. I'll report it now, and you'll be out of it."

"I don't even know where the alley is, though."

"I'll take care of it, Luther." Finn dialed 911 and walked into his bedroom. Luther started pacing and then went to the window. After a few minutes Finn came out of the bedroom.

"What did you tell them?" Luther asked turning around to face Finn.

"I gave them the general vicinity and said I saw a man running and I thought it looked suspicious."

"So you didn't pretend to have seen the stabbing yourself?"

"Uh, no."

"Well, that's not going to help that poor guy!" Luther shouted.

"Why are you mad at me?" Finn asked.

"I'm not. I'm mad at myself. I'm a fucking coward! It feels like I murdered the poor guy, myself."

Just then Finn's phone rang. "Hello? Yeah, that's me." Finn frowned. "Why? I didn't see it happen. No I'll come there. What's the address?" Finn took the phone into the kitchen and found a scrap of paper where he wrote something down. "I'll be there shortly."

"Was that Theo?" Luther asked.

"No. It was the cops. They want me to come to the police station to make a statement. They found the body."

"Dammit, Finn," Luther lamented. "You shouldn't have to do this. This is not fair to you. Now you might get in trouble."

"Why would I get in trouble?" Finn asked. "Just leave it alone, Luther. I'll be fine."

"I should come with you and be a man!"

"Oh for god's sake, you really want to go there? You're being stupid now. Be a man," Finn scoffed. "What does that even mean? That's the most ridiculous thing I've heard come out of your mouth."

Luther went back to pacing. He downed the rest of his whiskey and poured himself another drink. "What are you going to tell them?"

"Nothing much. I'll just say I wasn't close enough to see the guy who was running. Were you close enough? Could you describe him at all?"

"No. It was dark."

"I won't be much help, then. But neither would you have been if you'd called, since you can't describe him. So stop beating yourself up."

Chapter 13

THE NEXT MORNING FINN FOUND AN EMPTY BOTTLE OF WHISKEY ON THE COFFEE TABLE NEXT TO THE SOFA WHERE LUTHER WAS SLEEPING. He picked up the bottle, took it to the kitchen, made some coffee and toast, showered and dressed and was sitting at the kitchen table reading the Times when Luther finally stumbled into the kitchen. "How's your head?"

"Awful. Hurts like hell."

Finn nodded. "Well, sometimes you just need to give yourself a hangover."

"Not if it doesn't make you feel any better."

"It's not about how you feel the next day, Luther. It's about doing what you need to do when you need to do it. Even Buddha says to live in the present and not dwell in the past or worry about the future."

"But the title of your book . . . *Those Who Forget the Past are Condemned to Repeat It.*"

"I never said I necessarily believed that. It was a sign they had up in Jonestown. That's why I used it as the title of my book," Finn replied.

"So you don't believe it?" Luther asked.

"I think it's possible to believe both. There was also a saying after the holocaust – never forget. Those moments in history are not the same as our personal lives."

Luther was silent for several minutes and finally asked, "Got anything for a headache?"

"I've got aspirin and I've got vodka – which would you prefer?"

"Is that true? Drinking alcohol is the way to get over a hangover?"

"Hair of the dog. There are some who believe that."

"Do you?"

Finn shrugged. "Sometimes. Best would be a Bloody Mary with tomato juice, but I don't have any. Try a swig of vodka and see if it helps. Can't hurt."

"Are you sure it won't make it worse?"

Finn laughed. "Yeah, I'm sure." He took a Stoli out of the cabinet, poured some in a glass, and handed it to Luther. "You gonna be okay to come to the writing group?"

"I'll force myself," Luther replied after gulping down the vodka. "I want to see if Theo and Rocco show up."

"We have to leave early."

"Okay. Like what time?"

"Leave here about eleven." Finn glanced at the clock on the stove. "Can you be ready by then?"

"Yes, Finn. But where's the aspirin?"

"In the medicine cabinet." Finn opened the refrigerator. "You need food, too. Not that there's anything good here. We'll go to the Oyster Bar for lunch."

"Ooh, I don't think so, Finn. My stomach is pretty queasy."

"Just do what I say. You'll feel better. Anyway, you shouldn't take aspirin on an empty stomach."

"Since when did you become such a mother hen?"

Finn looked at Luther with the most serious expression Luther had ever seen on his face. "Since I had a daughter to raise by myself. That was sixty years ago." Luther started to speak, but then decided this was one of those times it was better to say nothing.

Luther was dressed and ready when Finn entered the living room. "So where is this Oyster Bar?"

"At Grand Central Station. It's a famous place."

"I have heard of Grand Central Station."

"I should hope so," Finn teased.

Luther followed Finn into the subway station and was glad to see that the train was not full so he didn't have to worry about losing Finn in the crowd. They got to Grand Central station and Luther was mesmerized by the amount of homeless people living in the waiting room. There were people sleeping on every bench, even a couple having sex on one. There were clotheslines strung across, packed with clothes hung to dry. Children played noisily, running back and forth with excitement. "Nobody kicks them out of here?" Luther asked.

"No point. They'd just come back."

"So where do people go to wait for trains?"

"I don't know. I guess they just hang around."

Luther marveled as they entered the Oyster Bar. "This place is amazing! Look at the tiled ceiling!"

"Hi Joe!" Finn waved at an older guy sitting at the counter.

"Finn! How ya' doin'?"

"Hey, join us at a table."

"Since when do we sit at a table?" Joe asked.

"Since today," Finn replied.

"Alright, I haven't ordered yet." Joe got up and joined Finn and Luther as the hostess sat them at a table.

"This is Luther."

"Nice to meet ya'."

A waiter who looked even older than Joe and Finn approached the table. "Well if it isn't the Bobbsey Twins. You getting the usual?"

"I don't know," Finn said. "Got to see what Luther wants to eat."

"Well, don't take too long. I wouldn't want you cheapskates taking up too much of my time."

The waiter left and Luther said, "That was kind of rude."

"Nah, Ernie was just joshing," Finn answered.

"Who are the Bobbsey Twins?" Luther asked.

Finn and Joe chuckled. "Those books weren't around when you were growing up."

"I guess you two come here often," Luther smiled.

"Probably been coming here for seventy years or so," Joe replied.

Luther's eyes popped out of his head. "How old are you, Joe?"

"Ninety-eight last August."

"Ninety-eight? Wow! You sure don't look it!"

"Are you having oysters?" Finn asked, ignoring Luther's wonderment.

"Uh, I guess I could look at the menu." Luther opened the menu. "They serve a lot of food here!"

"You like seafood?"

"I like everything."

"I'll order for you." Ernie came over. "Bring him a plate with an assortment of seafood," Finn said.

"Glad to see you're gonna spend some money for a change," Ernie grumbled. "I'll put lobster on it and then you'll really spend some."

Luther's eyes bugged out again. "Lobster?"

"What? You don't like lobster?" Finn said.

"I-I don't know. Never had it. I just know it's real expensive."

"Don't worry about it," Joe said. "I'm buying. I don't have much longer to spend all my money. If I don't spend it, it goes to the IRS."

"Why? Don't you have kids to leave it to?"

"Years ago my son-in-law the lawyer made a deal with the IRS. I owed a bit of money, they claimed. Since I was in my eighties at the time, they were game to let me write a will leaving everything to them. Hah! They figured I wouldn't be around much longer. Fooled them!"

Luther laughed. "Pretty clever. Why do they claim you owe them?"

"I had a fire adjusting business. I liked using cash and well, I forgot sometimes to write it down."

Luther looked into Joe's eyes, trying to figure out if he really forgot or conveniently forgot. "What's fire adjusting?"

"Your business or house burned, I was the guy who figured out what the insurance company owed you."

"I guess there are a lot of jobs I've never heard of."

"What's yours, Luther?"

Luther stiffened. "Oh. Uh, I work on a farm."

"A farmer eh? So what are you doing here?"

Luther took his time answering. "Um, just wanted to see New York."

"You're awfully evasive, young man," Joe said with a subtle smile. "But hey, I'm just making conversation. I don't need to know."

Their food came and Luther took one look at the platter of seafood in front of him and realized he was very hungry. "Wow! This is incredible! I don't know what half this stuff is!"

Finn laughed. "What's the half you don't know?"

"I guess I only know this is shrimp."

Finn pointed out the lobster, crab legs, mussels, clams and oysters. "Let me show you how to eat them." He picked up the tool and cracked open the lobster tail and crab legs. Then he took the tiny fork and took the meat out of the shells. "You can dip them into the melted butter or the cocktail sauce. The clams and mussels you can pry open easily. But watch me eat the oysters." He placed the crabmeat and lobster meat back on Luther's plate and took an oyster off his own. He squirted some lemon on it and then slurped it noisily.

Luther's eyes widened. "That's how you eat oysters?" Finn nodded and watched as Luther copied him. "Oh, these are good." Luther ate everything on his plate with relish. Joe and Finn looked on, amused. When they finished eating and the busboy had taken their plates away, Joe took out a newspaper. "What's that?" Luther asked.

"Daily Racing Form."

Luther and Finn watched as Joe read through the newspaper and wrote some things down. "Why is he doing that?" Luther asked Finn.

"Probably going to see his bookie after lunch."

"Bookie?"

"To bet on the horse races."

"Can you explain to me how you place the bets?" Luther asked.

"First off, you pick the horses based on their past performance, their pedigree, the jockey, the owner," Joe answered. "Then you decide which horse for win, place or show."

"What do you mean, place or show? I get what win means."

"Place is coming in second. Show is coming in third. You can also decide if you want to do exacta, trifecta and superfecta."

"What's that?"

"You'd figure out which horses to bet on and the order they'd come in. You could do it for one race or more than one."

"That sounds really complicated."

Joe looked up from the Racing Form and replied, "I've been doing this for seventy-five years. Not complicated at all."

When the bill came, Luther snatched it. "Let me pay for this." He glanced at the bill and exhaled sharply.

Joe cackled and grabbed the bill off the table after Luther had set it down to take out his wallet. "I told you that it's on me." Joe reached in his pocket and took out a money clip loaded with cash. Joe stood and said, "I need to get to my bookie before the races start."

Chapter 14

FINN AND LUTHER ARRIVED AT THE CHESS AND CHECKERS HOUSE IN THE PARK AND LOOKED AROUND FOR ROCCO AND THEO. "I don't see them," Luther said. "Do you think they'll show up?"

"I hope so," Finn answered. He started the writing group the usual way, asking for a prompt. No one raised a hand. "Okay. I'll go again. He looked straight at Luther. "The hardest thing to learn in life is which bridge to cross and which bridge to burn. Bertrand Russell said that. Write about a difficult decision you had to make."

Luther stared at Finn and then gave a slight nod. But he didn't start writing. He looked around and saw everyone else busily at work. He was tired of thinking about everything. He was tired of running . . . tired of being afraid . . . tired of feeling like a puppy dog following Finn everywhere . . . tired of being in this state of limbo. He just wanted to become involved in something. Maybe he needed a job to take his mind off his circumstances. Finn came over as he was brooding and stood over him. Luther looked up. "I guess I don't feel like writing."

"I know the feeling," Finn whispered. "Sometimes things are just a little too close to home and you'd rather not think about it. You just gotta roll with it. Writing and life."

"What about Theo and Rocco?"

"What about them? We can only wait for them to get in touch with us."

"Do you think something bad happened?" Luther asked.

Finn shrugged. "Probably."

"Maybe you could call the police and see if they know anything?"

"When we get home," Finn whispered, putting his finger to his lips. "Maybe they'll show up here yet."

"I guess so," Luther sighed.

Luther didn't write at all, but listened enthusiastically to those who read their prompts. When it was time to go into smaller groups, Finn gestured to Luther to join a specific one, but Luther shook his head no. Finn shrugged and circulated around all the groups, giving advice and critiques when asked. Luther just sat quietly by himself, occasionally looking out the window for Theo and Rocco. Four o'clock came and Finn and Luther were on their way home. "I wish you'd stop feeling sorry for yourself. Life could be a lot worse," Finn grumbled.

"Sorry." Finn gave him a cutting look. Luther knew Finn was annoyed with him, but he couldn't seem to get himself out of his funk. He knew Finn was right. Life could be a lot worse. Look at Rocco and Theo. They rode in silence all the way home on the subway.

"Can you get us a couple of whiskeys?" Finn asked.

Luther got the drinks and Finn joined him in the living room. "Should we call some hospitals?"

"Luther. We can't babysit those two. They reached out for help when they wanted it and they will again."

"Did you tell the police anything like that they might be missing?"

"I don't think reporting a homeless person as missing would get more than a chuckle from the police."

"I guess you're right," Luther sighed.

"Anyway, don't you have enough to worry about without worrying about those two?"

Luther's phone rang and he looked down at the screen. "It's Juniper! Hello?" Luther slumped into the sofa and his gaze went to the floor. "How bad?" he said softly. Finn watched silently. "Do you think he'll make it?" Luther glanced at Finn and shook his head. "Is he awake now? Can I speak to him?" Luther mouthed 'Homer' to Finn. "Hey Homer! Yeah, that's what Juniper said. Does Dutch have anything that helps? No, huh. I'm so sorry, man. I wish I were there. I know there's nothing I can do. Okay. You rest and I'll talk to you again soon. Bye." Luther hung up and inhaled deeply.

"What happened?"

"They want to keep Homer in the hospital for more tests. He's having trouble breathing and can't walk anymore at all. But the worst thing is he's become incontinent. Juniper thinks he's in the last stages now."

"Sounds like it." Finn shook his head. "Just as well. I can't imagine Homer allowing his friends to change his diapers." He stood and picked up the two glasses. "I assume you want a refill."

Luther was lost in thought when Finn returned with the drinks. "Worry is like a rocking chair. It won't get you anywhere."

"Good advice, but hard to follow," Luther said.

Finn's phone rang. He looked at it and saw another unfamiliar number. "I guess it could be Theo," Finn frowned. "Hello?"

"Is it Theo?" Luther asked.

"Okay. Nine a.m. Got it." Finn hung up and turned to Luther. "Theo's been arrested."

"Arrested? What for?"

"They didn't say exactly."

"Where's Rocco?"

"I don't know. That wasn't Theo. It was the detective I talked to when I went down there about the stabbing. He didn't say anything about Rocco. They're keeping Theo in jail."

"For what?"

Finn took a deep breath. "Murder."

"What?! Theo? You're kidding!"

"I'm not." Finn sat down and sighed. "He'll be arraigned tomorrow."

"What can we do?" Luther asked anxiously.

"Get him a lawyer I guess."

"Do you know any?"

"I'll call Joe. His son-in-law might be able to help."

"Damn!" Luther shook his head. "And we thought Rocco was the one in trouble."

"He may be too."

"Did they say who he murdered?"

"Why? Like we'd know them?" Finn scoffed. I'll probably find out in court tomorrow . . . if they even know the victim's identity." He paused and studied Luther. "I don't suppose you want to come with me?"

Luther sighed. "I'd prefer to stay away from anything to do with law enforcement."

Finn nodded. "Well, shall we pull something together for dinner?" He looked at his phone. "It's getting late."

"I guess so," Luther said. "But I'm not really too hungry. Let's just raid the fridge. Nothing fancy."

Finn laughed. "Fancy. Right!" They snacked standing up in the kitchen, saying very little, both lost in thought. Finn dropped plastic containers and utensils into the sink. "I guess I'll call Joe and get the number for his son-in-law." Finn went to his bedroom and shut the door. Luther did the dishes and went back to the living room to wait for Finn. But he never emerged from the bedroom so Luther lay down and closed his eyes, not expecting to sleep, but hoping for it nonetheless.

Finn was already in the kitchen dressed and drinking coffee when Luther woke the next morning. "Did you reach Joe's son-in-law?" Luther asked.

"Yeah. He'll meet me down there."

"I wish I could go with you, but I'm just too afraid."

"Well, I doubt anyone's going to arrest you at the courthouse in New York when you're wanted in Podunk, California, but it's your call."

Luther stared at Finn for a moment. "I guess you're right."

"But hey, I don't need you there," Finn added.

"Then I think I won't go."

"Suit yourself." Finn swigged the rest of his coffee and left.

Luther wasn't sure what to do while he waited to find out the outcome of Theo's arraignment. He also pondered Rocco's whereabouts. Had he been with Theo when he was arrested? Was he hurt or sick? Or dead? Then there was Homer who was probably going to die soon. Homer was like a grandfather to him. He picked up his phone and dialed. "Juniper? How's Homer?"

"The same," she answered. "Well, I don't know for sure. I haven't heard anything from the hospital this morning. But it is only six am here."

"Oh shit. I'm sorry, Juniper. I forgot the time difference."

"It's okay. It's nice to hear your voice first thing in the morning."

"Yeah. I miss you," Luther sighed. "I miss everyone at the farm. Are you going to the hospital this morning to see Homer?"

"I'll take the afternoon shift. Buster wants to get there early and stay all day, but they only let two people stay at a time. Dutch will bring Buster in as soon as visiting hours start. Then I'll go later on and stay with Buster til the end of visiting hours."

"I wish I could be there."

Juniper laughed. "Well how would we work it out? There aren't enough visiting slots."

Luther wanted to join in the laughter, but it wasn't happening. "I guess I'd better go. Call me from Homer's hospital room, will you?"

"Sure. Are you okay, Luther?"

"Yeah. I'm fine." He tried to say that with conviction, but he knew that Juniper wasn't buying it. "I'll talk to you later." Luther hung up and stared out the window. After several minutes, he got up and went into the bathroom. The least he could do is take a shower and get ready for the day, whatever the day was going to bring. He missed the everyday routine of working on the farm, doing the same things, with the same people. No worries. No changes. No expectations. He liked that way of life a lot more than this being in limbo stuff.

Chapter 15

FINN FINALLY RETURNED AROUND NOON AND FOUND LUTHER SITTING LISTLESSLY IN THE LIVING ROOM. "Well, you have a different shirt on, so you must have moved at some point this morning," he said as he passed by and made his way into the kitchen.

"What happened?" Luther asked, following Finn.

"He's staying in jail since he has no family to put up the bail."

"Did you get a chance to talk to him?" Luther asked.

"No. But I did ask Amos, Joe's son-in-law the attorney, to ask him where Rocco was."

"And?"

"He doesn't know for sure. When he called us, they were near the mission."

"Did he say what kind of trouble Rocco was in?"

"Theo has his own problems right now, Luther," Finn sighed and then took a deep breath. "The police claim Theo was the one who killed the guy you saw in the alley."

"What? No!" Luther yelled. "That's not right!"

"He told Amos that they picked him up because a witness said the murderer was wearing an Oakland Raiders Jersey #24 Lynch." Finn shook his head. "Where in hell did he get that? Like there are any Oakland Raiders fans in New York City . . ."

"Maybe he got it at a free store or homeless handout," Luther mused. "But it's freezing out. Wouldn't he be wearing a coat over a jersey?"

"Jesus, Luther! How the hell should I know?" snapped Finn. "Why don't you go down to the jail yourself and ask him!" He yanked open the refrigerator door and started rummaging.

"Well," Luther ventured in a small voice. "Do you think Theo has it in him to kill someone?"

Finn took a lid off a container and sniffed. "I don't really know him that well, Luther. By the time you reach my age you'll find people are mostly disappointing." He found a spoon, jammed it into the container, walked to his bedroom and shut the door.

Luther wasn't sure if Finn was mad at him or just wanted to be alone. He frowned and leaned against the sink, thinking about how nice Theo seemed and the weird specifics about the jersey until his stomach growled. He too went to the fridge, but found nothing appealing mid the odds and ends. He made himself a sandwich, sat at the kitchen table and slowly ate it. Eventually Finn returned with the empty container and put it in the sink.

"Are we okay, Finn?"

Finn sighed and looked out the window over the sink. "Yeah, why?"

"I don't know. You seem angry."

"I'm not."

"Oh, okay. Sorry."

Finn whirled around. "Dammit, Luther! Stop with the sorry! It's not always about you!" The hot, glazed look in Finn's eyes startled him more than his words. Finn wasn't so much angry as frustrated. Luther ducked his head and stared at the crumbs on the table.

They ignored one another for the rest of the day. Luther refocused his agitation on Homer in the hospital. He had texted Juniper a couple of times, but there was no response and that only served to worry him more. While Luther stared once again at his phone, Finn's rang. He watched Finn answer and his face growing dark as he quietly spoke into the phone. Finn ended the call and looked over at Luther. Luther was tired of his questions being shot down, so he silently waited for Finn to speak.

"Rocco," Finn finally sighed. "He's in the hospital."

"Is he okay?"

"He's well enough to give the hospital my number to call. They didn't say much, but it seems he tried to commit suicide. He's at Bellevue."

"Oh no!" Luther exclaimed.

"Do you want to come?" Finn asked.

"Absolutely!"

They left the apartment hurriedly and walked the mile or so up to Bellevue. Finn spoke to the person at the information desk and they were sent to the ICU where they found Rocco in bed, hooked up to several machines. His eyes were closed but he opened them when Finn and Luther walked in. "How are you feeling?" Luther asked. Finn gave Luther a piercing look.

"How do you think I'm feeling?" Rocco growled, turning his head towards the wall.

"What happened?" Finn asked.

"Do you know Theo's in jail?" Rocco's voice was very soft.

"Yeah. He called me. Were you with him when they picked him up?"

"They think he murdered someone," Rocco muttered. He turned back and stared at Finn. "But why Theo? The cops wouldn't tell me."

"A witness said the perpetrator was wearing a Raiders' jersey with the number 24. And Theo was wearing one."

Rocco started to cry. "I fucked up again."

"Talk to us," Finn gently murmured. "Tell us what has caused you so much pain?"

Luther and Finn both waited patiently while Rocco breathed heavily, trying to quell his sobs. "Could you find my backpack?"

"Is it here at the hospital?" Finn asked.

"I don't know."

Luther went to the door. "I'll ask the nurses." He came back a minute later. "They said it's under your bed." He took it out and put it on the bed next to Rocco. Finn and Luther watched as Rocco tried to maneuver his hands with IVs in them and to move his body so that he could unzip the backpack. "Do you want some help?" Luther finally spoke, unsure if it was cool to ask if he could look into someone's bag that held his entire life.

Rocco sighed loudly. "Get out my composition book."

Luther got it out, took the backpack off the bed, and handed the book to Rocco. He leafed through the it until he found what he was looking for and then handed the book back to Luther. Finn looked over Luther's shoulder and they read together silently. Luther closed the book and put it back into the backpack. He looked at Finn, hoping he would speak first. "I'm sorry this happened to you," Finn said gently, "but it was an accident."

"I murdered my own son," Rocco quietly sobbed.

A nurse came in at that moment. "I have to ask you gentlemen to leave. Rocco needs to rest."

"We'll be back, Rocco," Finn said. "I'll let you know what happens with Theo. Come on, Luther."

"But we——"

"We need to leave." Finn pulled on Luther's arm.

"See you soon, Rocco," Luther said as Finn pulled him out the door.

Finn and Luther walked home in silence, both lost in thought. Neither wanted to bring up what they had read in Rocco's notebook, at least not yet. They both went to the kitchen when they got home. Finn took out the Jameson and two glasses while Luther found some crackers and cheese. They sat down in the living room and sighed simultaneously. "That's quite a load Rocco's carrying on his shoulders," Finn said after they took several sips of whiskey.

"But he didn't murder his son," Luther replied.

"Certainly you can see why he thinks so, though."

"Well, I can see that he'd feel guilty. But it wasn't his fault." Finn didn't answer so Luther added, "Do you think it is?"

"There was a cause and effect in his son's death. Obviously it was an accident, but if fault is to be assigned, it would be with Rocco."

"Why would you say that?" Luther felt some anger and wasn't sure why. "That's like saying I was guilty because I chose to go with those guys to the convenience store!"

Finn raised his eyebrows. "You really think it's the same thing?" Luther was quiet. "I'm not blaming Rocco," Finn added. "It was obviously an accident, but he is certainly partly to blame."

Luther's phone dinged with a text. He looked at it and said, "It's Jed."

"Go ahead and answer him. There's nothing more to say here." Finn got up and went to his room.

Luther thought he'd call Juniper before answering Jed, but she didn't answer . . . again. He texted Jed that he had been unable to reach Juniper and Jed texted back that he was planning to go up to Garberville in the morning. He would let Luther know what was happening. This only made Luther more uneasy about whether he should go back to the farm. Juniper finally called and Luther asked anxiously, "Where have you been?"

"I've been busy," she answered irritably.

"I'm sorry," Luther said. "I'm just worried."

"We all are. Anyway, Homer wants to come home desperately and we are trying to figure out a way that he can do that. The doctors don't want to release him and we are all trying to decide if we should get him to sign an AMA."

"What's that?"

"It's a form that a patient signs when he goes against doctors' orders and asks to be released. Then the hospital can't be sued."

"I don't think he should do that," Luther replied firmly. "I mean the doctors know best, don't they?"

"We're having a meeting tomorrow to decide what to do."

"What do you think?" Luther asked.

"I'm torn."

"What about the others?"

"I can't answer that yet. That's why we're meeting tomorrow. Do you want to put in your vote now that you think he should stay in the hospital? Jed and Monica are coming tomorrow for the meeting."

"Jed texted me that he was going up in the morning, but not why. I don't know what I think. Can I somehow be part of this meeting?"

"Sure. I'll put you on speaker during the meeting."

"What time will it be?"

"It depends when Jed gets here," Juniper said with a catch in her voice.

"Are you okay?" Luther asked.

"No. Are you?"

"No," he sighed.

"Then why would you ask me that? Homer is dying." Luther wanted to say something consoling, but there was nothing to say. "Anyway, just to add to all the crap that we are all dealing with, that creepy cop is still showing up every single day, looking for you. He's really out for blood."

"You'd think he'd have other things to do."

"Apparently he's made you his vendetta. So stay where you are and stay under the radar."

Luther exhaled loudly. "I'll try." They hung up and Luther lay down on the couch. He tried to get his mind off Homer, but the thought of what Rocco had written in his composition book was so disturbing. He wasn't sure where he should let his mind wander. He hated thinking about Homer . . . Rocco . . . Theo . . . His own circumstances were bad enough.

Finn walked in just as Luther closed his eyes, trying to will himself to sleep. "Oops. Sorry. Are you sleeping?"

"No. Too much crap on my mind."

"You want to talk about Rocco?" Finn asked.

"Kinda."

Finn sat down and sighed. "I've heard stories about this happening."

"How do you forget your kid, though?"

"People get busy with their mind on other things. The kid was probably asleep in his car seat in the back of the car. Maybe Rocco wasn't used to bringing him to day care, so left him."

"I can't imagine how you go on living after that."

"Do you remember what Rocco wrote about committing suicide?"

"No," Luther replied. "I was too shocked to read the whole thing."

"He wrote he needed to suffer for what he did, and suicide would only end his pain. That's why he hadn't tried before."

"I guess he finally couldn't take the pain anymore," Luther sighed.

Chapter 16

"WAKE UP LUTHER!" FINN SAID AS HE SHOOK HIM.

"What time is it?" Luther asked, rubbing his eyes and yawning.

"It's half past hell. The hospital called. Rocco left."

"What?" Luther sat up abruptly. "He left? Why?"

"I don't know!" Finn answered impatiently.

"What are you going to do?"

"Look for him, I guess. He can't have gone far."

Luther rubbed his eyes. "So much for you not wanting to take care of all these homeless people."

Finn gave him a piercing look and then said, "Don't take everything I say seriously." Luther looked at him skeptically and shook his head. "Come on!" Finn shouted, shaking him again. "Get dressed!"

They arrived at the hospital and talked to the nurses on the floor Rocco had been on, but they were not much help. Apparently Rocco's bed was discovered empty just after midnight, and after a search by security and a review of surveillance cameras it was determined that he simply walked out with his backpack. Nothing more could be done, so Finn and Luther started exploring the neighborhood surrounding Bellevue. They decided to go back to the Bowery Mission where Rocco and Theo had been staying before being kicked out. "Walk or get a taxi?" Luther asked.

Finn hailed a cab without answering. They got in and started riding the nearly empty streets towards the mission. "Hey, you want this cat?" the driver asked.

"Huh?" Luther said.

The driver lifted a scrawny black kitten by its scruff from the front seat. "This cat jumped in my cab an hour or so ago. I can't keep a cat. My wife's allergic."

Luther looked over at Finn, but he just shrugged. "I don't know what that means, Finn. Is that a yes or no?"

Finn tipped his head aside. "Maybe Rocco would want it."

"Rocco? How can he take care of it? He can't even take care of himself."

"A lot of homeless people have pets. Jed had a cat on the boardwalk in Venice Beach. Her name was Mother. She was a great cat."

"I don't think we need to bring this up to Rocco right now."

"Yeah, you're right."

"So do you want to take this cat home?" Luther asked.

"Why not?"

"You just don't seem the type to have a pet."

"You really think you know me, don't you Luther."

"I'm just saying . . ."

"Yeah. Well, I didn't say it would be *my* pet, did I?" Finn turned to the driver. "We'll take it."

The driver opened the window between the front and back seats and again lifted the kitten by its scruff and shoved it through the window. Luther gingerly reached for it. "Boy, it is scrawny. We should probably take it to a vet."

"We'll just give it some food first," Finn answered. They arrived at the mission and Finn paid the driver. There was a sign on the door that said not to ring the bell between the hours of nine p.m. and seven a.m. "I guess we should have thought of that," Finn declared. "Let's just go home."

"We should have kept the cab," Luther replied.

"What's the matter? The cat too heavy for you?"

"No. It doesn't weigh more than a bag of chips."

"Then just carry it."

"What about cat food?"

"I'm too tired and cold to deal with that right now. I've got some tuna fish. I used to feed Mother eggs and she loved them."

Luther smiled. "You took care of Mother? I thought you said she was Jed's cat."

"Long story. Someday I'll tell you. Let's just get home. It's too damn cold out here."

They walked home and Luther found himself petting and cooing at the kitten. When they got in the apartment Finn opened a can of tuna and the kitten scarfed it up. "I guess we'll need a litter box too," Luther said.

"Yeah. And make sure it doesn't do anything on the floor. Cat pee stinks for a long time."

"What'll we name it?" Luther wondered aloud.

"Is it a he or she?"

Luther looked under the cat. "I don't know. It's kind of hard to tell with kittens this small."

"Then name it something neutral."

"So I guess Father won't work," Luther grinned.

"Hardy har har." Finn then scrunched his brow. "How about Bardo?"

"Bardo . . . hmmm," Luther mused. "I guess that's a cool name. Does it mean anything or did you just make it up?"

Finn laughed. "Well, there was Brigitte Bardot, but this Bardo is similar to the liminality we've been talking about. It's a Buddhist term for those times like what you're dealing with, when the normal sense of the continuity of your life is interrupted."

"Interesting. You never stop teaching me stuff."

"Once a teacher, always a teacher, as the saying goes."

Luther picked up the kitten. "What do you think? Do you like Bardo for your name?" The kitten purred and snuggled into Luther's arms.

"Alright, enough of this cutesy baby talk," Finn groused. "What time is it, anyway?"

Luther took out his phone and glanced at it. "Four."

"We should probably get a little shuteye and then buy some cat food, litter, and a litter box."

"Okay," Luther agreed, "but what are we going to do about Rocco?"

"Nothing we can do but wait for him to contact us. Goodnight, Luther." Finn went into his bedroom and Luther lay down on the couch with Bardo on his stomach. They all fell fast asleep and didn't wake up until well after eight.

Finn stumbled out of his bedroom and got to the kitchen just as Luther gulped down the last of his coffee. "Where's the closest store?" Luther asked. "I'll go out and buy the stuff for Bardo before he or she pees on the floor."

" You still got money?"

"Yeah."

"There's a CVS a few blocks down Eighth Street."

"Cool. I'll be back soon." Luther left and Finn took his coffee into the living room.

Just as Finn settled in with his cup and the morning crossword puzzle, his phone rang. He looked at the screen and didn't recognize the number. He began to snarl, then remembered the unknown number Theo had used in the past. "Finn here," he answered with a sigh.

"I'm in a bad way, Finn."

"Rocco! Why the hell did you leave the hospital? Didn't you appreciate having a warm bed and food?"

"I don't know. I couldn't take it, everybody poking at me and asking me all sorts of questions. And then they said I had to talk to some psychologist. Shit! They're gonna commit me or something. I couldn't handle that.

And that medication they gave me made me feel even crazier. I don't need that shit."

"Oh for Christ's sake, Rocco. These people are just trying to help you. You tried to commit suicide. You're depressed. You're angry. Where are you now?"

"I'm at the mission. They let me use the phone to call you, but they won't let me stay here."

Finn exhaled sharply. The last thing he wanted was another houseguest. "Look, I'll make some calls and see if I can find you another place to stay."

"You mean like a shelter?"

"What did you think? You think I'm going to call a four star hotel? You should have stayed in the hospital. You're not ready to be out on the streets."

"I'll find a place myself. I'm sorry, Finn. I got to get myself together to help Theo."

"How are you going to help Theo? I already got him a lawyer."

"Theo ain't no murderer! That's for damn sure!"

"That may be true, but he's in jail and he's going on trial and a jury's going to decide that."

"We gotta get him out of there!" Rocco cried. "Jail is no place for him. I've been there. He's just a young kid."

"You were in jail?"

"I murdered my son! Remember?"

Finn sighed. "We're working on helping Theo. Listen, get yourself somewhere you can rest and call me again."

"Okay, Finn. Thanks." They hung up and Finn went back to his puzzle, but he couldn't concentrate. There were too many damn people relying on him and needing too much from him. He threw the newspaper and pen across the room and glanced over at Bardo. "And now I've even got a damn cat to join that distinguished club!"

Luther arrived with cat supplies. "Where should I put the litter box?"

"In the bathroom, where'd you think?"

After Luther set up the litter box he brought Bardo into the bathroom to show it to the kitten. Then he poured kibble into a bowl and put some canned cat food onto a plate and set them down in the kitchen. Bardo ate ravenously again and then settled into Finn's lap. "Bardo seems to be right at home here," Luther smiled.

"Rocco called," Finn said while absentmindedly petting the cat.

"Where is he? Is he okay?"

"He's not okay."

"Well . . . what did he say? And what did you say?"

"He's worried about Theo. And I offered to help him find a bed in a shelter, but he wasn't interested."

Luther waited a minute for Finn to say more. "So, how did you leave it with him? Are we going to help him?"

"I don't know how we can help him if he doesn't want our help," Finn replied irritably. "Let's move on, shall we? I'm pretty much done with those two." Finn put Bardo on the floor and retrieved his newspaper and pen to continue the crossword.

Luther and Finn spent the rest of the morning doing their own things. Luther had bought some cat toys along with the necessities so that took care of his couple of hours. Finn went into his bedroom after finishing the puzzle and Luther could hear him talking on the phone. When he came out of his bedroom, Luther wanted desperately to ask him who he'd been talking to, but knew better. "I'm going out," Finn said as he went to the door.

"Uh, okay. Are you teaching today?"

"No," Finn said as he slammed the door behind him.

Chapter 17

LUTHER WAS SOUND ASLEEP ON THE COUCH WHEN HIS PHONE STARTLED HIM AWAKE. "Luther? It's Gordon," the man on the other end of the phone said. "I have great news for you."

Gordon had been Luther's lawyer from the Innocence Project, the group who had gotten his prison sentence exonerated. "Hey, Gordon," Luther replied, trying to get his bearings. "I could sure use some good news."

"What's going on?" Gordon asked.

"Why don't you tell me the good news first."

"Okay. Your money has come through."

"My money?"

"I told you there'd be a large sum coming your way from the state of California. You're entitled to more than a million dollars!"

Luther jumped up and dropped the phone while Bardo scampered away and hid under the coffee table. "A million dollars? Are you shitting me?" he shrieked into the phone after he retrieved it.

"It's one hundred forty dollars a day so that's fifty-one thousand dollars a year or one million twenty-two thousand for twenty years they kept you in prison."

"Oh my God! I had no idea it would be that much!"

"You're not going to get it all at once. I have to find out the exact particulars, but I think they'll at least give you the fifty-one thousand now. Of course, there will be taxes taken out of it, probably around ten thousand."

"This is unbelievable!" Luther paced the living room, grinning and picked up Bardo. "Oh man, do I ever need this now."

"Doesn't Dutch pay you enough? Just kidding."

"Actually I'm not at the farm. I'm in New York." As soon as he said it, he regretted it. He should be keeping it a secret. But then he remembered that Gordon was his lawyer and anything said would be kept confidential.

"New York? What the hell are you doing there?"

Luther exhaled sharply, his good mood suddenly dissipating as he remembered the fix he was in. "Oh man. The cops found a dead body near the farm and think I did it. I decided to get the hell out of there before I would end up in jail again for a damn murder I didn't commit!"

"Why are they accusing you? Just because they found the body near the farm——"

"Gordon, there's like a half dozen Blacks in the whole county . . ."

"Why didn't you call me?"

"They haven't actually arrested me so I didn't see anything you could do."

"Well, we do have expert lawyers here, you know . . ." Luther did not laugh. "You're not the first to go through this." Still no response from Luther. "Are you okay?"

"Yeah. I'm staying with an old fart named Finn, but he's a good guy underneath."

"Good. Uh, look, I need to wire this money to your account." Gordon hesitated. "You have a bank account, don't you?"

"I guess I can open one. I have a little money Dutch gave me for the trip."

"Go do that and then call or text me the account number. Are you going to stay in New York?"

Luther sighed. "I don't know. Homer, the old guy on the farm who has Parkinson's, is probably going to die pretty soon. I want to get back there and see him before he's gone, but I'm afraid to show my face there since the cops are actively looking for me."

"Well, call me if you find your way back there. We've still got your back." Gordon waited for a response. "At least money won't be an issue for you," he added.

"Yeah." Luther dragged himself out of his worried thoughts. "Wow. Thanks for everything, Gordon."

"It's my job. Now go open that bank account so I can wire the money and you can go celebrate. New York's a pretty good place to party."

Luther laughed. "I think it will probably be Finn and me at the White Horse Tavern drinking some fine Irish whiskey."

"You? Drinking whiskey? Pretty funny."

"Finn's got me eating Jewish food too."

"When in Rome . . ."

"Huh? I'm in New York."

"It's a saying," Gordon explained. "When in Rome, do as the Romans do."

"Oh. I get it."

"Take care. How's the weather?"

"Cold."

"Button up when you go out. Talk to you later."

They hung up just as Finn came in the front door. "What are you grinning about?" Finn asked.

"Gordon, my lawyer from the Innocence Project called. I'm getting a million dollars from the state of California!"

"Whoa. A million dollars?"

"Well, not all at once. For now I'm getting about fifty thousand, and then after taxes it'll be more like forty."

"A million bucks huh! What are you going to do with it?"

Luther shrugged. "I mean, it helps to have money, but not when you don't know where to go or what to do."

Finn laughed. "Only you would create a crisis situation out of a windfall. Just appreciate it and stop the damn worrying. You'll figure it out and it's not like you have to be anywhere or leave here, for that matter. Sorry you have to sleep on the couch and all, but it's not like you're in a jail cell."

"Oh no, Finn. I'm very appreciative. You, Dutch, Jed . . . you've all been so generous and––"

"Enough already," Finn interjected. "I have some news also."

"You do? Did you find Rocco?"

"Rocco went to the police and confessed."

"Confessed?" a bewildered Luther asked. "To what? The death of his child years ago? The police already knew about that."

Finn scoffed and shook his head. "Yeah and put him in prison for it. But he confessed to the murder that Theo was arrested for."

"Are you serious? What the . . ."

"It's crazy. He said Theo was wearing his shirt and that he had thrown it away after killing the man."

"This is nuts!" Luther exclaimed. "So Rocco's in jail and Theo's out of jail?"

"Yup."

"Have you talked to Theo?"

"Haven't talked to either of them. Joe's son-in-law Amos called and told me. I guess the lawyer is who they contact."

"So now we know where Rocco is but not Theo?"

"Something like that. But hey, I really don't want to get more involved. I got Theo a lawyer. Rocco can figure out his own representation since he's crazy enough to confess. He'll just get his wish, I suppose."

"You mean suicide by cop?" Luther asked.

Finn nodded. "In a roundabout way. So, what's for dinner?"

"Is it that time already?" Luther looked at his phone.

"It is if you're hungry."

"I just want to call the farm and tell them about my windfall."

"Take your time. I don't need you for cocktail hour." Finn went to the kitchen and Luther took out his phone to call Juniper.

"Hey, I've got great news!" he exclaimed into the phone.

"We could all use some good news around here," she replied. "Jed and Monica are going to be late so we haven't had our meeting yet."

"Oh jeez. I totally forgot. So much has been happening here. How's Homer?"

"Still hanging on. So what's your good news?"

"I got a call from Gordon. The compensation money has come through from the state for keeping me in prison all those years. It comes out to more than a million dollars!"

"A million dollars? Oh my God! Did you know it was going to be that much?"

"Nope. I don't get it all at once, though. Gordon's still finding out all the particulars, but I'm going to open a bank account so he can put in the first year's amount, around fifty thousand minus taxes."

"I'm happy for you, Luther."

"For us, Juniper. We're a couple. It's ours, not just mine."

Juniper sighed. "It's yours. You have a lot of life to live. Enjoy the money. I don't need it. I'm perfectly happy here on the farm."

Luther was flabbergasted. "What are you saying, Juniper? Are you breaking up with me?"

"No. Just let's look at this time as a break of sorts. You're there and I'm here. That's all."

"I don't understand what you're saying," Luther said, bewildered.

"Do you still want to be part of this meeting about Homer?" she asked.

"Yes! Call me when Jed and Monica get there."

"Okay. Bye Luther."

Finn came out of the kitchen. "Women troubles?" Luther gave him a look. "Yeah, I know. No privacy."

"I don't know," Luther admitted. "I can't figure it out."

"Well, here." Finn handed Luther a glass of whiskey. "Forget your troubles and celebrate your millionaire status."

Enough whiskey was consumed so that Luther completely forgot about the meeting at the farm. After a dinner of whatever was in the refrigerator, Luther glanced at his phone and noticed a missed call from Juniper. "Oh shit!" he exclaimed.

"What?" Finn asked as he washed the last of the dishes.

"I missed the call from Juniper––two hours ago!" He dialed, but it went to voicemail. "Hey, sorry, I missed the meeting. I didn't hear the phone. What did you all decide? Please let me know. Say hi to everyone and tell them I miss them. Uh . . . look forward to hearing from you soon." He hung up, worried that she wasn't answering his call on purpose.

"You've got enough on your own plate and Homer has plenty of people taking care of him. He's old. He's sick. He's had a good life. Let it go."

Luther bristled. "How can you be so heartless?"

"I'm not being heartless," Finn replied coolly. "Just realistic. I'm sure Homer would agree with me. I think you and I need a vacation."

"Vacation? Are you finally drunk?"

Finn narrowed his eyes. "No. It may come as a shock to you, but it's just as easy for me to fall into the same traps you do, worrying about everyone else. You think I don't care about Rocco and Theo? Or Homer for that matter? Sometimes you just plain have to focus on yourself. I may not have the police on my tail, but I've only got a few healthy years left if I'm lucky. Carpe diem, Luther. What do you say? You up for a trip?"

"I think you're already on one."

Finn burst out laughing. "Sock it to me!"

Luther managed to grin. "You mean . . . like Hawaii?"

"Oh Jesus Christ . . ." Finn gasped. "All the drinks there have fruit and flowers and umbrellas." He took a deep breath. "I was thinking of more like a road trip."

"Hm. That sounds kinda fun."

"You want to get back to Garberville. I'd like to see my daughter and Jed before I kick the bucket."

Luther's mouth dropped open. "A cross-country road trip?"

"Yeah," Finn smiled. "You need a chaperone and I need a driver." He crossed the room towards his bedroom, pausing to push up Luther's slack jaw with a knobby finger. "Pleasant dreams."

Chapter 18

FINN AND LUTHER BOTH TOSSED AND TURNED ALL NIGHT, OBSESSING OVER THIS NEW IDEA. They were up early and sleepily grinned at one another as they reached for cups of coffee.

"Well," Finn said to start the conversation. "You can probably get a pretty decent used car with some of the money you got."

"A car?"

"Well, we're not going to hitchhike."

Luther chuckled. "Yeah I know. But I don't want to spend the whole thing."

"That's why I said *used* car."

"So how much should I spend? We'll need money for motels and food and––"

"Luther! I'm not destitute. I'll pay my way. But I don't have a driver's license so I can't buy a car. And you realize you'll have to do all the driving."

"Oh, I figured that," Luther said with a mischievous look. "I guess buying a car would be the first step. What should I buy? And how do I do it?"

"I don't know. I never drove."

"Never?" Luther was incredulous.

"A lot of people in New York don't drive."

"And we need to figure out a route to take," Luther added.

"Let's just start driving."

Luther grinned, surprised and pleased to see Finn enthusiastic about anything at all. "You're much more adventurous than I thought."

"Yeah. You know me so well!" Finn said sarcastically. "We probably need to drive a southern route because of weather," he added.

"Maybe we should visit some used car lots," Luther mused.

Finn looked at him skeptically and shook his head. "There really aren't used car lots in Manhattan. We need to go to Queens or the Bronx, or even Staten Island."

"Queens is where the airport is, right?"

Finn smiled. "You're learning, you're learning. Do you know enough about cars so you won't get ripped off?"

"Not really. I always relied on Homer and Buster to help me when the truck had a problem."

"Hmm," Finn mused, drumming his fingers on the table. "I have a thought."

"Yeah?"

Finn went into his bedroom without answering. Luther fed Bardo and cleaned out the litter box. He sat back down to start Googling on his phone when Finn entered. "We are going on a train ride to Yonkers."

"There are used car lots in Yonkers?"

"No. I mean yes, but I've got something better. A friend of mine's late husband's car. He died––oh, a couple of years ago, and knowing her, it's probably still sitting in the garage. At least I saw it there a few months after his death."

"That sounds promising. How much?"

"I don't know. She's going to meet us at the train station."

"Do you know what kind of car it is?"

"No, but does it matter? As long as it's cheap enough and it runs well."

"I guess. So what time is the train?"

"Pretty much whenever we get to Grand Central. They leave every half hour or so."

"Grand Central huh. Maybe we should have lunch at the Oyster Bar," Luther added.

"Sure. I just told her I'd call when we got on the train."

"Is this a girlfriend?" Luther grinned.

"I don't have time for that nonsense anymore. Come on, let's go if we're going to eat first."

"Oh no!"

"What?"

"My lawyer Gordon told me I needed to have a bank account so he could transfer the money to me. I was going to do that yesterday. Do you have an account?"

Finn rolled his eyes. "No, Luther, I live in a dumpster."

"Huh? Oh––," Luther chuckled. "How about I just ask Gordon to transfer the money to your account?"

Finn shrugged. "That'd work, I guess. But don't you want to join the real world and have a bank account?"

"I guess," Luther replied reluctantly.

Finn rubbed his head. "Beside, I'm not sure how a chunk of money like that passing through my account would affect my taxes. Come on. Let's get ready. There's a Chase branch a couple of blocks from here."

"I'm pretty sure there isn't a Chase in Garberville."

"Doesn't matter," Finn said, getting up and taking the last swig of his coffee. "You bank on your phone. That's what folks your age do. And use ATMs."

"Hooray for technology," groaned Luther.

"Come on, old man," Finn sighed, giving him a playful shove. "Wash up. We've got a car to buy."

They were soon sitting at the desk of the assistant manager. "You don't have a bank account and you've never had one?" the woman asked incredulously.

Luther remembered getting his phone when he was first released from prison and the person there had been just as condescending. "I haven't needed one," he answered, trying not to show his annoyance.

"Do you have identification?" Luther took out his driver's license. "How about credit cards?" she continued.

"No."

She peered over her glasses. "Do you have any credit?"

"No."

She typed on her keyboard the answers Luther gave to her questions: name, address, phone etc. "How much are you planning to put in to open the account?"

Luther took out his wad of cash and looked at Finn for help. "Put in a hundred," Finn said.

"There will be fees involved for keeping such a low balance," the woman warned.

Luther squeezed the cash in frustration. "It won't be low for long," he mumbled. He then forced himself to look her in the eye. "I–I'm expecting a payment from––the government."

Her eyebrows rose for a moment, but then her expression softened. "Well, wouldn't it be nice if we all could be so lucky."

"Lady," Finn growled. "Luck had nothing to do with it."

A trace of color showed through her makeup. "Pardon me."

Luther suppressed a grin as he peeled off a hundred dollar bill and handed it to the woman. She took it and printed the papers for Luther to sign. "Do you want any checks?" she asked.

"Just give him a few," Finn replied. "He won't need a checkbook or anything."

"There will be a charge to print checks."

"Yeah, yeah. Print him two, then."

The woman typed again and then went off to collect the checks off a different printer. Luther glanced over at Finn. "Is it just me or is she a bitch?"

Finn chuckled. "Money is the root of all evil." He watched her as she started back towards them, her high heels clicking. "Aw, she's alright. Just not used to people like us."

The woman handed Luther a blue plastic envelope. "Here you go. Thank you for choosing Chase, gentlemen."

Finn and Luther rose and left the building. "Phew," Luther said. "Glad that's over."

"Me too. And I'm starving. Let's hit the subway."

They got on the subway, got off at Grand Central, and made a beeline for the Oyster Bar. "I don't see Joe," Luther said looking around the restaurant.

"It's probably too early for him. That's okay. We should eat quickly."

"Yeah. And I don't need that whole platter of seafood like the last time."

"You know what you like so just order that."

Luther read through the menu carefully, trying to decide. "I still can't believe these prices," he finally said.

"Jeez, Luther. You're a rich man now. What are you worried about prices for?"

"I don't know. I never had money before. We need to buy the car and then stay in motels and stuff."

Finn exhaled loudly and grabbed the menu out of Luther's hands. "We'll order the shellfish platter and split it, okay?"

"Sure. But I'm paying."

"That's fine, Luther, but I want you to understand that I'm not destitute and you don't owe me for staying at my apartment. It's not a burden." Then Finn smiled. "I like the company."

Luther smiled back. "Me too." The waiter came, they ordered, ate, paid the bill and were on the train an hour later.

Chapter 19

THE SCENERY FROM LUTHER'S WINDOW SEAT WAS A FAR CRY FROM THE QUAINT BROWNSTONES OF GREENWICH VILLAGE, THE SKYSCRAPERS OF MIDTOWN, AND THE HUGE APARTMENT BUILDINGS ON CENTRAL PARK. The train rumbled through Harlem and the Bronx before getting to Westchester. The tenements had clotheslines strung from window to window, so close to the railroad tracks that Luther felt like he could touch them. A break in the laundry revealed a huge neoclassical building about a block away. "That's Yankee Stadium," Finn said.

"Oh yeah? Looks more like a courthouse or something," Luther mused. I'm not much into baseball."

"Just adding to all the famous sights you've been so enthralled with since you arrived."

Luther looked at Finn quizzically. "Was that sarcastic?"

"Gee, Luther," Finn replied, rubbing his chin. "I guess it was. Please don't take offense."

Luther snorted. "Just checking, Mister Tour Guide."

Luther turned back to looking out the window. They went through the Bronx and then hit a few small towns before finally reaching Yonkers. As the train ground to a stop he noticed an elderly woman standing on the platform, short and round, with fluorescent red hair and matching nails and lipstick. "Is that your friend?"

"Yeah. That's Miriam." Finn chuckled. "She's hard to miss." They got off the train and Finn and Miriam hugged. "This is Luther."

"Very nice to meet you," Luther said, reaching out to shake her hand.

"Oh stuff and nonsense," she said, reaching around to hug him. "Any friend of Finn's . . . so you want to buy my husband's car?"

"Well, I guess, but I need to know something about it first."

"It was my Herb's pride and joy."

"What kind of car is it?"

"Chrysler. It's a convertible. I think it's called a Le Baron. I can't remember what year it is. You'd have to look at the registration, but it's pretty old."

"Like how old?" Finn interjected.

"He bought it new . . . oh my," she sighed. "Maybe almost forty years ago."

"In the eighties?" Luther's eyes popped out of his head. "Whoa. That's old."

"He took very good care of it."

"Let's go look at it," Finn said, taking Miriam's arm. "We can talk about the particulars when we see the car."

"This way, honey," Miriam smiled, guiding him towards a taxi parked at the curb.

"I thought you'd drive to pick us up," Finn said with surprise. "We could have taken a cab to your house."

"Oh, I don't drive anymore, but I needed to get out of the house. It's pretty boring getting old."

Finn patted her arm. "Yeah, but at least we have our health, right? You are doing well, Miriam?"

"Just the usual aches and pains. Nothing I can't handle. You okay too, Finn?"

"So far." They got in a taxi and Miriam gave the address to the driver.

"Can you tell me more about the car?" Luther asked.

"It's a real beauty," Miriam sighed. "I wish Herb was here to explain it better. Except he'd be giving me hell for selling it."

"Well, how much are you asking?"

Miriam shrugged. "I don't know. What do you want to pay?"

Luther looked at Finn. He had no idea and didn't know how to find out. Finn wouldn't know either, of course. "Uh, what do you think it's worth?"

"It doesn't matter what it's worth to me. What matters is that you're a friend of Finn's, you need a car, and will take good care of it."

Luther tried to decide whether he needed to tell her his story and how he came upon forty thousand dollars. And that's when he realized he didn't actually have the money yet. "Shoot. Finn, I never called my lawyer with my account number."

"Call him now," Finn replied as Miriam glanced between them with interest. "Get one of your checks out and read him the account number on the bottom."

"Okay." Luther took out the blue envelope containing his two checks and juggled it with his phone.

"Wait. No. Do it when we get to Miriam's. The cab driver doesn't need to know your account number." Luther nodded and put his phone back in his pocket along with the check. An awkward silence fell inside the cab, which Finn tried to cut by musing aloud, "We should probably have a mechanic look at it."

"Sure," Miriam said. "Take it to Horowitz. That's where Herb always went. I have receipts." She turned to Luther. "You don't know how to fix a car? I thought all young men were into cars."

Again Luther looked at Finn. Should he tell her his story? Finn smiled at him and shrugged. He knew what Luther was asking with his eyes, but he wasn't going to answer for him. "Um, not really. I've kind of been out of commission for some time."

Miriam gave him a quizzical look, but didn't ask him what he meant. "Well, you can drive it to Horowitz."

"I didn't think Jews became auto mechanics," Finn said.

"Hah! Nor the Irish!" Miriam replied.

"Why do you say that?" Luther asked.

"Just a joke," Finn answered.

They arrived at Miriam's and Finn quickly paid the cab driver before Miriam could protest. She took them into the kitchen and then to the door leading to the garage. The car was indeed in pristine condition: white with wood panel sides, a white top, and brown leather interior. Luther opened the door and sat down in the driver's seat. "Wow! This is incredible! Power every-thing?"

"Yeah," Miriam answered. "The top goes up and down by itself and the seats and windows do too."

"Get in Finn. See how it fits you."

Finn got into the passenger seat. "Pretty comfort-able."

"I'll get the key." Miriam left and returned with the key and handed it to Luther. He put it in the ignition, but nothing happened when he turned it.

"Do you think Horowitz would come here or would we have to have it towed?" Finn asked.

She shrugged. "All we can do is ask. Let me get the phone book."

They followed her into the kitchen and she took a phone book out of a drawer and handed it to Luther. He found Horowitz's Garage and dialed the number. "I have an old car that hasn't been driven for a while and won't start. Can you come here and look at it?"

"I have to send my tow truck driver. I can't leave the shop."

"Okay." Luther sighed, thinking about the cost. He turned to Miriam. "What's the address?"

"Give me the phone." Miriam gave her address to the mechanic and said, "Okay. Half an hour." She handed the phone back to Luther. "I don't know how to turn this thing off, anyway. Now, come and sit down while I get us some noshes."

"Oh that's not necessary," Finn protested.

Miriam glared at him. "Of course it's necessary. You don't visit an old Jewish lady without eating something."

Finn and Luther both laughed. "I guess that's true," Finn acquiesced.

Miriam told them to sit in the living room and she'd be right out. She joined them shortly with a plate of assorted cookies, a pot of coffee, a pile of plates, some cups and saucers, a sugar bowl and pitcher of cream on a tray. "Did you bake all these?" Luther asked.

"Of course not," she scoffed. "We have a wonderful Jewish bakery in town." She turned to Finn. "I know you'd rather have a glass of whiskey——"

"Not now," Finn interrupted. "Coffee's good."

Luther chuckled and whispered, "I don't think I've ever heard you say no to whiskey." Finn sneered back at him.

Luther took a cookie off the plate. "That's it? One cookie?" Miriam exclaimed. Luther shrugged and took a couple more. "That's better. Cream and sugar?" she added as she poured coffee into one of the cups, placed it on a saucer and handed it to Luther.

"Sure."

"Finn?" Miriam asked, handing him his coffee.

"Black is fine." Finn took a plate and a couple of cookies, as well.

"So," Miriam began as she sat down with her plate and cup. "What's in this for you, Finn?"

"Luther and I are planning a cross country trip."

"Again? You can't make up your mind what coast you want to live on?"

Finn laughed. "I'm just going along for the ride."

Miriam turned to Luther. "So you're the one wanting to go to California?"

"Well, um, I live there. I'm just visiting Finn."

Miriam looked from one to the other. "You're full of dreck. You think I'm a putz?"

Finn laughed and Luther looked at him, totally perplexed. "Just tell Miriam the truth, Luther. She's a good person."

"Ha! I was right. This is fercockt!"

"What? I——"

"Yiddish!" Finn and Miriam laughed in unison. Miriam continued, "Tell me the real story, honey."

Luther took a breath. "I was in prison for a murder that I did not commit. I got out twenty years later when The Innocence Project lawyers were able to prove I didn't do it. Then I went to live on a farm and uh . . ." He looked at Finn who nodded to him. "They found a body near the farm and they've accused me——"

"Why?" Miriam interrupted.

"Because I'm Black and I was in prison."

"But you were exonerated."

Luther paused for a moment. "As I said, I'm Black and I was in prison."

"Oh, yes," Miriam sighed. "I know all about labels. So why are you going back?"

Luther exhaled. "I don't know. I want to go home, but I'm not sure if that's the right decision."

"Since when did you make a decision?" Finn interjected.

"What do you mean?"

"Are you going back to the farm?" Finn asked.

Luther shrugged. "I don't know."

"So the only decision is that you are buying a car and you and I are going on a trip. And who knows where we'll end up?"

"Well, we need some kind of plan, don't we?"

"Der mensch trakht un Got lakht!" Miriam added. "Man plans and God laughs."

Finn smiled. "My son-in-law's favorite quote."

"You have a Jewish son-in-law?" Miriam asked.

Finn smiled again and looked at Luther. "Nope. A southern Black."

"I didn't know that," Luther chuckled, shaking his head.

"Apparently I have to keep reminding you that there's a lot about me you don't know."

Chapter 20

MIRIAM, FINN, AND LUTHER WAITED ANOTHER HOUR BEFORE THE DOORBELL RANG. Miriam pulled back the curtain from the window next to where she sat. "The tow truck is here," she announced, and the three of them went to the door.

"You called for a tow?" the driver asked.

"Yeah," Miriam answered. "Come this way. It's in the garage."

When Miriam opened the garage door, the tow truck let out a low whistle. "Whoa. Have I died and gone to Lee Iaccoca heaven?" He ran a hand over a faux wood panel. "Nuff plastic here to build a Kia." He patted the hood. "So it won't start?"

"Hasn't been driven since my husband Herb got sick. It's been a couple of years."

"Oh, he's doing better?"

"He's dead," Miriam said simply. "But this young man wants to buy it."

The driver nodded. "Oh, sorry ma'am. Well, Mr. Iacocca wouldn't like me to just crank his baby after sitting so long. Gotta drain out old gas and make sure the oil hasn't turned to tar. I'll just tow it to the station."

Finn and Luther got in the cab along with the driver after hooking up the car. They pulled into the garage and a middle-aged Black man in greasy blue overalls came out from one of the bays, wiping his hands on a dirty red rag. "Are you Horowitz?" Luther called out, holding the pile of receipts Miriam had given him.

The man lifted his chin as if he had been hit and started laughing. "Do I look like a Horowitz? What are you doing with Schwartz' Town & Country anyway?" He turned to Finn. "You a Schwartz?"

"Nope. Irish."

The mechanic started laughing again. "Hell, it's like we're on the floor of the United Nations. So, what can I do for you?"

"I'm looking for the owner of this shop, Horowitz," Luther said, tapping the pile of receipts. "Thought I'd have him go over some of these with me."

"Well, I bought the business from Horowitz, so now you're stuck with me," the mechanic grinned.

"You didn't change the name?"

"He had a good reputation here. I don't need to have my name on the door."

"So how did you know whose car this was?" Luther asked.

"Daddy said to always look people in the eye and remember their names and you'll get far in business and pleasure, even if Daddy's business was mostly pleasure.

Anyway, I was here when Mr. Schwartz used to come in for his annual check-up and boy did I have to jump to keep his business. But we worked it out and when he picked up his car he sorta apologized for being an old fart."

"I never apologize for being an old fart," Finn chimed in, trying to keep a straight face.

The mechanic shot him a look, but refrained from any number of smartass remarks running through his mind. "Anyway, we started talking man to man and sharing our slights of life. He even showed me his tattoo before he left."

"Tattoo?" Luther asked

"Ya know, camp numbers."

"Come on, Luther. You know," Finn sighed. "*Concen-tration* camp."

"Oh." Luther looked down.

"He taught me the Yiddish word for Black is Schvartze. But he said it was derogatory, so if I ever heard anyone say it to me, I should call them a Kike."

"That's no way to get someone's business," Finn chuckled.

"I think he was joking. So," the mechanic went on, looking at Luther. "What do you want to know?"

"I want to buy this car," Luther replied in a small voice, "And I want to know if it'll make it to California."

The mechanic let out a guffaw. "Yeah, but I suggest you don't drive through Mississippi." Luther looked down, embarrassed. "Ah, c'mon, buddy," the mechanic said, clapping a hand on his shoulder. "It's a joke, but also sound advice. Let's go inside and work on the computer. It'll be quicker to show you everything than going through this pile." He stuck his hand out. "I'm Damon."

"Luther," he replied, shaking Damon's hand. "And the old fart is Finn."

Damon let out a peal of laughter. "Now that's more like it!" Damon led them to the office. "Coffee? Just made a fresh pot. Momma says never let anyone drink out of a nasty old pot."

"Don't mind if I do," Finn said, reaching for a cup and the carafe as Damon went over to the computer.

"So," Damon began, "Is this gonna be like that movie, 'Driving Miss––"

"Yeah, yeah," Finn snorted. "But more whiskey, less perfume."

Damon just grinned as he scrolled. "Schwartz, Schwartz, Schwartz. Here we go. '83 Chrysler LeBaron Town & Country convertible. He brought it in every mid-summer or so for a checkup. He used to do his own oil until a few years ago. Boy did he gripe about what we charged for synthetic. I replaced the PVC valve and three vacuum hoses, and a light tune up. I cleaned the plugs and made sure it was within tolerances on the diagnostics. A few years back we replaced the water pump and gave the cooling system a good flush and fresh coolant. Those are the kind of things you have to watch for in old cream puff like this. Hoses, valves and fluids deteriorate whether you use the car much or not. Got AAA?"

"Uh, no," Luther replied.

"It's not a bad idea," Damon said, casting an eye at Finn. "Anyway, I think you'll do fine if you treat her nicely. No hot roddin' and shit like that. Just pretend you're Mr. Schwartz. Keep an eye on the oil level. Check it every morning and top her off if she uses it. I can give her a good look over, but I'm pretty busy today."

"How much?" Luther murmured.

"Oh, get me a combo pizza for dinner and a couple hundred bucks for labor. Won't know what the parts will cost until I look. And you better send me texts and photos of the trip."

"Especially if we get stuck somewhere west of Laramie," Finn smirked.

Damon shook his head as he tapped on the keyboard. "I'm more worried about Luther than the Chrysler, old fart."

"How are we going to get to the train station?" Luther asked Finn.

"I'll have Bruno give you a lift, if you don't mind riding in the tow truck again. Let me just get your phone number." Luther gave it to him.

"When you planning on leaving?" Damon asked.

Luther shrugged and glanced at Finn who let out a chuckle. "Doesn't matter," he replied. "We have no agenda and no place we have to be."

Damon smiled at them. "Now that's the life!"

"Ain't liminality great," Finn smiled back.

Damon looked at him quizzically, but let it go. "What time is the train?"

Finn shrugged. "Doesn't matter. We can wait at the station. There are a lot of them into the city aren't there?"

"At this hour there's a shitload coming from the city. I don't know about the other direction. Bruno can take you when he gets back from his latest call. Meanwhile, I need to get back to work. I'll look at your car tomorrow."

"Thanks," Luther answered. He and Finn started to walk outside.

"You can wait inside," Damon called after them. "No need to be out in the cold."

Bruno arrived a few minutes later and Damon told him to take Finn and Luther to the train station. They waited there for about half an hour and both fell asleep on the ride back to Grand Central. When they got home, Finn looked at the clock. "Jesus! It's already eight o'clock. I need to eat something." He opened the refrigerator and took out some eggs and cheese.

"You're really going to cook now?" Luther asked.

"Why not? Pour me a glass and I'll make us some omelets." Luther did as he was told. "No drink for you?"

Luther shook his head. "I don't know how you do it, Finn. You're twice my age but you have twice the energy."

"Must be the whiskey," Finn winked.

Bardo appeared, meowing and rubbing on Luther's leg. "Oh man!" Luther exclaimed. "I forgot about Bardo." Luther got out the cat food and poured it into a bowl. "Here you go Bardo. I'm sorry that I forgot about you."

"Hey, don't worry about it. She has a warm place to sleep and food to eat. She's happy."

"How are we going to figure out how much to pay for the car?" Luther asked.

"First of all, we're going to have to see if anything's wrong with it. Then I guess we can ask Damon what he thinks we should pay."

"Maybe we can look for other cars like it and what people are asking for them," Luther added.

"That's an idea. Why don't you Google it."

"Finn, I'm really not good with computers. Could you do it?"

Finn grinned and shook his head. "It's not rocket science to type words into Google, but I'll do it in the morning."

"I bet Buster or Dutch would know," Luther murmured.

"Would know what? How to Google?"

"No. How to figure out what to pay."

"Then call them," Finn answered.

Luther looked at the clock and said, "I guess I could call Dutch, but I didn't want him to know anything yet, so he wouldn't have to lie to the police."

"You don't have to tell him where you are or where we're going. Just ask him how much to pay for the car."

"I 'm not sure he'd know."

Finn shrugged. "Maybe not, but he'd probably have an idea how to find out."

"Okay." Luther dialed Dutch's number, but it went to voicemail. "Hey Dutch, it's Luther. Um . . . do you know how to find out what a car is worth? Uh . . . like who to ask or something? You could just text me. Thanks." He hung up and Finn laughed loudly. "What's funny?"

"You probably should give a little more information, even if you're not telling him the whole story. Like what kind of car or at least that it's an old one. I really doubt his phone is tapped if that's what you're afraid of."

"It's not that. I just don't want to put him in an awkward situation."

Finn shook his head and turned back to the stove and his omelet-cooking. Luther got a glass out of the cupboard and poured himself a couple of fingers. "Joining me after all?" Finn asked.

"Living with you brings it out I guess."

"Well, well, well. Looks like I'm having an influence on you after all. Drinking and being a smart ass."

Luther smiled wanly and gulped the rest of his drink down. "I guess I'm learning from the top dog." He heard a ding and looked at his phone. "It's Dutch. He says to look at Kelly Blue Book and Edmunds."

"There you go. I tell you what, we'll eat first and then we can look online together. Fair enough?"

"Sounds good." They sat down and ate quickly and were on Finn's computer a few minutes later. "Here's that Kelly Blue Book site," Finn said. "KBB dot com. Let's see. There's used car values. Okay. They want the year, make, and model. Uh oh."

"Uh oh what?" Luther asked.

"They don't go as far back as 1983."

"Then try that Edmunds one."

Finn typed some more. "Same problem."

"Crap. What now?"

"I told you to tell Dutch it was an old car."

"I'll text him. Oh man! I forgot to ask about the meeting with Jed about Homer. They didn't call me when Jed got there."

Finn raised his eyebrows. "Is that because Juniper's mad at you?"

"She's not mad at me. I don't know why." Luther looked down at his phone. "Oh. Wait. There's a voicemail." He listened and frowned. "They tried calling, but I didn't answer."

"It was probably when we were on the train underground. So what did the voicemail say?"

"They were meeting then, so they hadn't made any decision."

"You can ask Dutch when you tell him the year of the car."

Luther texted and Dutch answered right back. "He said they would honor Homer's wishes to be home. That there were enough of them to give him round-the-clock care."

"And?"

"And what?"

"What about another place to see the value of the car?"

"Oh yeah." Luther looked down. "Autotrader."

Finn typed and read out the results. "Well . . . they certainly run the gamut. None are 1983. They're 1985 and 86."

"How much?" Luther asked.

"They go from six thousand to fifteen thousand."

"What are the differences? Do they all run well and look good?"

Finn read for a minute. "Yeah."

"So what do you think?"

"I say if everything checks out well, give Miriam ten thousand. That's in the middle range and seems fair."

"Okay. Oh brother. I forgot to give Gordon my account number.Luther called Gordon, Finn did the dishes, and Bardo jumped up on the keyboard that Finn had just finished using and curled up to sleep.

Chapter 21

DAMON CALLED THE NEXT DAY WITH GOOD
NEWS. They could pick up the car that afternoon and it
would be ready to go. He started to list the things that
he fixed, but Luther stopped him. "Can it wait until we
get there? I think I'd understand more if you just
showed me what you fixed on the car."

"No problem, man," Damon chuckled. Maybe I
should go with you, just to make sure you get there."

"Well, uh——"

Damon burst out laughing. "Man, I'm just kiddin'.
Two Black dudes with an old White guy in the back
seat, we'd be busted in no time."

"Oh, ha. Yeah." Luther turned to Finn. "What time do
you think we can be there this afternoon?"

"That's alright," Damon interjected. "It doesn't
matter. It'll be ready anytime you come. I close at five.
Don't forget the pizza."

"Oh right. What kind was that again? And, uh, where
should we buy it?"

"We can figure that out when you get here. Maybe
we'll all go out to dinner and celebrate."

Luther didn't know if he was kidding or not, so he decided to just acquiesce without committing to anything. "Okay. See you this afternoon." He hung up and turned to Finn. "Are you teaching today?"

"I'm supposed to."

"Should we wait to pick up the car on a day you're not teaching?"

Finn shrugged. "I don't drive. Do you really need me along?"

Luther's eyes almost popped out of his head. "Yes! I don't know my way around here. I'm nervous about driving in the city. And where would I park when I get back?"

Finn grinned. "Gee, Luther. You're a forty-year-old man. How are you going to drive across the country if you can't drive here?"

"By staying away from big cities. I'm used to driving out in the country. Who wants to fight traffic anyway?"

Finn laughed. "I tell you what. I'll ask Miriam if we can leave it at her house until we're ready to go. I'm sure it will be fine. You call Damon and ask him if we can leave it there until we can get up there to drive it to Miriam's."

"Good idea. Do we have any idea when we should leave?"

"There are no shoulds. We'll go after I've let them know at both my gigs that I'll be gone."

"What about Theo and Rocco?" Luther asked.

"What about them?"

"I don't know. Do you?" Luther asked.

Finn shrugged. "I don't think cats do well in cars, though."

"Well then, what'll we do?"

"Give the cat away or take Bardo, anyway."

Luther shrugged. "I don't know. Can I think about it?"

Finn laughed. "Sure." He opened the door and they went inside.

They finished their banking business and asked about how to pay for the car and were told that a cashier's check was best and they could get one at the bank branch in Yonkers. They left for home, discussing their lunch plans. "Shouldn't we eat up any food left in the fridge?"

"Good idea. See that, Luther. You're turning into a regular person, planning ahead and being thrifty."

Luther wished he was quick with snappy, sarcastic replies, but he wasn't. He just frowned and kept quiet and left the sarcasm to Finn. They walked home in silence, each contemplating what lay ahead with a bit of trepidation. "I think we should take Bardo," Luther said as they opened the door to Finn's apartment and Bardo greeted them with meows and leg-rubbings. "Should we take the litter box or treat Bardo like a dog and use a leash when we stop?"

"We'll just let Bardo out."

"I'd be worried."

"I don't know. I mean, are we going to just leave them both in the lurch?"

"What lurch? Rocco made his decision. Joe's son is taking Rocco's case. And we have no idea where Theo is or how to get in touch with him."

"I guess you're right," Luther sighed.

"You know, they're not our responsibility. Theo's young and healthy. He'll be fine."

"I guess I feel for him because he's kind of in the same circumstances I am. He was in jail for a crime he didn't commit."

"We don't know if he committed it or not. Just 'cause Rocco confessed doesn't mean Theo didn't do it."

"Really?" Luther was shocked. "You believe that?"

"I didn't say I believed it," Finn answered. "I said we don't know. Just leave it. Anyway, are you coming with me today?"

"I guess so. Hey Finn? What else do we have to do before we leave?"

Finn shrugged. "Go to the bank and get you some traveler's checks."

"Traveler's checks? What are those?"

Finn scoffed. "You know––." Then he frowned. "You don't have a credit card. I guess we can use mine and you can get a debit card and cash."

Luther nodded. "What time should we leave for the writing class?"

"We'll go to the bank first. Let's leave here about 11:30."

"How do we pay for the car?"

"We'll ask at the bank. Probably a cashiers check."

"I don't know what that is, but okay."

Finn started to make a flippant remark, but stopped himself. "I'm sorry, Luther."

"What? You're saying you're sorry?"

"Yeah. I am. I forget that you were in a jail cell and then a farm where you didn't have to do much of anything independently. I don't mean it disrespectfully. Really. I don't apologize often. Take it and don't comment."

"Okay. Thanks."

Finn went to his room and shut the door, leaving Luther to ponder what was going on with Finn. He wanted to call Juniper and talk about what was happening between them, but it was too early in California . . . so much for calling Jed either. Well, he could call Damon back at least. "Hey Damon. Would it be possible for us to come another day?"

"That's fine for now. I've got room to leave it for a few days."

"Thanks. I'll pay you extra."

"No need. Just let me know when you're coming. It'll be parked in the back of the garage."

They hung up and Luther contemplated what Finn had said earlier about being a forty-year-old man and afraid to drive in cities. Finn was right. But Luther had fears beyond driving in cities. He had finally gotten used to the farm and what goes along with a rural life-

style. Having grown up in a city, he hadn't thought urban lifestyle would affect him. But New York was cry from San Francisco in more than just populatic and food choices. Luther found there was much to afraid of after most of your life had consisted of a in, closet-sized cell. He tried to suppress them or a least hide them from others, but his fears were nu ous and diverse.

Finn and Luther took off for the bank, discussi what, if anything, they would need to buy for thei They didn't come up with much since neither of t was particularly adept at traveling. Finn had done share, but always by plane and always to and fron large enough to provide everything he would nee Luther had nothing to offer, never being anywhe northern California. He had taken a quick trip to Phoenix once, to the Musical Instrument Museu he was with Dutch and had left all planning and cisions to him. Their final determination was tha would take some snacks, whiskey and plenty of get anything they had forgotten.

"What are we going to do about Bardo?" Finn just as they approached the door to the bank.

Luther stopped in his tracks. "Jeez, I don't kn had forgotten about that. What do you think we do?"

"Do you want the cat?" Finn asked.

"You mean forever?"

"Yeah. That would give us our answer."

"There you go again, Luther. Do you always look for the worst case scenario?"

"No, but––"

"I'm kidding," Finn interrupted. "I don't relish bothering with a litter box in the car," Finn interrupted. "If Bardo runs away, there's nothing we can do about it."

Luther sighed. "I guess you're right."

Finn looked at the clock. "We'd better gobble something down and get on the way to the park for the writing group."

Luther opened the refrigerator and took out some cheese, lettuce, pickles and mustard. "I'm making a cheese sandwich. Want one?" Finn nodded and took out the bread to give to Luther.

The writing class went well and just before it was time to clean up, Finn stood up to address the group. "I'll be going on a trip and I'll be gone for a while. Keep writing and I'll let the powers-that-be know when I'm back and they'll put up a sign on the door."

There was much chatter at that point and several people threw out questions and disappointed comments. Finn ignored them all, to Luther's surprise. Just as they finished tidying up the room, the door opened and Theo burst in. "Theo!" Luther cried out and strode quickly over to him with a grin on his face.

"Oh man, I'm so glad you're still here!" Theo said breathlessly.

"Are you okay?" Luther asked.

"I guess. I don't know what to do about Rocco. He didn't murder that guy either! He just confessed to get me out of jail."

"We know that," Finn said, gently pushing the other two toward the door.

"How can we get him out of jail?" Theo asked. "We can't leave him there."

"Nothing we can do," Finn replied. "It's up to the lawyer now to work with him. And there's more to it than just his wanting to free you. He thinks he should be punished for what he did years ago. The guilt overwhelmed him and he probably somehow feels better being in jail, strangely enough."

Theo glanced at Luther who nodded in agreement with Finn. "Rocco has to do this himself. We can only hope that he finally realizes that he can't continue to beat himself up over an accident."

"Well, I don't know if he'll ever get to that point," Finn added, "but perhaps he will realize that this is not the way to live out the rest of his days . . . in a jail cell."

"But now I feel guilty!" Theo shouted.

Finn put his hands on Theo's shoulders. "Listen to me, Theo. You did nothing. He did it to himself."

Theo started to cry softly. "I miss him. He was like my Dad." Luther and Finn exchanged glances.

"Where are you staying?" Finn asked.

"At the Bowery Mission."

"Is that a good idea?" Luther asked abruptly. "I mean, after all that's happened."

Theo looked at Luther questioningly. "Well, it was Rocco that got us kicked out."

"I mean since that's where you were when that guy was murdered near there."

"It doesn't matter anymore, now that Rocco's taken the rap. The cops don't care about me. Right?"

"I wouldn't be so sure. They might think you were in on it with Rocco."

"You'll be alright," Finn broke in and glared at Luther.

"Aren't there other homeless shelters Theo could go to?"

"Go talk to the folks at Covenant House," Finn responded. "They can help you."

Theo shook his head as he wiped his tears with his sleeve. "They have a waiting list. I'll be okay." He started to leave.

"Hey Theo!" Luther called out. "Um, take this." He took a couple of twenties out of his wallet and handed them to Theo.

"Huh?"

"Get a meal or something."

"Uh, thanks." Theo sighed. "I guess I lost my job taking care of Rocco."

"You need a phone, Theo," Luther said.

"Where's the nearest phone store to your apartment, Finn?"

Finn smiled at Luther and shook his head. He turned to Theo. "Meet us tomorrow morning at ten at the Verizon store on Eighth Street, a block or so from Broadway."

"You gonna buy me a phone?" Theo asked, incredulously.

"We can get you a burner with some minutes," Luther said. "Then you'll need to put more minutes on as you need them. That's what I did when I first got out of prison."

Theo's eyes widened. "You were in prison?"

"I was arrested for a crime I didn't commit. Same as you."

"I'd like to get the hell out of here if you don't mind," Finn said sharply.

"Thanks guys." Theo hugged them both and ran off.

"You are a piece of work, Luther." Finn patted his back.

"A good piece or a bad piece?" Luther asked with a smirk.

"Well, I don't think you should have frightened Theo about staying at the mission, but you made up for it."

"So I'm both a bad guy and a good guy?"

"You tell me."

"Nah, I'll keep you guessing."

"I will say, Luther, you seem to have joined the cantankerous cynics club."

Luther laughed. "Thanks, Finn. That means a lot."

They spent the evening poring over maps after cleaning more food out of the cabinets and refrigerator. Their dinner was a hodgepodge, but they didn't care. They were both starting to get excited about the trip. "Are you going up to Yonkers with me to buy the car?" Luther asked.

"Yes, Luther," Finn answered with a sly grin. "We can go after you buy Theo his phone."

"Did you talk to Miriam about leaving it in her garage?"

"Yes. But I'll call her in the morning and let her know we'll be bringing it to her tomorrow afternoon. I also need to stop by the Covenant House and inform them that I'll be gone."

"Are you supposed to be there tomorrow?"

"Yeah. We can stop on our way to Grand Central."

"Are we having lunch at Oyster Bar? After all, you need to let Joe know you'll be gone too."

"We don't usually keep tabs on each other, but okay if you want an excuse to eat at the Oyster Bar."

"I know you want to be spontaneous and all, but when do you think you'd want to leave?"

"Couple of days. We should probably watch the weather too."

"Have you told your daughter yet?"

"No. I'll call her when we're ready to leave."

"Should I tell Jed and Dutch?"

"Jed, for sure. You don't need to tell Dutch yet. You're not going up to the farm, are you?"

Luther shrugged. "I want to see Homer before . . ."

"Up to you, Luther, But why not wait and see."

Luther nodded. "Good advice, that wait and see stuff. Apparently that's your mantra."

"Hasn't always been. It's just the wisdom that comes with age. You might as well learn it before I did. On that note, I'm going to bed."

Finn left and Luther took out his phone. He could at least find out how Homer was doing. He texted Juniper who texted back that Homer was home and doing okay. She asked about his buying a car. Luther wanted to tell her so badly what was going on, but knew he needed to still stay under the radar. Instead he just texted back that it was a good deal and he knew he'd need one eventually. That sounded vague enough, he thought. He waited several minutes for a response from her, but nothing came. He sighed and put his phone down. He'd try to sleep, but he wasn't sure how successful he would be.

"I don't know. I mean, are we going to just leave them both in the lurch?"

"What lurch? Rocco made his decision. Joe's son is taking Rocco's case. And we have no idea where Theo is or how to get in touch with him."

"I guess you're right," Luther sighed.

"You know, they're not our responsibility. Theo's young and healthy. He'll be fine."

"I guess I feel for him because he's kind of in the same circumstances I am. He was in jail for a crime he didn't commit."

"We don't know if he committed it or not. Just 'cause Rocco confessed doesn't mean Theo didn't do it."

"Really?" Luther was shocked. "You believe that?"

"I didn't say I believed it," Finn answered. "I said we don't know. Just leave it. Anyway, are you coming with me today?"

"I guess so. Hey Finn? What else do we have to do before we leave?"

Finn shrugged. "Go to the bank and get you some traveler's checks."

"Traveler's checks? What are those?"

Finn scoffed. "You know––." Then he frowned. "You don't have a credit card. I guess we can use mine and you can get a debit card and cash."

Luther nodded. "What time should we leave for the writing class?"

"We'll go to the bank first. Let's leave here about 11:30."

"How do we pay for the car?"

"We'll ask at the bank. Probably a cashiers check."

"I don't know what that is, but okay."

Finn started to make a flippant remark, but stopped himself. "I'm sorry, Luther."

"What? You're saying you're sorry?"

"Yeah. I am. I forget that you were in a jail cell and then a farm where you didn't have to do much of anything independently. I don't mean it disrespectfully. Really. I don't apologize often. Take it and don't comment."

"Okay. Thanks."

Finn went to his room and shut the door, leaving Luther to ponder what was going on with Finn. He wanted to call Juniper and talk about what was happening between them, but it was too early in California . . . so much for calling Jed either. Well, he could call Damon back at least. "Hey Damon. Would it be possible for us to come another day?"

"That's fine for now. I've got room to leave it for a few days."

"Thanks. I'll pay you extra."

"No need. Just let me know when you're coming. It'll be parked in the back of the garage."

They hung up and Luther contemplated what Finn had said earlier about being a forty-year-old man and afraid to drive in cities. Finn was right. But Luther had fears beyond driving in cities. He had finally gotten used to the farm and what goes along with a rural lifestyle. Having grown up in a city, he hadn't thought an urban lifestyle would affect him. But New York was a far cry from San Francisco in more than just population and food choices. Luther found there was much to be afraid of after most of your life had consisted of a walk-in, closet-sized cell. He tried to suppress them or at least hide them from others, but his fears were numerous and diverse.

Finn and Luther took off for the bank, discussing what, if anything, they would need to buy for their trip. They didn't come up with much since neither of them was particularly adept at traveling. Finn had done his share, but always by plane and always to and from cities large enough to provide everything he would need. Luther had nothing to offer, never being anywhere but northern California. He had taken a quick trip to Phoenix once, to the Musical Instrument Museum. But he was with Dutch and had left all planning and decisions to him. Their final determination was that they would take some snacks, whiskey and plenty of cash to get anything they had forgotten.

"What are we going to do about Bardo?" Finn asked just as they approached the door to the bank.

Luther stopped in his tracks. "Jeez, I don't know. I had forgotten about that. What do you think we should do?"

"Do you want the cat?" Finn asked.

"You mean forever?"

"Yeah. That would give us our answer."

"I don't know. Do you?" Luther asked.

Finn shrugged. "I don't think cats do well in cars, though."

"Well then, what'll we do?"

"Give the cat away or take Bardo, anyway."

Luther shrugged. "I don't know. Can I think about it?"

Finn laughed. "Sure." He opened the door and they went inside.

They finished their banking business and asked about how to pay for the car and were told that a cashier's check was best and they could get one at the bank branch in Yonkers. They left for home, discussing their lunch plans. "Shouldn't we eat up any food left in the fridge?"

"Good idea. See that, Luther. You're turning into a regular person, planning ahead and being thrifty."

Luther wished he was quick with snappy, sarcastic replies, but he wasn't. He just frowned and kept quiet and left the sarcasm to Finn. They walked home in silence, each contemplating what lay ahead with a bit of trepidation. "I think we should take Bardo," Luther said as they opened the door to Finn's apartment and Bardo greeted them with meows and leg-rubbings. "Should we take the litter box or treat Bardo like a dog and use a leash when we stop?"

"We'll just let Bardo out."

"I'd be worried."

"There you go again, Luther. Do you always look for the worst case scenario?"

"No, but––"

"I'm kidding," Finn interrupted. "I don't relish bothering with a litter box in the car," Finn interrupted. "If Bardo runs away, there's nothing we can do about it."

Luther sighed. "I guess you're right."

Finn looked at the clock. "We'd better gobble something down and get on the way to the park for the writing group."

Luther opened the refrigerator and took out some cheese, lettuce, pickles and mustard. "I'm making a cheese sandwich. Want one?" Finn nodded and took out the bread to give to Luther.

The writing class went well and just before it was time to clean up, Finn stood up to address the group. "I'll be going on a trip and I'll be gone for a while. Keep writing and I'll let the powers-that-be know when I'm back and they'll put up a sign on the door."

There was much chatter at that point and several people threw out questions and disappointed comments. Finn ignored them all, to Luther's surprise. Just as they finished tidying up the room, the door opened and Theo burst in. "Theo!" Luther cried out and strode quickly over to him with a grin on his face.

"Oh man, I'm so glad you're still here!" Theo said breathlessly.

"Are you okay?" Luther asked.

"I guess. I don't know what to do about Rocco. He didn't murder that guy either! He just confessed to get me out of jail."

"We know that," Finn said, gently pushing the other two toward the door.

"How can we get him out of jail?" Theo asked. "We can't leave him there."

"Nothing we can do," Finn replied. "It's up to the lawyer now to work with him. And there's more to it than just his wanting to free you. He thinks he should be punished for what he did years ago. The guilt overwhelmed him and he probably somehow feels better being in jail, strangely enough."

Theo glanced at Luther who nodded in agreement with Finn. "Rocco has to do this himself. We can only hope that he finally realizes that he can't continue to beat himself up over an accident."

"Well, I don't know if he'll ever get to that point," Finn added, "but perhaps he will realize that this is not the way to live out the rest of his days . . . in a jail cell."

"But now I feel guilty!" Theo shouted.

Finn put his hands on Theo's shoulders. "Listen to me, Theo. You did nothing. He did it to himself."

Theo started to cry softly. "I miss him. He was like my Dad." Luther and Finn exchanged glances.

"Where are you staying?" Finn asked.

"At the Bowery Mission."

"Is that a good idea?" Luther asked abruptly. "I mean, after all that's happened."

Theo looked at Luther questioningly. "Well, it was Rocco that got us kicked out."

"I mean since that's where you were when that guy was murdered near there."

"It doesn't matter anymore, now that Rocco's taken the rap. The cops don't care about me. Right?"

"I wouldn't be so sure. They might think you were in on it with Rocco."

"You'll be alright," Finn broke in and glared at Luther.

"Aren't there other homeless shelters Theo could go to?"

"Go talk to the folks at Covenant House," Finn responded. "They can help you."

Theo shook his head as he wiped his tears with his sleeve. "They have a waiting list. I'll be okay." He started to leave.

"Hey Theo!" Luther called out. "Um, take this." He took a couple of twenties out of his wallet and handed them to Theo.

"Huh?"

"Get a meal or something."

"Uh, thanks." Theo sighed. "I guess I lost my job taking care of Rocco."

"You need a phone, Theo," Luther said.

"Where's the nearest phone store to your apartment, Finn?"

Finn smiled at Luther and shook his head. He turned to Theo. "Meet us tomorrow morning at ten at the Verizon store on Eighth Street, a block or so from Broadway."

"You gonna buy me a phone?" Theo asked, incredulously.

"We can get you a burner with some minutes," Luther said. "Then you'll need to put more minutes on as you need them. That's what I did when I first got out of prison."

Theo's eyes widened. "You were in prison?"

"I was arrested for a crime I didn't commit. Same as you."

"I'd like to get the hell out of here if you don't mind," Finn said sharply.

"Thanks guys." Theo hugged them both and ran off.

"You are a piece of work, Luther." Finn patted his back.

"A good piece or a bad piece?" Luther asked with a smirk.

"Well, I don't think you should have frightened Theo about staying at the mission, but you made up for it."

"So I'm both a bad guy and a good guy?"

"You tell me."

"Nah, I'll keep you guessing."

"I will say, Luther, you seem to have joined the cantankerous cynics club."

Luther laughed. "Thanks, Finn. That means a lot."

They spent the evening poring over maps after cleaning more food out of the cabinets and refrigerator. Their dinner was a hodgepodge, but they didn't care. They were both starting to get excited about the trip. "Are you going up to Yonkers with me to buy the car?" Luther asked.

"Yes, Luther," Finn answered with a sly grin. "We can go after you buy Theo his phone."

"Did you talk to Miriam about leaving it in her garage?"

"Yes. But I'll call her in the morning and let her know we'll be bringing it to her tomorrow afternoon. I also need to stop by the Covenant House and inform them that I'll be gone."

"Are you supposed to be there tomorrow?"

"Yeah. We can stop on our way to Grand Central."

"Are we having lunch at Oyster Bar? After all, you need to let Joe know you'll be gone too."

"We don't usually keep tabs on each other, but okay if you want an excuse to eat at the Oyster Bar."

"I know you want to be spontaneous and all, but when do you think you'd want to leave?"

"Couple of days. We should probably watch the weather too."

"Have you told your daughter yet?"

"No. I'll call her when we're ready to leave."

"Should I tell Jed and Dutch?"

"Jed, for sure. You don't need to tell Dutch yet. You're not going up to the farm, are you?"

Luther shrugged. "I want to see Homer before . . ."

"Up to you, Luther, But why not wait and see."

Luther nodded. "Good advice, that wait and see stuff. Apparently that's your mantra."

"Hasn't always been. It's just the wisdom that comes with age. You might as well learn it before I did. On that note, I'm going to bed."

Finn left and Luther took out his phone. He could at least find out how Homer was doing. He texted Juniper who texted back that Homer was home and doing okay. She asked about his buying a car. Luther wanted to tell her so badly what was going on, but knew he needed to still stay under the radar. Instead he just texted back that it was a good deal and he knew he'd need one eventually. That sounded vague enough, he thought. He waited several minutes for a response from her, but nothing came. He sighed and put his phone down. He'd try to sleep, but he wasn't sure how successful he would be.

Chapter 22

LUTHER AWOKE TO BARDO PURRING ON HIS CHEST. "Hey, Bardo," he murmured. "You want to go on a trip?" Bardo stretched and bumped noses with him. He stroked the cat for a few minutes and then got up and went to the kitchen to get some food for her. Finn was up, pouring himself a cup of coffee.

"Hey, sleeping beauty. It's already nine o'clock. I'm working on my third cup."

"I better hustle then," Luther yawned. "I didn't sleep too well." He put some food down for Bardo and went to shower.

"Did you call Jed last night?" Finn asked when Luther returned to the kitchen, clean and dressed.

"No, did you?"

"I thought you should."

"Okay." Luther looked at the clock. "Kind of early. I'll do it later."

Finn nodded. "We'd better get down to the Verizon store." They left and found Theo waiting at the door of the store, smiling and waving. "He looks happy," Finn said.

"I'm sure he's excited to have a phone of his own," Luther replied. "I know I was."

"You realize that Theo wasn't there when I told the group that I was going on a trip."

"I know," Luther answered. "Well, we can tell him now and at least he'll have a phone so we can be in touch with him."

Finn nodded and greeted Theo. They went inside and told the clerk that they wanted a burner phone. "Oh, a prepaid plan?"

"Uh, yeah."

"Do you have a phone?"

"No."

"We have some great new models over here." The clerk led the threesome to the displays of different phones.

"Oh man!" Luther bellowed. "These are expensive. When I got mine, the store had some old used ones in the back. Do you have any?"

"I'm afraid not."

"Hold on," Finn interjected. "I have an idea. There's a thrift shop down the street. Maybe they have a phone."

"I don't think it's a good idea to get one at a thrift store," the clerk cut in. "You really want to find one somewhere that sells electronics."

"Hey guys?" Theo interjected. "I can get one."

Luther and Finn exchanged glances, wondering if he was going to steal one. "Where's that?" Luther asked warily.

"I know a guy who has one and is looking to sell it cheap. He'd rather have money than a phone."

Luther turned to the clerk. "If we buy this guy's phone, can you clear it all up? I mean, erase this guy's stuff?"

"Sure."

"How much does this guy want for his phone?"

"I don't know. I thought I'd just offer him something."

"What should we pay?" Finn asked the clerk.

"Depends on the phone. If it's an iPhone——"

"It's not," Theo interrupted.

"Then offer fifty bucks," the clerk said.

Luther peeled off fifty dollars from his wad and handed it to Theo. "Oh man, thank you so much!" Theo said.

"When can you get it?"

"I'll go now and meet you here later."

"Make it tomorrow morning at ten," Finn said. "We've got business to attend to."

"Okay. See you here tomorrow at ten." Theo ran off.

"I hope you don't get screwed out of fifty bucks, Luther," Finn said as he watched Theo run down the street.

Luther shrugged. "You know what, Finn? I don't really care. If all I did was give Theo fifty bucks, it doesn't matter."

"Well, aren't you generous."

"So are you, Finn. Giving your time to teach writing to the homeless, taking me in."

"We both learned from the king."

"Huh? You're a religious man?" Luther laughed. "I didn't see that coming."

"Not Jesus or God or whoever," Finn snorted. "I'm talking about the king of kindness. Jed."

"Ah, yeah. He is that."

"Let's go to Covenant House and lunch at the Oyster Bar," Finn said. "Then we have a car to buy."

Finn told the Covenant House that he would be gone for awhile and they were at the Oyster Bar at noon. It was crowded, but they found Joe at the counter. "Well, look who's here!" Joe exclaimed.

"Join us at a table?" Finn asked. Joe got up and followed them. "I'm buying this round," Finn added. "We'll have the seafood platter," he said to Ernie the waiter.

"What'd you do? Win the lottery?" Ernie replied. "You old geezers never spend this much."

Finn smiled at Luther. "Something like that. Anyway, we'll take some drinks to celebrate our big winnings. I'll take whiskey straight up. What do you want, Joe?"

"Cognac for me."

"I'll just take a beer," Luther said.

Ernie stood there, staring hard at Luther. "You gonna tell me what kind?"

Luther sighed. "I don't know, what do you have?"

"You really gonna make me get the beer menu?" Ernie grumbled.

"Do you have Budweiser?"

"All these fancy beers and you're gonna have a Bud," Ernie scoffed as he walked away.

The drinks arrived and Luther proposed a toast. "To new friends and new adventures!"

"Hah!" Joe exclaimed. "I don't see too many new adventures up ahead for me and Finn, but here's to you Luther!"

Luther looked at Finn, waiting for him to answer. Finn smiled and said, "Aw Joe, we're never too old for a new adventure. Luther and I are embarking on a cross country road trip."

"What the hell for?"

"Why not?" Finn responded.

"I'm buying a car and I want to get back to California," Luther explained. "Finn wants to go see his daughter and old friend, Jed."

"So take a plane."

"We thought it would be more interesting to drive," Luther replied. "I haven't, um, seen much of the country."

"Hey, I lived ninety-eight years and have hardly been out of New York or, at least, the East Coast. Who needs it?"

"Hey, Joe," Finn scoffed. "Different strokes for different folks."

Their food arrived and the conversation switched to politics and horse racing. Luther didn't have much to say, knowing little about politics and nothing about horse racing. But he was content to enjoy the food and listen to the two old men grumble over just about everything. "So when are you two leaving?" Joe asked when the check came.

"Not sure when, but soon," Finn answered.

Joe got up from the table. "Well, thanks for the meal. And Luther, take care of this old guy."

They went to check the train times to Yonkers and Finn called Miriam. He told her they'd be going straight to Horowitz's to pick up the car and then bring it to her house.

"The car looks so shiny!" Luther exclaimed when they got to the garage.

"Washed and waxed, as well as fixed," Damon replied. "No extra charge."

"So everything's working well?" Finn asked. "We're not gonna get stuck out in the middle of nowhere?"

"Well," Damon chuckled. "I can't guarantee that, but it won't be any fault of mine or Schwartz. It was about as tiptop as any old car could be. I just did things that needed doing because it sat for a while." Damon opened the hood.

"Even the engine looks clean!" Luther exclaimed.

"I changed the oil and replaced the filter. I replaced the transmission, brake and power steering fluids and the radiator coolant. Then I pumped out the old gas and put in some fresh. I checked the drive belts and the wiring. Rodents have been known to chew them, but all was okay. I replaced the fuel pump just because it's been sitting a while. I checked for leaks and nothing was out of the ordinary."

Luther frowned. "It seems like you did a lot of work."

"You're going on a long trip." Damon cast a shy grin over at Finn. "I don't want you stuck in Laramie."

"So what do I owe you besides the pizza?" Luther asked uneasily. Damon handed Luther the bill. "Oh. This isn't bad at all."

"Let me see," Finn said, snatching the bill from Luther's hand. He looked at the bottom line and handed it back. "How about I pay this since you're buying the car. Seems only fair."

"But it will be my car, Finn. I don't mind."

"Let me do my part."

"You've done plenty already, Finn."

"Oh let him pay for it," Damon intervened. "Humor the old fart."

They all laughed. "Oh fine," Luther consented. Finn paid the bill and Luther turned to Damon. "So where do you want us to buy that pizza?"

"Oh, I'm too busy now. Just keep me posted on how the trip's going. Hey, maybe I'll come visit you in California."

"That would be great," Luther said. "Okay," he said, looking at Finn. "How do we get to Miriam's?"

"You don't have GPS on that fancy smartphone of yours?"

"Yeah." Luther was quiet for a moment. "But I don't know how to use it."

"Of course not!" Finn scoffed.

Damon started laughing. "This is going to be some trip, alright! Here, let me show you," he said, reaching for Luther's phone.

Finn gave him his phone instead. "I guess I'll be the navigator on this trip since I'm not driving."

Damon showed him how to use Google Maps. "Got it, old man?"

"Yeah, I think so," Finn replied. "Maybe there's a good old fashioned map in the glove box."

"No, man! You gotta get used to this. It'll tell you where to eat, sleep, road conditions. Everything." Finn peered at the map on his phone and shrugged. Damon took the phone out of his hand and looked at it. "Take a left at the end of the street and go about two miles. The rest is up to you, Finn."

"Thanks so much, Damon," Luther said as he shook his hand.

"Seriously, call me if you get stuck. I don't want you to get taken by some mechanic. Make sure to run it by me first . . . whatever they claim."

Luther sat down in the driver's seat and beamed. Finn and Damon winked at each other about the pride emanating out of Luther. Finn got in the passenger seat. Luther put the key in the ignition and turned the key.

"Fasten your seatbelt." Both Luther and Finn practically jumped through the roof.

"What the hell?" Luther shrieked.

Damon started laughing hysterically as Finn opened the door as if to escape. The same voice came back on and said, "A door is ajar."

"Oh, man!" Damon choked through his laughter. "I guess you haven't met EVA."

"Who the hell is EVA?" Finn demanded.

"Some eighties Chryslers had Electronic Voice Alert. It also tells you not to forget your keys and that you left your lights on."

"Jesus Christ!" Finn exclaimed. "Can you turn the bitch off?"

"She's a good thing," laughed Damon. "You'll get used to it."

"Let's just go, Finn," Luther muttered, now embarrassed by their reaction. "Damon's right. We'll get used to it."

Luther turned the key and the engine purred. He took off but stopped abruptly with a jolt as he attempted to turn onto the street. "Hey, easy on the brakes!" Finn bellowed.

"I'm not used to these power brakes. The truck I drive at the farm is a far cry from this."

"Well, don't kill us before we even get out of Yonkers!"

Finn found that he was perfectly capable of getting them to Miriam's and they arrived there about fifteen minutes later. She came out the door to greet them. "The car looks good on you, Luther!" she called out.

"It's a beauty! Damon fixed it all up and even washed and waxed it!" Luther gushed.

"Come on in. I have some noshes for us."

Finn and Luther smiled at each other, too polite to admit they were still quite full from lunch. Miriam poured some coffee and sliced them each a piece of cake. "This is delicious," Luther said as he took a bite. "What's it called?"

"Babka," Miriam answered.

"You made it?" Luther asked.

"I told you. We have a wonderful Jewish bakery in town."

"That's right," Luther grinned.

"We'd like to leave the car here until we're ready to leave," Finn said after they'd finished their coffee and cake.

"That's fine. It's been in the garage all these years. What are another few days? You are talking a few days, right?"

"Yes. And we'll bring you a cashier's check when we pick it up. How does ten thousand sound?"

"Ten thousand? Are you kidding me?"

"Too little? I'm sorry––" Luther began.

"No!" Miriam interrupted. "Too much!"

"We looked it up," Luther replied. "That's kind of a middle price."

"Well, I'm not taking that much from you."

"Hey, Miriam," Finn broke in. "You're not living up to your heritage."

"Finn!" Luther was flabbergasted that Finn would say that.

"She knows I'm joking," Finn replied. "What do you think it's worth, then?"

Miriam thought for a moment. "All right. Give me eight."

"Eight thousand?" Luther asked.

Miriam snickered. "Well, I certainly didn't mean eight dollars."

"Okay. It's a deal." Luther hugged Miriam. "I'd shake hands on it, but you said you don't do that."

Finn gave Miriam a hug, too. "Thanks bubala." He turned to Luther. "We need to get to the station. We'll be in touch to let you know when we'll be leaving, Miriam."

Chapter 23

THE NEXT MORNING WAS A FLURRY OF ACTIV-
ITY. They needed to meet Theo at ten and had an
appointment at a vet for Bardo. Besides a health check
and possible shots, Bardo's gender would finally be
revealed. "So, is there any reason to wait or are you
ready to leave?" Finn asked as he went through the
refrigerator, looking at expiration dates.

"Maybe we should leave when all the food's been
eaten in the refrigerator!" Luther replied dryly.

"Hey, I just don't want to come back to rotting food."

"Maybe you should just throw it all out. Do you even
know when you'll be back?"

Finn grinned at him. "Carpe diem. Whatever happens, happens."

"Maybe you should give it to Theo."

"Great idea. He can just put it in the mini fridge he
carries around with his sleeping bag."

Luther frowned. "Are we really just going to leave
him like this without Rocco?"

Finn narrowed his eyes and glared at Luther. "What
are you saying? You want to take him with us?"

"No, I just feel bad for him. He's so young."

Finn shrugged. "You can't save everybody, so stop trying."

Theo was waiting outside the Verizon store at ten when Finn and Luther got there. "Did you get the phone?" Luther asked.

Theo took an older phone out of his pocket. "I offered thirty and he took it." He took a twenty out of his pocket and tried to hand it to Luther.

"Keep it. I don't need it." Luther smiled at Finn. "Boy, I never thought I'd be able to say that."

"Thanks, man." The clerk unlocked the door and let them in. "Here's the phone!" Theo gave him the phone with a huge smile.

"Oh, okay. I'll erase and restore for you. And you want to buy minutes for it, correct?"

"Uh, I think so. Right Luther? How do I pay for that?"

"You can set it up with a credit card or your bank account to pay monthly."

Theo laughed. "Well, I don't have either of those."

The clerk looked at Luther and Finn. "Can't we just pay for minutes now and then Theo could go into a Verizon store and pay for more minutes when he needs them?"

"We need a credit card or debit card connected to the phone."

"Go ahead, Luther," Finn said. "You wanted to do something for Theo."

"I'll pay for the minutes every month. I promise!" Theo said.

"Could you connect the phone to Luther's debit card, but Theo comes in to the store to pay?" Finn asked.

"I don't see how I can do that."

"How much a month is it?" Luther asked.

"Depends if you want Auto Pay and how many gigs you want."

"Well, how many gigs do you suggest?"

The clerk shrugged. "We have 5, 15 or unlimited."

"What are the prices?"

"Twenty-five, thirty-five and fifty."

"Just get me 5, Luther," Theo said. "I'll give you the money."

"The problem is I won't be in New York for much longer."

"You won't?"

"I'm from California. I'm just visiting."

"I could send it to you."

The clerk sighed. "You should try one of the other places. They might have plans that would work for him."

"Like what?" Finn asked. "Where do we find these other places?"

"Look. Can't you just do this in some way?" Luther asked in exasperation. "Put my card on the account, but when Theo pays, you could credit me? And if he doesn't pay, cancel the plan?"

The clerk was quiet for a minute. "Let me call my manager." He went into the back.

Luther looked over at Finn who was grinning slyly. "You finding something funny?" Luther asked.

"Not funny. Just, I don't know, noticing, or maybe appreciating, that you have reached some kind of milestone."

"What milestone is that?"

"You have a debit card and a bank account and are being assertive."

The clerk came back out and said, "My manager said we could do that."

It took about twenty minutes to finish the transaction and Theo immediately put in Finn and Luther's phone numbers. They did the same with Theo's. "Oh man. Thanks so much Luther."

"It's okay. Just remember there's only a month's worth of minutes on it so you have to pay it next month."

"I won't forget."

"Okay, Theo," Finn said. "We have to get the cat and bring it to the vet."

"You have a cat? What's its name?"

"Bardo."

"Cool name! I like cats a lot."

Theo was obviously wasting time, trying to hang out a little longer. "So, uh, we'll see you later." Finn patted Theo on the back and pulled Luther's arm.

"Thanks again Luther!" Theo called after them as they walked down the street.

"I guess it does feel pretty good," Luther said with a slight smile.

They picked up Bardo and got to the vet just before they were closing for lunch. Luckily, they were willing to take a look at the cat anyway. "Definitely a she and about ten weeks old," the vet said. "Will you want us to spay her?"

"Oh yeah. That's a good idea," Finn replied. "And give her whatever shots she needs."

"You'll need to leave her here overnight."

"And then is there anything special we have to do after spaying?" Luther asked.

"It's pretty hard with cats, but try to keep her from jumping if you can. Did she eat this morning?"

"Not much. A little dry food."

"Okay. Pick her up tomorrow late in the day."

"What time do you close?" Finn asked.

"Five-thirty."

They left Bardo and got back home in time to empty out some more of the refrigerator. Finn's phone rang as they sat down to eat. He took it out and looked at the screen. "I don't recognize this number."

"Well we know it isn't Theo since his name would come up now."

Finn didn't answer and waited to see if they left a message. They did. He listened to it with a solemn face and put the phone down and turned to Luther with a frown and a sigh. "That was Amos."

"Amos . . ." Luther paused. "Oh, Rocco's lawyer."

Finn nodded. "Rocco committed suicide in jail."

Luther dropped his fork and sat back in his chair. "Are you shitting me? How did he do it?"

Finn stared out the window and sighed loudly. "Hung himself."

"Jesus!" Luther picked up his fork again and poked at the food before him. "I guess I'm not surprised, though. Are you?"

"No, I'm not," Finn replied. "Telling Theo won't be easy and we should do it soon while we're still here. He's going to need some support."

They ate the rest of their meal in silence and Finn went into his room. Luther called Jed, wanting to tell him everything, but he didn't pick up. He left the message just to call him back when he could. He tried Juniper again, but her phone went to Voicemail also. He picked up one of Finn's books, but couldn't concentrate on reading. He thought about Theo and realized that Finn had not told him that he would also be going on a trip. Just then Luther's phone rang. He looked at the caller ID, hoping it was Jed or Juniper, but it was Theo. Luther hesitated and then mustered a cheerful attitude. "Hey Theo, everything okay?"

"I went to the writing group but you guys weren't there. I saw a sign on the door that said Finn would be gone for a while. He's going with you?"

"Uh, yeah. Just for a visit. His daughter and a good friend live in California."

"Oh, man." Theo wailed.

"Finn will be back."

"When?"

"Um, I don't know." Theo was quiet. "Hey, you'll be okay. Go to Covenant House and talk to them. They'll connect you to groups you can hang out with."

"It's just that with Rocco in jail . . ." Theo's voice trailed off and Luther heard him stifling a sob. "Okay. Thanks again Luther. I really appreciate it." Theo hung up, leaving Luther feeling like crap. What would be the best way to break the news of Rocco's suicide?

Finn came out of his room. "Was that Jed?"

"No. Jed didn't answer. It was Theo."

"Great," groaned Finn. "What did he want?"

"He went to the writing group and saw the sign on the door. He's really upset."

Finn just nodded. "Did you tell him about Rocco?"

"No." They looked at one another, and Luther finally spoke softly. "I think we should tell him in person."

"Yeah," Finn sighed. "You're right." He shook his head. "Poor kid."

Chapter 24

FINN'S PHONE RANG JUST AS HE AND LUTHER GOT HOME WITH BARDO THE NEXT AFTERNOON. "I think this is Rocco's lawyer, Amos. I'll take it in the bedroom." Finn left Luther to fawn over Bardo who wanted nothing more than to be left alone to sleep. A few minutes later Finn reappeared.

"What did he want?" Luther asked.

"The police released Rocco's backpack to him. He wanted to know if we knew his next of kin."

"Do you?"

"No. It isn't likely he was still in touch with anyone. It's not like there's anything valuable anyway."

"Theo would probably like his journal."

"Yeah. I figured I'd get the stuff and see if Theo wants it."

"Poor Theo," Luther murmured, shaking his head.

"Amos also told me that Theo had told him that he found the Raiders jersey in a trash can and put it on. He's sure Theo is telling the truth and he's requesting a DNA test be done on the shirt to see who else's is on it."

"Oh, that would be great," Luther smiled. "Then Theo won't have to be looking over his shoulder for the rest of his life."

"Anyway, Amos said he'd drop it off because he's going downtown to the courthouse."

"Should I call Theo?"

"Sure. Might as well get it done so we're free to leave."

Theo answered Luther's text right away. He'd love to come over so Luther gave him Finn's address. He then went in search of Bardo who had disappeared. "Oh, here she is, behind the sofa."

"I wonder why," Finn replied dryly. "Just let her be until the medication wears off. I have some phone calls to make and I'll need to stop at the post office to have my mail held."

"How would you know if something important comes?"

"I don't get anything important anymore. People that matter email or call me."

Theo arrived first, dirty and looking hungry. "Sorry, guys. I couldn't find a good place to sleep last night. The mission was full and Covenant House is trying to squeeze my age out of me."

"Huh?" asked Luther.

"I'm under eighteen," Theo explained with a frown. "The social workers are always trying to send me back to my family."

Luther glanced at Finn, wondering if he should ask the obvious question. Finn shrugged. "Well, where is your family?"

"What family!" Theo scoffed. "The brother who's a meth addict? The mother who drank herself to death? The father who never showed up?"

"How long have you been on your own?"

"All my life, really, but away from them, about three years."

"How old are you?"

"Sixteen."

"You were thirteen and living on the streets?" Theo nodded. "How long were you with Rocco?"

"Oh, I dunno. Most of that time. He took me under his wing. Didn't want me to end up in the sex and drug trade."

"We have something to tell you," Finn said, glancing at Luther. "Rocco committed suicide in jail."

Theo took a deep breath and wiped a tear off his cheek. "I guess I'm not surprised."

Finn reached out and touched his arm. "Would you like to take a shower? It would make you feel better."

Theo mustered a little smile. "I'd love to take a shower."

"Well, Finn said, eyeing Theo's dirty clothes. "I can probably find some sweats for you to wear, if you don't mind wearing old man clothes."

Theo almost laughed. "I'm way beyond being embarrassed about what I wear. I'll take anything clean. Thanks."

As Finn showed Theo the bathroom and gathered up a towel and some clothes, Amos arrived. Luther introduced himself. "I-I've had lunch with your father-in-law a few times," Luther said awkwardly.

"So you know he's an old pain in the ass," Amos grinned. "Great guy, but . . ."

"Same with Finn, "Luther chuckled.

"What's the same as me?" Finn called from the hall.

"Nothing!" both replied in unison.

Finn appeared and shook Amos's hand. "Theo is in the shower. He should be finished soon. Are you in a hurry?"

"I've got a few minutes." Amos handed Rocco's backpack over. "Here's the sad little end to that tragedy."

"Yeah," Finn replied, handling the pack gingerly.

"Hopefully, with time, Theo will find some comfort in having something of Rocco's," Amos said.

"Is his journal in it?" asked Luther.

"Yes. Theo will like some of the things he wrote n there. Rocco told me himself that he loved Theo like a son. A little light in their dark lives, I'd guess."

"Hey, these aren't sweats." Theo appeared, tucking a long sleeve shirt into a pair of khakis.

"My sweats looked worse than what you wore when you came in," Finn grinned. "Pretty good fit."

Theo buttoned the cuffs. "Am I ready for Wall Street?"

They all laughed. Finn lifted Rocco's backpack and handed it to Theo. Theo bit his lip and looked over at Amos. "Thanks." He slowly unzipped it and started sifting through it.

"Do you want us to leave you alone?" Amos asked.

"No," Theo replied, his voice cracking. "You're my only friends now." He pulled Rocco's journal from the pack.

"Have you read it?" asked Luther.

"No. He was always pretty secretive about what he wrote." Theo leafed through it and stifled a sob. "Sorry. I liked taking care of Rocco. He could be real funny when he wasn't brooding."

"What are you going to do now?" Amos asked.

Theo shrugged. "I'm pretty used to being on my own. I'll figure it out as long as the social workers leave me alone."

"They're just trying to help," Amos responded.

"I know. But I don't want to go to some foster home."

"Don't you want a home?"

"Sure but only with someone I like."

Finn and Luther frowned at each other, both thinking the same thing, but neither wanting it to happen. "How do you know you wouldn't like the foster family you were placed with?" Finn asked.

Theo gave him a hard look. "Believe me. I know what most of them are like. They don't really care about the kids. They just want the money."

"Sad but true," Amos said. "Sorry to cut out but I need to get to the courthouse. He paused and then asked, "Theo, would you give me a call later this evening?"

"What for?"

"I have an idea but I need to check something out."

Theo looked at Finn for advice. "Go ahead, Theo. Give him your number and Amos can call you too. He's not going to rat you out to the powers that be."

Theo gave Amos his number and put Amos' in his phone. "I'll talk to you later, Finn. Nice meeting you, Luther."

Theo started rummaging through the backpack again. "Oh, I'll just take the whole backpack. It'll be nice to use his." Theo emptied out his backpack and stuffed all the items into Rocco's. He got up to leave. "Thanks again for everything. Do you know when you'll be back, Finn?"

"Nope. But I'll let you know."

Theo lingered and Finn and Luther glanced furtively at each other. They both felt bad for Theo, but hesitant to say anything. Was he looking for an invitation to go with them? Or was it that he didn't know where to go? Luther finally broke the silence. "Hey, you want something to eat before you go? We don't have much, but we're trying to empty out the fridge."

Theo's phone rang before he could respond to Luther. "Hello? Oh hi, Amos. I guess so. Them too? Let me ask them. Hey, Amos wants to meet us all for dinner at a restaurant."

Finn and Luther looked at each other, perplexed. "Uh, sure," Finn replied. "Where?"

Theo spoke into the phone. "They said ok. Where?" He turned to Finn. "He said he'll be picking up Joe and he wants to go to Pete's Tavern. Do you know where that is?"

"Of course I do! Let me talk to Amos a minute." Theo handed Finn his phone. "What's this about?" Finn smiled. "Ah, got it. Okay. See you there in about half an hour." He gave the phone back to Theo and grinned at Luther.

"What's going on, Finn?" Luther asked.

"You'll see. Let's go. It's not too far. We can walk."

"Where's Pete's Tavern?" Theo asked.

"Irving Place and Eighteenth Street. Near Gramercy Park." Finn turned to Luther. "Now you can see another New York Landmark."

Luther laughed. "So I've seen all the famous New York restaurants, but none of the famous New York sights."

"It was your call, Luther. You weren't interested."

"Okay, okay. You're right."

They arrived at Pete's before Joe and Amos. "I've never been to any place this fancy before," Theo said.

"Before I met Finn, me neither," Luther said. "I guess this is part of our education."

"This is hardly fancy," Finn said.

Theo looked at the menu. "Who's paying for all this?"

Finn and Luther looked at each other. "We'll probably all split it," Luther said.

"Or Joe will have a little less to give to the IRS," Finn added.

The hostess sat them at a table and Joe and Amos arrived momentarily. "Theo, this is Joe, my father-in-law."

"Nice meeting ya' Joe," Theo replied.

"Yeah. My son-in-law thinks I need a caregiver," he grumbled.

"Yeah," Amos chuckled. "You've had practice with Rocco. Dad's a pain in the ass, but he also has an extra bedroom and I read him the riot act. Either he moves in with my wife and me or he gets help."

A mix of emotions flashed across Theo's face. "Wow. I don't know what to say." He turned to Joe. "I won't be a bother."

"Damn right you won't! Now, how do I get a drink around here?"

They ate, drank, and laughed at Joe's stories of all the times he met important people, none of whom Theo and Luther had ever heard of. When Joe excused himself to the restroom, Amos leaned forward and said low, "Dad knows the case——" He looked directly at

Theo. "Knows all about Rocco. That bond was the clincher for him. Deep down he's a sentimental sap."

Theo lowered his eyes. "I hope I can do this."

"I'll grant you that he's a different personality than you're used to being with, but you'll be okay," Amos reassured. "You can always call me for advice. You're not alone in this."

"Okay." Theo smiled. "I do appreciate it very much. Thanks."

Later Finn and Luther watched Amos, Joe and Theo ride off in a cab. "Phew!" exclaimed Luther. "Glad Amos came up with that solution."

"Yup, we can assuage our guilt."

"You feel guilt?" Luther teased.

"Here you go again. Thinking you know me so well. Anyway, you ready to hit the road?"

"Anytime. You're the one who has places to go and people to see."

"I just have a few things to finish taking care of to-morrow. What do you say we leave the day after to-morrow?"

"Should we get the car tomorrow or just leave from Miriam's the next day?"

"Too hard to park. It's not like we're taking much luggage so we can just take the train to Miriam's day after tomorrow."

"Cool."

Chapter 25

THE NEXT DAY FINN SCURRIED AROUND THE CITY ON SOME LAST MINUTE ERRANDS. Luther followed him like a puppy, not wanting to spend his last day in New York just sitting around the apartment. He did like the excitement that emanated from the streets, if not sightseeing in particular. He wouldn't miss it, however. Five o'clock rolled around just as they walked in the door. "Cocktail hour," Finn said as he went to the kitchen to pour drinks.

"Is there anything left in the refrigerator?" Luther called from the living room.

"Not much. Unless you want to eat condiments."

Luther plopped himself down on the sofa next to Finn. "So what New York specialty are we going to have for my last dinner here?"

"Up to you. I'll be back. You won't."

"I don't know. Let's just do what's easiest. I'm pretty tired. It's not easy keeping up with you, old man. I don't really want to sit in a restaurant. Any place that delivers?"

"In New York, everything can be delivered," Finn answered. "Chinese food? Pizza?"

"You choose."

"Chinese food. We might be eating a lot of pizza on our trip. Chinese food is probably harder to come by in the middle of the country. I've got a menu somewhere." Finn went into the kitchen and started sorting through a drawer.

"Here." Finn handed the menu to Luther. "Pick out what you want."

"What's good here?"

"No idea. They just leave these menus on everyone's doors."

"So you've never eaten anything from this place?"

"What difference does it make? How bad can it be? Just pick out what you want."

"How about barbecued spare ribs, egg rolls and wonton soup?"

"Real distinctive."

"What do you mean?"

"Just ordinary stuff. But it's fine. Is that enough or you want some chicken chow mein too?" Finn teased.

"I don't understand," Luther scowled at him.

"Just joking. But seriously, is that enough food?"

"Okay. And chicken chow mein."

Finn laughed heartily. "You're a kick, Luther."

Luther started to retort, but decided against it. Instead he asked, "You wanna call it in or do you want me to do it?"

"I'll do it." Finn made the call. "They'll be here in half an hour."

"Wow that's quick!"

"They're just a block or so away."

They cleaned out the refrigerator, dumped the garbage, Finn packed his bag, and they went on Finn's computer to look at maps. "Should we check the weather too? We talked about going south before . . ." Luther's voice trailed off.

"You afraid to do the southern route?"

"Not afraid exactly. I just don't want to be hassled."

Finn grinned. "I'll protect you."

Luther rolled his eyes. "Yeah, right!" The doorbell rang. "Do I pay now?"

"I paid with my credit card."

"Ooh. Cutting edge."

Finn snorted. "No, I wanted my food. It was that or some app shit to get it."

Luther opened the door and took the bag from the delivery guy. Luther started closing the door, almost on the guy's expectant face. "Oh, um, just a minute." Luther took out some cash and handed over a ten-dollar bill.

The delivery guy smiled broadly. "Thanks, man."

Luther closed the door and turned around to see Finn laughing. "What?"

"I already tipped when I ordered. Good thing we're leaving 'cause he had us pegged as suckers."

Luther shrugged and smiled. "His lucky night."

Finn laughed again and slapped him on the back. "Atta boy. Just roll with it!"

They ate and discussed their itinerary. "Let's plan on leaving from Miriam's by noon," Finn said. "We can drive southwest and stop after about five hours."

"Where would that be?" Luther asked.

Finn took out his phone. "Good. This is a chance for me to practice using this GPS shit. You want to see Washington DC while you're on the East Coast? It says four hours thirteen minutes. I think we'd go through Philadelphia. You could see the Liberty Bell on our way and spend the night somewhere near DC. What do you think?"

"I'm kinda nervous about driving in big cities."

"Okay. I don't care. I've seen it all. You want to stay on back roads?"

"Probably. It's what I'm used to."

Finn shrugged. "Doesn't matter to me. It'll take us a lot longer, but we're not in a hurry."

"We're not? I mean . . . I don't know. Whatever. What was that thing Miriam said? Man plans and God laughs? Let's just drive on roads that are going in the right direction and that I'm comfortable driving on."

"You do realize that all the roads getting out of Yonkers and through New Jersey are going to be highways. You okay driving on them?"

"Yeah, I'll be okay. Just get me out of the New York area."

"Well, it looks like the New Jersey Turnpike is the best route to get out of here quickly." Finn scrolled around the map. "Before New Brunswick we can get on–– "

"Finn!" Luther interrupted. "Just get us out of all these cities as quickly as possible. As long as I'm on a highway I'll be okay. We can just stop at a motel when I get tired of driving."

"Aye-aye-sir. You're the boss since you're the driver."

They slept, finished the Chinese food for breakfast, took out the garbage, locked the apartment, and scooped up Bardo and a bag of kibble. They hailed a cab and were on the train to Yonkers by nine a.m. Miriam had coffee, sandwiches, fruit, and bakery goodies in a paper bag for them. "You never know if there will be a place to stop so you need to be prepared."

"Such a Jewish mother!" Finn said in his best New York Jewish accent.

They took the bags from Miriam and the trio went to the garage to load up the car. Luther grinned when he saw it again. "Damon did such a great job making her look good."

"Herb took meticulous care of this automobile!" Miriam said sharply.

"Oh, I know he did," Luther said apologetically. "I didn't mean to imply otherwise."

"Did you get the registration and insurance changed?" Miriam asked.

Luther looked at Finn who shrugged. "Uh, no. Neither of us has ever bought a car before."

"Oy vey! Okay. I'll call my insurance guy and you can talk to him."

"What address should I use?" Luther asked.

Miriam sighed. "I see this is going to take a while. I tell you what. As a little parting gift you can leave it all in Herb's name until you get home to your farm. Then you can change it."

"Thanks Miriam. I promise I'll drive carefully."

"Let's see how Bardo likes the car," Finn said. He put the cat in the back seat and she scurried around, sniffing and inspecting.

"The cat needs a bed," Miriam said. "Just a minute." Miriam left and returned with a blanket. She put it on the back seat and Bardo jumped on it and lay down.

"Thanks Miriam," Luther said. "But are you sure you don't need this?"

"At my age I have to get rid of stuff. If I thought I needed it, I wouldn't have given it to you."

Luther started to apologize again and realized that New Yorkers, whether they were Jewish or Irish, were a special breed. They said what was on their mind without hesitation and apologies were unnecessary. "Thanks for everything, Miriam," Luther said.

"You take care of Herb's car, now. Zei Gezunt." She hugged them both.

"What does that mean?"

Miriam shrugged. "Safe travels. To your health."

Luther got in and stuck the key in the ignition and jumped when the car told him to put his seatbelt on. Finn laughed. "You'd better get used to it. This car is quite talkative."

Miriam laughed. "I never did get used to it."

Finn got in the passenger seat and Miriam pressed the garage door opener. They waved goodbye, Bardo jumped onto Finn's lap and purred, and they were off.

Chapter 26

FINN TURNED OUT TO BE A MORE THAN COMPE-TENT NAVIGATOR, STEERING LUTHER ONTO THE HENRY HUDSON PARKWAY WITHOUT INCIDENT. The map app also proved to be a good distraction from any perceived flaws in Luther's driving, as Finn was often well ahead of the car, plotting lane changes through the heavy traffic. Soon they were passing over the George Washington Bridge and merging onto the New Jersey Turnpike, eventually fulfilling Luther's wish not to be in the thick of a city for a while.

Once they were through Philadelphia, Finn reported they were past the worst. Traffic thinned and picked up speed, passing the Chrysler as Luther relaxed and settled back into the leather seat. Occasionally a driver or passenger stared curiously as they came alongside the convertible. A dusty rose hump-backed Cadillac Seville of similar vintage appeared, the older Black man driving doing a double take at Luther and slowing down to give an enthusiastic thumbs up. Luther laughed and returned the gesture. Finn looked up from his phone. "Jesus, it's like being in a parade."

"You're missing all the fun, staring at your phone," grinned Luther.

"Well, you're the one who wants to get off the four lane," Finn frowned, again looking down at his phone. "Any interest in going to Lancaster?"

"What's in Lancaster?"

"It's Pennsylvania Dutch country. You know, the Amish." Luther gave Finn a questioning look. "You never heard of the Amish?"

"No. What is it?"

"More like who are they?" Finn replied.

"Okay. Who are they?"

"They're a religious group that eschews cars and technology of any kind, although in this day and age that might have changed. They dress old fashioned and farm and make furniture. They're kind of like hippies in a commune, only better dressed and less hairy."

Luther laughed. "Oh yeah. Maybe I saw them on TV or something. They ride in those black horse-drawn buggies, right?"

"Yup. Might be interesting to take a little detour through there."

"Sure," Luther answered. "It sounds interesting."

"Right up your alley, farming and all."

"Just tell me where to go." It wasn't long before they were in Lancaster. "Hey," Luther complained. "This is just another city I have to drive through. I thought you said the Amish lived in the country."

"Take a look over there." Finn pointed to a family walking down the street. The girls and women were dressed in long dresses and had white bonnets on their heads, while the men were in black suits with large black hats. "I guess they come to town to buy what they need."

They drove further and saw a Costco. "Look at that!" Luther exclaimed. "They have designated parking for horse and buggies!"

Finn laughed. "Hey, pull over a minute." Luther pulled into the Costco parking lot. Finn got out of the car and went up to a Costco employee who was moving the shopping carts. Luther watched as the employee pointed in two different directions.

"What were you asking him?" Luther asked as Finn got back in the car.

"He said to go to either Bird-in-Hand Farmer's Market or Julius Sturgis Pretzel Bakery in Lititz."

Luther laughed. "It's always about the food with you."

"Look. I don't care about trinkets and we don't have much time to be here because it'll be dark in a couple of hours and we have to eat something. Anyway, local food is how you really get to know a place."

"I don't know if that's true, Finn, but I'm fine with eating. I'm pretty hungry."

"Let's try the farmer's market in Bird-in-Hand." Finn looked at his phone. "He said it's on the Old Philadel-phia Pike."

"Bird-in-Hand is the name of a town?" Luther asked. "That's a weird name."

Finn shrugged. "You get to be my age and nothing's weird anymore." He directed Luther and they arrived at the farmer's market about fifteen minutes later. They parked and went inside. Most of the workers were Amish. They bought some apples and soft pretzels, which they munched on as they walked back to the convertible. "The kid at Costco said you could see how they make pretzels in Lititz," Finn said with a mouthful.

"I'll pass," Luther replied. "I'm just happy to eat them. Where to now?"

"Just drive around a bit so we can get a flavor."

"So I should just drive down any road?"

Finn sighed. "You got somewhere you gotta be?"

"Well, you were the one who said it'll be dark in a couple of hours––whoa!" Luther stepped on the brake as he came upon a horse and buggy on a curve. "Oh wow. Now this is more like it."

"Quaint, eh?" Finn responded. "I'll bet these farms are beautiful in the spring. All green. Now it's mud season."

"What's mud season?" Luther asked.

"What do you think? End of winter, snow melted, but sun hasn't dried it out yet. You know, a lot of California doesn't exactly have four distinct seasons. The northeast has about six, mud season being one of them."

"Well, Garberville had a mud season too this year," Luther scowled. "It's just earlier than this," They drove around a bit more, enjoying the peace and quiet. "It's getting dark, Finn. Let's get past Washington and Baltimore and then look for a motel. How can we do it so I don't have to deal with traffic?"

Finn looked at his phone for several minutes. "Want to go to Gettysburg? Might as well see something historical. It skirts the big cities and it's about an hour and a half away."

"Great," Luther deadpanned. "I can see where my people were set free."

Finn snorted a laugh. "Sarcasm becomes you, sir."

"It rubs off sooner or later," Luther replied in the same manner. "So, how do we get to Gettysburg?" Finn directed Luther onto Route 30 and within an hour they found themselves cruising by motel after motel. They chose one at random that looked nice but affordable and checked in. "Believe it or not I'm hungry," Luther announced. "What's Gettysburg famous for food-wise?"

"I don't know," Finn replied. "I'll go ask at the office." He left and returned. "There's an Irish pub called Garryowen. Might as well give you a taste of my old country."

"And let me guess, there's a good selection of Irish whiskeys."

Finn winked. "Probably so."

"What's Irish besides corned beef and cabbage?" Luther asked as they got back in the car.

"Shepherd's pie, bangers and mash, soda bread, ulster fry . . . of course there's Irish stew. Lots of meat and potatoes, especially bacon and sausage."

They arrived at the pub and even Finn was taken aback at the amount of Irish whiskeys on the menu. "What are you going to order from this huge whiskey menu?" Luther asked.

"No idea. Guess I'll have to ask the waiter or bartender to recommend one. You want whiskey or beer?"

"I think I'll stick to beer," Luther answered.

"Well at least make it a Guinness."

The waiter brought them their drinks and Finn took a sip. "Jesus this is good!"

"Are you going to ask the waiter for food recommendation too?" Luther asked.

"Let's keep it simple. Shepherd's pie for you, bangers and mash for me. We can share."

The food and drinks went over well with the hungry pair and they got back to the motel ready to plan the next day. It was a noble effort, but Luther's eyes closed and he was snoring softly before any planning got done.

Chapter 27

FINN SQUINTED AT THE RISING SUN COMING THROUGH THE WINDSHIELD AS HE TOOK A SIP OF MOTEL COFFEE. "Jesus," he sputtered. "I think this was brewed on the battlefield back in 1865!"

Luther swung the Chrysler around the parking lot and started heading west. "Ah, the flavor of history. Who needs it? Let's skip the battlefield."

Finn shot him a look. "When's the next time you're going to have an opportunity like this?"

"I don't really care, Professor," Luther replied surly. "It's just an idea you came up with almost eighteen hours ago. We hadn't planned out a thing, so what's the big deal about a veto?" The car hit a chuckhole, spraying dirty water high in the air. "Anyway, it'll be soggy and cold and boring."

"Well, Mary Mary Quite Contrary," Finn sniffed. "The sun is out for now. You might as well take advantage of it."

Luther glared at him. "What advantage? I can't even put the top down. Just tell me how to get out of here, will you?"

"Well," Finn replied, wincing over another sip of coffee. "If you don't want to see historical sites, and it's too cold to go to national parks, and you don't want to drive through big cities, I'm not sure how to direct you."

Luther sighed with annoyance. "Well, so far this whole trip for me has been about food and drink. Even when we were in New York, you took me to famous restaurants. It was the right pizza. Jewish food. Chinese food. Then it was about German pretzels in Lancaster and Irish food in Gettysburg, even though I doubt that the Irish have anything to do with Gettysburg historically."

Finn shrugged. "One's gotta eat. Might as well make it a destination, since you're not giving me much choice in the matter." When Luther didn't reply Finn added, "At least you're going in the right direction." Finn pulled out his phone and started scrolling and tapping. After a few minutes he said, "How about making Bardstown, Kentucky our next stop? It's about eight and a half hours on I-79."

"Sounds dull."

"It's Appalachia."

"That too."

"Mountains, rivers, moonshine . . ."

"In the day, perhaps."

"If you know where to look."

Luther looked over. "You're talking drink, aren't you?"

"Me?"

"And in Bardstown there will be . . .?"

"Bourbon."

"Of course."

"Food, too, I imagine."

Luther sighed. "Lead the way."

Soon they were sailing over I-79, climbing and dropping into valley after misty valley. Rivers reflecting the silver gray sky. "Not half bad," Finn murmured, closing his eyes.

"Where is everyone?" wondered Luther. "This interstate is almost empty. Why was it even built?"

"Politics," muttered Finn. "And to get to The Bourbon Capital of the world."

"Well, New Jersey sure could use it."

"Among other things." Finn was quiet for a moment, and then asked, "Happy, Nature Boy?"

"Uh, I guess . . ." Luther paused. "What do you mean?"

"Just thinking about your future. You probably should avoid cities."

"When did I ever say I wanted to live anywhere besides Dutch's farm?"

"You didn't," Finn admitted. "You have some money now. You should get a country life of your own and make it work for you."

"Thanks for the advice, Dad," Luther replied disdainfully. "Whatever happened to doing nothing when you don't know what to do?"

"Talkin' ain't doin'––Jesus, I sound like I live here now." Finn took a breath. "I just felt you were driving and thinking of short term unknowns instead of long term possibilities."

Luther moped, annoyed that Finn could read his thoughts. Driving through the empty, quiet countryside was different from the distractions of traffic and what exit to jockey for next. What lay ahead . . . the impending death of Homer and the unknown that was Juniper, had started running like a loop through his mind. He felt inexperienced and totally unequipped to face either situation. The future––the independent future Finn spoke of––never entered his mind.

The Chrysler crested another range of mountains, revealing another misty valley. He started seeing the clearings for the first time: the trailers and the junk, and the occasional proud columned home with a white fence and a "Vinyl is Final" sign stuck in the greening lawn. Luther almost chuckled aloud, recalling all the old PVC crap he came across working on the farm. Nothing is the final fix. There are only periods of coasting, like the Chrysler was doing at that moment. The convertible swept past seventy, the tires whining, not quite overriding Finn's gentle snore. Coasting. So relaxing. So fleeting. Luther would never admit how far into the future he went, how far he went in his mind with a woman who was not Juniper. It was EVA who jolted him back into the present with the admonishment, "YOUR FUEL IS LOW."

Finn stirred and Luther felt flush, as if Finn could read his mind in his sleep. "Need a bathroom, old man?" Luther asked a bit too brightly.

"Yes," Finn yawned. "And lunch."

Luther nodded and pulled off at the next gas station and glanced around. "No restaurant around here. You'll have to make do with snacks."

Finn scoffed. "Probably just as well." He got out and went inside while Luther filled up the tank.

When Finn returned Luther was putting in the mileage on an old calculator he found in the glove box. "Twenty-two point nine miles per gallon. Not bad." Finn mumbled something and Luther continued, "What did you get us?"

"Just bananas. One's for you and the bag of nuts is big enough. I thought you might want some pork rinds or Flamin' Hot Cheetos, but then I remembered you're already mad at me."

Luther's mind flashed back to the future and he felt that tingle again. "I'm not mad at you."

Finn eyed him and gave him a half-smile. "Then I guess a banana won't offend," he said flashing the fruit in front of Luther's face.

Luther grinned and leaned back. "No man, he laughed nervously. "Unless you say, 'here you go, porch monkey."

Finn burst out laughing. "Oh God, you're killing me!" he gasped. "That's truly awful, and it came right out of your mouth."

Luther grabbed the banana and started peeling it. "You're a bad influence. What else did you get?"

"Another banana, for the sake of racial equality, and a big bag of peanuts."

"That ought to hold us over." Luther paused, then added, "But I could use a cup of coffee."

"Can do, my friend, can do." Finn went back into the station and returned with two big cups of coffee. "This will assure us of another pit stop in an hour."

"Better hold back on the splash of whiskey, then," Luther said solemnly. "You don't want to fall out of the car when we stop."

"What a great idea!"

"Falling out of the car?"

"Whiskey, dammit! And I shall exit the car as gracefully as Fred Astaire." Luther gave him a blank look and Finn added, "Do not ask who's Fred?"

"Okay," Luther sighed. He took a deep breath and said firmly, "Honestly, officer, Fred here hasn't an open bottle."

Finn slapped Luther's knee. "We'll go a long way, baby!"

"We've been a long way," Luther groaned.

"Alright, alright. I can hold off for straight bourbon." Finn took a sip of coffee. "Hey, this isn't bad at all. Want some peanuts?"

Luther steered the Chrysler back onto the Interstate and they munched for a while in silence. Luther finally spoke. "You got me thinking . . ."

"What? You don't want to go to Disneyland, do you?"

Luther shot him a look. "The future--"

"Tomorrowland is long gone."

"My future."

"Now that's more like it," Finn nodded, popping a peanut into his mouth.

"Congratulations on making a move in liminal space."

"Huh?"

"Westward Ho! Where shall we go?"

"Well, uh--"

"I know my looks have faded, but you know I can cook."

"Are you sure you didn't put anything in your coffee?"

"Oh, I get it. Who needs food when you can--"

"GET MY INDEPENDENCE!"

"Right on, brother, right on!"

Luther breathed out loudly. "God, I'm exhausted now."

"And you haven't even started plowing. Or have you?"

"Shut up!" Luther laughed. "You creep me out."

"Thank you."

Luther chuckled. "It's like you can read my mind or something," he muttered.

"Nope," Finn said, taking a swallow of coffee. "It's just that I was a young man once, too."

"I'm forty."

"Going on twenty."

Luther sighed. "I guess you got that right."

Finn tapped the side of his head. "Wisdom. Also known as cobwebs."

"Shhh!"

Finn gazed at him admiringly and whispered, "Independence."

They drove in silence for some time. Eventually Finn looked at his phone and said, "It's another three hours to Bardstown, Kentucky. You want to stop sooner and find a meal and a motel?"

"No. Do you?"

"Hey, I'm not the one driving. If you're okay, I'm okay." He ate some more peanuts and handed the bag to Luther.

They arrived in Lexington, Kentucky at sundown. "Now this is really beautiful!" Luther marveled.

"Bluegrass country. Joe would be having us exit now for all the famous race horse farms."

"Juniper would love it here then, too. She has a horse named Zorba."

Finn frowned, wishing Luther wouldn't fall back into old patterns as Bardo jumped on his lap. "Hey there," Finn said as he petted her. "I'll bet Bardo would be happier with her own place in the country."

"Oh she'll be fine on Dutch's farm. She'll have company with Minnie the cat and Gypsy the dog."

"Whatever," Finn replied glumly. "I didn't even tell Kate we had a cat with us."

"Will she mind when we show up?"

"Oh, it shouldn't matter for a little while," Finn shrugged. "Bardo's no problem. We've sneaked her into the motel rooms without incident."

Luther laughed. "She really has been easy. And she seems to like being in the car."

"Lucky for us we found her in a taxi, preconditioned to life on the road."

They arrived at a motel on the outskirts of Bardstown at dusk, everyone road weary, including Bardo. They immediately asked the desk clerk for a good place to taste bourbon and get a meal. He directed them to The Blind Pig Speakeasy. "Best bourbon flights in town," he told them.

They had a hard time figuring out how to get inside the speakeasy, however. It was apparently part of the mystique to have a password to get inside. Eventually they gained entrance when another customer arrived and gave them the word. The interior was dimly lit with dark paneling and beautiful furnishings. "This place is like all those places you took me to in New York," Luther murmured,

"Yeah, straight out of prohibition days."

"You were around then?" Luther asked incredulously.

"I only look over a hundred," Finn smirked. "That was the 1920s, you know."

Luther took a look at the bourbon menu. "There must be a thousand bourbons on here! Not to mention all these fancy drinks with bourbon in them."

"We're here to taste the bourbon," Finn scowled. "We're not here to drink stupid umbrella drinks."

Luther looked around at the tables under pools of light. "I don't see any drinks with umbrellas."

"Ah, hell. You know what I mean. No mixed drinks."

"Well then, you order for us. I haven't a clue what to order."

"I don't either, Luther. It's not like I'm a bourbon connoisseur."

"So how should we order?"

"I guess pick some names you like."

Luther looked at Finn skeptically. "We're going to order because of the names?"

"You got a better idea?" Finn asked.

"Well, how much should we spend? They have it divided by price."

"Give me the menu!" Finn snapped, grabbing it from Luther's hand. "We'll get two flights. That way we can taste six different ones."

The waiter arrived and Finn rattled off the order. "We'll get one sow flight and one boar flight. For the sow we'll have Chattanooga Whiskey 111 proof Cask Strength, Redemption Wheated, and Tin Cup American Whiskey. For the boar we'll have Kentucky Owl Confiscated, Rabbit Hole Dareringer, and Whistle Pig Roadstock Rye Whiskey." He handed the waiter the menu and sat back with a smug smile.

"Those are some wild names," Luther said.

"What do you expect for 111 proof," replied Finn.

"A headache?" Luther shook his head. "I thought they would have food here. I need to eat, Finn. I can't hold my liquor so well on an empty stomach. And if you recall, a banana and some peanuts is not much of a lunch."

"Yeah, I'm hungry too. We can ask the waiter for a recommendation or just find the closest restaurant when we're done."

"The closest restaurant, please!"

The waiter brought the flights and the taste test was on. After much consideration, they both agreed that they liked Redemption Wheated the best. "An appropriate name, don't you think?" Finn asked as they paid the bill.

"What? Redemption?"

"Yes. Don't take offense, Luther. Everyone is looking for redemption. It's a funny word with a lot of meanings."

Luther decided to leave well enough alone. Anyway, he was more interested in finding food. His head was spinning and his stomach was growling. They walked around the neighborhood a few minutes and found Mammy's Kitchen. "How about some southern food?" Luther asked.

"Sure," Finn replied.

They went in, were seated and Luther glanced quickly through the menu. "I'll have a southern burger."

"What makes a burger southern?" Finn asked.

"Pimento cheese and fried green tomatoes."

"Hmm. Well I'm going to continue the bourbon motif." The waitress appeared. "I'll have bourbon-grilled chicken breasts smothered in Uncle Marty's bourbon glaze and topped with Swiss cheese and fried onion straws."

"You get two sides with that," the waitress said.

Finn looked at Luther. "You want fries and green beans?"

Luther shrugged. "Sure. But——"

"I have plenty to eat," Finn stopped him. "I don't need sides."

They ate heartily and were quite full when they finished, but they split a piece of coconut cream pie anyway. Now stuffed, they rose, Luther relieved that he felt steady again. They wandered back to the Chrysler, drove back to the motel, and crawled into their beds.

Chapter 28

"FASTEN YOUR SEATBELT."

"Yeah, yeah," muttered Finn as he fumbled with the buckle. "Someday I'm gonna belt you EVA."

"I see that crappy breakfast in the motel lobby didn't improve your mood much," Luther grinned.

"What does Little Debbie know about breakfast?" demanded Finn. "Sounds like a lap dancer in a gentlemen's club."

"Uh huh. But you were just there for the whisky."

"Bourbon. And that was a speakeasy, not a gentlemen's club."

"Right," Luther replied, rolling his eyes. "Sweet Little Debbie has melted your brain. We'll get some real breakfast on the road soon enough. Where are we headed today?"

Finn pulled out his phone and scrolled and tapped. "Little Rock is about five hundred miles. We could get through there and stop in the next smaller town and look for a motel."

"Sounds good. I guess we'll still be dining Southern style. What's the specialty in Arkansas?"

"I don't know. Catfish, okra, hushpuppies, collard greens, chitterlings, and grits?" Finn speculated. "Uh," a grin crossed his face. "Shouldn't you know better than me?"

"Oh, sure. That's all we ate in the projects. Especially collards. We'd just go out into an empty lot, kick aside the beer cans and dirty needles and pick us some."

Finn blinked. "Am I supposed to laugh or cry?"

"Neither."

Finn glanced down at his phone. "Well, the fastest route is I-40, but you go through Nashville and Memphis. You could take the Western Kentucky Parkway. It's a little longer, but you don't go through cities. Unless you want to listen to Country or Blues?"

"Huh?" Luther asked. "You want to go to a club or something?"

"Who me? Nah. But I thought you might. That Buster character and Dutch might question how you could be so close to these cities and not partake of the music."

Luther sniffed. "I don't need to impress anyone."

"Okay, big shot. Then you'd better decide now so I can direct you."

"I thought I did. The parkway sounds like it'll be a prettier ride."

Finn nodded and directed him. They drove for about an hour and saw a diner with a flashing pink and green neon sign amidst the oaks. Luther swung the Chrysler into a crowded parking lot and they went inside. The menu turned out to be pretty ordinary, but scrambled eggs, bacon and toast were a welcome remedy to the motel fare. They ate and were back on the road quickly, admiring the scenery. "Have you texted the farm or Jed lately?" Finn asked after a while.

"No. I thought I'd hear something from Juniper if there were any changes. And to tell you the truth, I'm not sure how she feels anymore. I'm kind of waiting for her to make the next move."

"A wise decision," Finn grinned, "but you could ask Dutch how Homer's doing."

"I could. But I guess I don't really want to know."

"Dying is a part of life. You'll be witness to that over and over again. My address book is all crossed out."

Luther looked over at Finn. "Really?" Finn nodded solemnly. "Well, I think I'll wait."

"Sure. They die with or without you."

Luther pretended to be intent on the road. Finally he said, "I wonder how Theo's doing with Joe. Have you heard anything from them?"

"No. But I can ask." Finn typed into his phone. He laughed. "Never thought I'd be such a part of this technology generation, but I have to admit that I like texting. Never been one for long phone conversations. With texting you can just say what you want and you don't need to listen to anyone's long ramblings."

"I agree but don't you talk to your daughter?"

"Sometimes."

"Do you miss her?"

"Of course. But we didn't do that well when I lived with her in Venice Beach."

"But it would be nice if you lived near her, wouldn't it?"

"Are you trying to get me to move back to Los Angeles?" Finn asked warily.

"No. I just thought . . ." Luther's voice trailed off.

"What? That I'm getting old and might need her help?"

"I didn't say that."

Finn started to speak, but was interrupted by his phone dinging. He looked down at it and chuckled. "Theo says they're doing really well together. Joe's a character and makes him laugh. And he's loving a warm bed, a TV and the great food Joe's introduced him to."

"What is it with old men and food?" Luther sighed.

"Not much left to live for, buddy. And it's an excuse to get together. Anyway, I'm glad it's working out for them. Theo must be pretty good at looking interested. Joe loves an audience."

A few hours later a line at a walk up hamburger stand in a small town caught their attention. After a tasty lunch and Finn's customary nap, Luther asked, "Have you found us a motel just past Little Rock?"

"I'll look." Finn scrolled down the map. "It seems that Benton might be a good place to stop. But it's not a small town. You okay with that?"

"Well, it's not a city like Little Rock, right?"

"Population of thirty-five thousand. But there's a restaurant there called Eat My Catfish. Sounds like it's what we're looking for."

"Okay. I can handle that."

They arrived at Eat My Catfish in Benton at dusk. Luther enjoyed the greasy, spicy food while Finn complained throughout his meal. "I'll need a liquor store before we find a motel. Only thing I can think of to settle my stomach after that mess of fried everything!"

Luther laughed. "Well, at least you can say you've tried southern delicacies."

"Hah! I'd hardly call these delicacies!"

Luther pulled into a parking space in front of a liquor store. "We'll try to find a gourmet restaurant for tomorrow's big meal." Finn gave Luther a disdainful look and went inside the store. He returned with the proverbial brown bag and took a swig as soon as he got in the car. "Hey, man!" Luther exclaimed. "We are in Arkansas and I don't want anybody stopping little ol' Black me with an open bottle."

"I would guess that in Arkansas it's not illegal."

"I'd prefer not to take a chance so please put it away."

Finn took another swig. "Well, well, well. Look at Luther taking a stand and being assertive."

"Oh shut up, Finn." They found a motel a bit south of Benton in Malvern. After registering and going to their room, Luther said, "I'll sneak Bardo in now."

"Well, I'm going to shower and enjoy my Southern Comfort. It's a little sweet for my taste, but I figured that was the appropriate drink in these environs."

Luther shook his head, went out to the car and hid Bardo under his coat. Just as he passed by the registration desk, she squirmed out of his arm and jumped to the floor. He glanced furtively at the clerk who winked at him and came around the desk to pick up Bardo. "I don't give a rat's ass if you got a cat," she drawled. "What's its name?"

"Bardo." Luther said apprehensively.

"Mm, that's an interestin' name," the clerk replied, unimpressed. "Where you headed?"

"Los Angeles . . . eventually."

"Yeah, you got a ways to go. You seein' the sights along the way?"

"Not really." Luther chuckled. "It's kind of turned into a food and drink trip. You know, trying whatever is the specialty of wherever we are."

"Well, that's different. Where you headed next?"

"Texas, I think."

"Well you gotta do barbecued ribs in Lubbock."

"Oh yeah?" Luther said. "You got any recommendations?"

"J&M or Rooster's. But I think Rooster's is only open for dinner on weekends."

"Okay. Thanks. We'll try J&M."

The clerk lifted Bardo before her face. "You be a good pussycat, ya hear?" Bardo meowed on cue. "Yeah, I know ya are." She handed her back to Luther and smiled. "Think of me when you have those ribs. J&M was my aunt's favorite."

"Will do," Luther smiled. "Thanks again," he added, lifting Bardo for emphasis before tucking her back into his coat.

Chapter 29

THE NEXT MORNING THEY AVOIDED THE CONTI-
NENTAL BREAKFAST AT THE MOTEL AND SOUGHT
OUT BOWLS OF GRITS AT A CAFE. "Mm," Finn said as
he took another spoonful. "This is very much like a rich
risotto."

"What's risotto?" asked Luther as a he savored
another mouthful.

"Italian rice dish. Very creamy like these grits."

Luther sighed as he swallowed. "I sense an Italian
restaurant in our future. That is if there's one as good as
any in New York."

"Not likely," Finn replied as he stirred in the melting
butter.

"I wonder what Buster would think. You think he
ever had risotto?"

"Well, he toured a lot, didn't he?"

"Sure," Luther replied as he took another mouthful.
"But it was only recently that he was finally recognized
as a trailblazing artist."

"Maybe not, then. I imagine his performances are
served with a side of green tomatoes. It's what his fans

expect. And he might not care either way. Some people merely eat to live."

"Like Little Debbies?" Luther grinned.

"That's a death wish!" laughed Finn.

After breakfast they settled into the Chrysler for a long day's drive. "So we're off to Lubbock and ribs for dinner," Luther announced.

"Oh, are you navigating now?"

"No. You still have to find our way to J&M's. That's where the motel clerk told me to go."

"Hmm," Finn responded as he started fiddling with his phone.

"I know it's hard for you to take direction from others," Luther smiled, "but I enjoy telling you what to do."

"Well don't get too used to it." They took Interstate 30 and drove an hour or so, lost in their own thoughts, before Luther reached for the radio controls. "Remember, we're in Arkansas," Finn warned. "The music may not be to your liking."

Luther hit the scan button and the first station was Christian. The second was Country. The third was Country Christian. Finn started laughing. "Maybe we'll get some Blues once we cross into Texas."

"We may have missed that by not going through Mississippi or Memphis," Luther chuckled.

"Well, that was your choice." After Texarkana, Finn directed him onto US 82. "This will be more to your liking. And you get to see Paris!"

"France?"

Finn looked over at him. "You're kidding, right?"

"Yeah," Luther replied, feigning innocence. "Sure. Just want you to maintain your superior intellect."

"Well, thank you." Finn then consulted his phone. "I knew there was a Paris, Maine but little did I know that there are at least twenty-three towns named Paris in America. We missed the mini Eiffel Tower in Paris, Tennessee."

"Do they sell mini croissants under it?"

Finn flipped his phone around. "Doesn't look like it. Too bad. An opportunity for the Pillsbury Doughboy to expand."

"Well, I forgive your navigation error then. Just this once."

Finn shut his phone. "I'm so relieved."

The countryside was flattening, the oaks were sparse, but the grass was greener. "Maybe tomorrow we can put the top down," Luther mused aloud. He glanced up at the roof lock and saw red and blue lights flashing in the rear view mirror. "Shit!"

"What?"

A siren squawked. "Cops!"

"You weren't speeding were you?"

"Nope," Luther replied as he slowed and moved onto the broad shoulder. "Just driving while Black."

"Screw 'em," Finn growled. "Let this old White man handle them."

"You don't want to test them, Finn. Just do what they say." Luther looked in the rear view mirror again and saw two cops get out of the car. One was older and portly––to put it nicely. The other looked like a teenager just out of acne. "Get the registration out of the glove compartment now and have it ready so they don't think we have a gun hidden in there."

"A gun? Good lord." Finn shuffled the contents of the glove box, looking for the registration.

"Oh shit!" Luther suddenly exploded. "They're going to think we stole the car because it's registered to Miriam's husband."

"Well I don't have a driver's license so they can't ask me for mine," Finn replied confidently. "I'll just tell them I'm Herb Schwartz."

Luther looked at Finn skeptically. "I don't think you look Jewish."

"You really think cops here know what a Jew or an Irishman look like?"

Luther snickered. "Outside of Lucky Charms, no. But if they believe you, they'd have another reason to beat on us: Black and Jewish."

"Hah! Sounds like the start of a joke: a Black and a Jew get stopped by a cop . . . Hey, maybe that's why they're stopping us: the New York plates. They probably wonder why a couple of New Yorkers would drive in this godforsaken place."

"You're such a snob, Finn, but you're probably right."

The cops approached the car with their hands resting on their holsters. "Damn!" Luther exhaled loudly. "You distracted me. I should have gotten my license out of my wallet before they got here so they don't think I'm reaching for a gun in my pocket!"

"Jesus Christ, Luther, stop enacting the worst case scenario. They're not gonna shoot us."

"Hopefully not, as long as you don't pretend to be Herbert Schwartz."

The younger cop stood by Luther's window and motioned to roll it down. The older one stood by Finn's. "How ya 'all doin'?" the younger cop said after the glass whirred down the door.

"Uh, fine," Luther mumbled.

"Why'd you stop us?" Finn asked. "He wasn't speeding."

Luther frowned and shot a look of daggers at Finn. He turned back to the cop and smiled. "Um, my license is in my wallet which is in my pocket. Do you want me to get it out?"

Finn decided distraction was the best move and thrust the registration onto the older cop standing at his door. Luther sighed and clearly rolled his eyes so the cop at his door could see his frustration. The older cop glanced over the registration with a skeptical look. "Which one of you is Herbert Schwartz?"

"He's dead and we bought the car from his wife who is a friend of mine," Finn explained. "She suggested we keep the registration as it is until we get settled in California."

"Humph," he replied. "That's a trusting friend." He stared at Finn for a moment and then added, "We don't see New York plates here much." Finn kept cool and finally the cop glanced over the Chrysler. "This car reminds me of one my Daddy had."

"Hold on Travis," the younger cop spoke up. "We still need to see driver's licenses."

"Dammit, Clem," the older cop barked. "How many times have I told you to call me Sergeant Williams in these situations."

"Well, we still need to see their licenses!"

"Well, duh, Clem."

Luther tried to mollify the young cop. "I need to reach in my pocket and get my license out."

Clem took his gun and held it, although he kept it pointing at the ground. "Get out of the car slowly."

Finn looked up at the older cop who was frowning at the scene unfolding. "I don't have a license," Finn said. "I don't drive."

"That's alright, old man. You're not being transported against your will, are you?"

"Most of the time, no."

The older cop guffawed and looked back up sharply as Luther opened his door and put his hands in the air. "What pocket is your wallet in?" the young cop asked, raising his gun and aiming it at Luther.

"Back right."

"Get it out slowly."

"For Pete's sake Clem," the older cop sighed. "Lower the gun."

The younger cop gave the older cop a dirty look, but did as he was told. Luther reached into his pocket slowly and took out his wallet. He handed Clem his license and waited while the younger cop looked at it. "I thought you said you're from New York. This here says you live in California."

"Finn is from New York. I flew in to, uh, visit him and now I'm driving home to California."

"We just need to check on this registration to make sure this baby isn't stolen," the older cop said quietly.

"No problem," replied Finn. "You can talk to Herb's wife, Miriam," he said pulling out his phone.

"Freeze!" yelled the young cop. Everyone jumped as he aimed at Finn inside the car.

"Clem! Lower your gun!" the older cop ordered. He then looked down at Finn. "Go ahead, old man, make your call." Then with a jerk of his head, he said crisply, "Clem, can I speak to you?"

The two cops strode off a few paces, the young one surly, his gun back in his holster, but his hand ready. Finn found the contact and nodded to the older cop that Miriam had answered. Travis handed over the registration to Clem so he could call it in and took the phone from Finn. After a brief explanation and a few yes and no ma'ams that suggested that Miriam was giving him a piece of her mind, he handed the phone back to Finn. "Hey Miriam," Finn said to announce his return. "Yeah, there's a first time for everything. We're okay and the car is running like your Mama's sewing machine. Talk to you more soon."

Travis had been walking around the car, stooping and leaning in to admire it from every angle. "What a beauty. That Schwartz guy kept it immaculate, just like my Daddy. Shoulda kept it. Does it talk to you?"

Finn laughed and Luther managed a grin. "Hell yeah," Finn replied. "And I talk right back at her!"

Travis roared. "That's the right attitude. Scared the hell out of me first time I heard it. Gives more orders than the chief of police! But it was cutting edge technology back in the day. How does it ride?"

"Real smooth," Luther managed to say. "Like a bigger car."

"Yeah, that downsized luxury was a hard sell. Luckily everyone was doing it. Imagine——" he paused as an SUV flashed by, "trying to sell that now." He pointed to the dashboard. "Look at that speedo topping out at 85 MPH. That guy was probably doin' that before he saw us. He then stood up and shouted, "Hey, Clem, how's that registration?"

"As presented," he called back dully.

"Good work," he yelled back. He turned to Luther and Finn. "Where you heading today?"

"Lubbock," Luther replied, finding his voice again. "Heard there's a great barbecue joint there. J&M's."

"Oh yeah. And no matter how full you are, make sure you save some room for peach cobbler."

"Will do!" Finn chimed in.

"Drive carefully and have a nice day." He raised his head and shouted, "Let's go, Clem." Soon the police car sped off with a spray of gravel leaving Luther to drop wearily back into the car.

"Phew," Luther said, grabbing the steering wheel. "Now I have something to text Damon about besides food and mileage."

"Who knew a knock off of The Three Stooges could be so frightful," Finn replied.

"You didn't act frightened."

Finn shrugged. "I was. A bit. And I was going to be an ass, until you told me to behave. Better to fake a friendly yet slightly cantankerous old man."

"You fake that?"

Finn grinned. "C'mon. Let's hit the road."

Luther started the Chrysler, EVA admonished and soon they were cruising down the highway again. He hit the scan button on the radio and got a Blues station. "That's better," he murmured.

"And appropriate," Finn replied.

They arrived in Lubbock at dusk and went directly to J&M Barbecue. Finn reported there were a couple of motels within walking distance, so they got a room at the Days Inn and secured the curtains so Bardo wouldn't put on a show in the window. They cleaned up and walked to the restaurant, happy to stretch their legs. The ribs and sausage were delicious, and they had ordered cole slaw and mashed potatoes instead of fried okra and fries so they could squeeze in some peach cobbler. J&M didn't serve hard liquor, so Finn had to join Luther in ordering beer. They enjoyed bottles of Shiner Bock from Shiner, Texas, to keep with the local food and drink theme. "Do you want to stop at a bar for whiskey?" Luther asked as they paid the bill.

"No need. I still have some in my suitcase."

"Shit, Finn. You had an open liquor bottle? What if that young asshole cop would have searched the car?"

Finn shrugged and smiled. "Well, he didn't."

Chapter 30

"SO WHERE ARE WE GOING TODAY?" FINN ASKED OVER A PLATE OF CORNED BEEF HASH.

"As far away from Texas cops as we can," Luther replied, dipping a wedge of toast into his egg yolk.

"Aw, I'm starting to recall Officer Travis quite fondly."

Luther eyed him. "You finished off the bottle of whiskey, didn't you?"

"Nope. I was Mister Moderation last night."

"Well, I should congratulate you, but we'd be safer if you drank it all."

"I don't think this joint would appreciate me spiking my coffee."

"Your suitcase is going in the trunk."

"Yes, Mother," Finn replied meekly. He pulled out his phone and started tapping. "How about Flagstaff?"

"Is that in the right direction."

"Yeah, but are you going to be okay driving through Albuquerque?"

Luther frowned. "Aren't you getting kinda tired of asking that big city question?"

Finn stuck out his lower lip. "Just checking because Los Angeles is pretty damn big."

"Hey, you think I'm going to be your chauffeur when we're in Los Angeles?"

"Hell if I know you'll even make the sixty miles from San Bernardino to the Westside."

"Thanks for the vote of confidence," Luther chuckled. "Let's stick to getting to Flagstaff today."

"Yes sir!" Finn studied his phone. "Got to find US 84 to Clovis."

Luther turned and looked out the window. "Mm, step up, Finn. I need more details than that." Finn started reading off the turn-by-turn directions in a remarkable imitation of the electronic guidance voice. "Okay, okay," muttered Luther, embarrassed by a few looks in their direction. "How long will it take?"

"It's long. About nine and a half hours."

"Oh well," sighed Luther. "If I get tired of driving, we can just pull into any old motel. No need to get to Flagstaff––unless there's something you must eat there."

"Ha, ha, ha. I can't think of any food or drink specific to Arizona."

"What about Native American food" Whatever that would be . . ."

"Whoa, I'm impressed, Luther. I'll look that up." Finn took some time Googling and scrolling. "Interesting. You ever heard of Tepary Beans?"

"Of course not."

"It says here it's an ancient superfood of the Sonoran Desert."

"Where's the Sonoran Desert?" Luther asked.

"Way south of where we're going," Finn replied, studying his phone. "South of Phoenix, I think. But at least it's an Arizona food. And there's corn, of course. Also wild rice that they call manoomin. And a thing called fry bread. I guess maybe they make a taco-like thing with the beans, rice and corn inside the fry bread."

"That would be worth trying."

"I'll see if I can find us a restaurant in New Mexico or Arizona that serves fry bread. Probably have to be on or at least near a reservation." Finn spent several minutes on his phone. "I don't see any place in Flagstaff. We might have to stop somewhere on the way to get that fry bread." He continued looking and finally said, "Here's a place that has a fry bread stand. Chee's Indian store and gift shop."

"Where is it?" Luther asked.

"A town called Houck, before we get to Flagstaff. It's right off Interstate 40, the road we'll be on."

"How far from here?"

"About seven hours."

"Nothing sacred about Flagstaff," Luther said.

"Then let's make that our next destination. We can eat that fry bread and then find a motel."

"I'm sure there'll be a liquor store near the Indian reservation."

"Now there's a sweet little stereotype," Finn replied dryly.

"What? Only Whites are allowed to stereotype?"

Finn laughed. "Be my guest."

Soon they were cruising along, quietly listening to the radio, lost in their own thoughts. When they stopped for a gas/bathroom break Luther decided to call Juniper and find out what was happening at the farm. He didn't care for the barren cotton stubble fields they were driving through. He missed the trees and foliage near Garberville. If he couldn't stay on the farm, he at least knew he didn't want to be in a city or the desert. Juniper didn't answer, so he left a message. They continued driving for a while. "Hey Finn?"

"Yeah?"

"I think I've traveled a bit further on this road of liminality."

"Meaning?"

"Well, if you don't know what you want, it helps to know what you don't want. It makes me feel like I'm closer to some kind of decision."

Finn nodded. "What have you figured out that you don't want to do?"

"It's more about where, not what. I know I like forests. I don't like deserts, plains or cities."

"That's good that you know where you don't want to live." Finn chuckled. "But I don't think you want to wander around the forest eating whatever you can find."

"Are you teasing me, Finn?'

"No. I'm not. I'm trying to be encouraging. Really."

Luther nodded. "Then thanks."

"So you're not planning to go back to the farm any-time soon?"

Luther didn't answer right away. Then he sighed and said, "It was a perfect place for me. Now . . . I don't know. I mean . . . it's like a cocoon . . . warm and cozy . . . but very confining."

"That's why butterflies break free."

"And I don't know what is happening in my relation-ship with Juniper. It would be pretty awkward living there if we're not together."

Finn studied Luther for a moment. "Does acknowl-edging that make you feel more mature?"

"Yes, somehow."

"I mean I am very sorry about anyone's idyll ending, but you're absolutely right about everything you said."

Luther shrugged. "Thanks. At least I have some money now to do something on my own." After the sprawl of Albuquerque and miles and miles of some-times-colorful desert, they reached Chee's Indian Store and Gift Shop. They found the place quite busy with tourists. "Do you want to look around the store?" Luther asked as they parked in front of the fry bread stand.

"No. I'm way more interested in eating."

They ordered their fry bread and sat down at an out-door picnic table to eat it. "Tastes pretty much like a taco to me," Luther said.

"I haven't eaten much Mexican food," Finn responded. "That's a California thing."

"There's got to be plenty of Mexican restaurants in New York."

"I'm sure there are, but I don't frequent them."

"You lived in California a while too."

"Yeah, and I actually knew someone who owned a Mexican restaurant, but I just went there for beer and chips. And to wash dishes."

Luther was about to take a bite of his fry bread, but paused with his mouth open and stared at Finn. "You what?"

"I washed dishes at Luis' restaurant. So did Jed."

"Why? You were down and out and needed money? I knew Jed was, but I thought you were a best selling author."

Finn scoffed. "Very few people get rich being a best selling author."

Luther took a bite of his fry bread. "Well, you're sure right that there's a lot about you I don't know."

"Let's just say it wasn't my finest hour."

"How far is it to Flagstaff from here?"

Finn looked at his phone. "A couple of hours. Hey, we'll be going by the Petrified Forest." He laughed. "I doubt it's your kind of forest, though."

"I'd just as soon stop next at a motel. I'm kind of sick of driving."

"I wasn't saying we should go there. Let's just find a rest room and get going before it gets dark." They continued west as the sun sank and colored the sky and clouds. The Chrysler's prismatic hood ornament changed like a kaleidoscope until dusk settled and the juniper covered hills merged with the night.

"Finally!" Luther said as they approached the lights of Flagstaff.

Finn looked at him. "You were that excited to get to Flagstaff?"

"I'm talking about the pine trees and mountains."

"It's dark. How are you seeing pine trees and mountains?"

"I can smell 'em, Finn. I can feel 'em." Luther stopped short. "Hey, do the headlights look dimmer to you?"

"I don't know. Maybe a little. We haven't used them much, you know. But Damon checked everything out."

"I know, but things could happen. We've driven a lot of miles."

"Let's just find a motel and give the car a rest," Finn replied.

"Do we have a dinner plan for Flagstaff?"

Finn shrugged. "I wouldn't mind some regular old American food."

"Well, I wouldn't mind just getting some fast food or something and eating in the motel. It's late and I'm tired."

"I tell you what. Let's find a motel with some kind of restaurant next to it where I can go eat and drink. I can either bring something back for you or you can get your own fast food."

"Are you sure you don't mind?"

"No offense, Luther, but it might be nice to get away from you for a couple of hours."

Luther laughed. "Yeah. I haven't spent this much time with the same person since my cellmate."

"Look here. There's a bunch of motels and a place called Dirty Birdie's Sports Bar and Grill across the street. You pick a motel."

Luther drove into a parking lot of a cheap chain motel and they were checked in quickly. "I guess I'll go with you to Dirty Birdie's."

"Can't stand to be away from me?"

"Yeah. That's it, Finn. I'll just take my dinner to go and bring it back here. You can stay and drink to your heart's content."

When they walked in, they were greeted by several televisions, each turned to a different sport. Some loud college-aged kids played pool and loud music permeated the ambience. "You really want to eat here, Finn?"

"Absolutely. This place is right up my alley. Might even play a few games of pool with these youngsters. Show them how the game should be played."

Luther shrugged. "I'm going to order some food to go and I'll have a beer with you at the bar while I wait."

They sat down at the bar, facing about twenty-five beers on tap. "Which ones are the local beers?" Finn asked the bartender. Then he turned to Luther. "Got to keep with the theme. After all, this is our last day on this scintillating vacation."

"Lumberyard is one of our local breweries," the bartender replied. "We have a couple from there."

"I'll have the Hazy Angel IPA."

"What'll you have?" the bartender asked Luther.

"That's fine for me too. I'd like to order food to go."

The bartender brought menus and Finn said, "I'll eat mine here. I'll have the meat loaf dinner."

"And I'll have the shrimp basket," Luther said.

"Sticking to the fried food motif, I see. Fried shrimp and French fries."

Luther glowered at Finn silently. When the food came Luther downed the rest of his beer and took his bag and left without a word. Finn ordered another beer and enjoyed his solitude, even if he was in a noisy sports bar.

Chapter 31

THE CHRYSLER WAS PACKED, BARDO WAS ABSCONDED FROM THE ROOM, AND A TYPICAL MOTEL BREAKFAST WAS EATEN. "Just stay on 40?" Luther asked as he buckled his seat belt.

"Yep. All the way and no big––"

"Yeah, other than Los Angeles," Luther scoffed as he turned the key in the ignition. Nothing happened.

"What's going on?" Finn asked.

"How the hell should I know?!" Luther snapped as he twisted the key again. Again nothing. "Maybe the battery is dead. Remember the lights were dim last night."

"I guess that's one way to shut EVA up," Finn harrumphed. "Now what?"

Luther fell back against the leather seat and shrugged. "I guess we need to get a new battery."

Finn looked up and down the street. "Where are we going to buy one?"

"We have to get it towed to a garage, Finn," sighed Luther. "It's not like I know how to put one in, even if there was a store that sold them across the street."

"Okay-y," Finn drawled as he pulled out his phone. "Who do I call?"

"I dunno," Luther replied sullenly. "Look online. For towing, I guess. We should have listened to Damon and got that AAA thing."

"Well, it's too late for that," Finn replied as he squinted at his phone. He tapped and was now telling someone about their situation and where they were. "Said they'll be here in about half an hour," Finn finally reported.

"Damn! I hope it's a quick and easy fix."

"I thought you liked it here. You know, all those trees and stuff," Finn teased.

Luther rolled his eyes and got out of the car. "I'm going to take Bardo for a walk."

"See you on the evening news," Finn called out. He went back into the motel for another cup of coffee and sat in the lobby. He took a sip and wondered if his sense of taste was failing. Not bad. He took another sip and pulled out his phone. "Hey Kate. We're in Flagstaff, but the car won't start. We're waiting for the tow truck. I'll keep you posted, but I doubt we'll be in Los Angeles tonight." He hung up after leaving the voicemail and then dialed Jed. He didn't answer either, but this time Finn didn't leave a message.

The tow truck driver arrived and jump-started the car. "Is that all?" Luther asked hopefully.

The driver gave him a look. "No. Unless you want to be stuck somewhere between here and Kingman. At least I don't have to tow you to the garage, so I'm saving you some money. Follow me and we'll test the battery, but I'm guessing the real problem is the alternator."

"Is that a big deal?" Luther asked.

"You mean money-wise?"

"Well, yeah, but I mean will it take a long time to fix?"

"Not to fix it, but we might have to order the part." The driver began to chuckle. "I've never seen an '83 Chrysler before. I have no idea if anyone here in town has an alternator that will replace OEM."

"OEM?"

"Original Equipment Manufacturer," explained the driver. "Maybe this car is simple enough that a universal can be used."

"Your electrical equipment is malfunctioning," EVA suddenly admonished. "Prompt service is required."

"What the fuck?!" the driver yelped, jerking back from the Chrysler.

Luther and Finn burst out laughing. "That's EVA, my nemesis," Finn said. "That bitch is always telling us what to do."

"Well, it would have been nice if she told us that last night," Luther sighed.

The driver stood there, shaking his head. "Whatever. I grew up on reruns of 'Knight Rider.' This is sorta like KITT for old people."

Finn waggled his eyebrows and pretended to take a cigar from his mouth. "I resent that remark!"

The driver blinked at him. "This may be more compli-cated than I thought."

"Tell me about it," Luther muttered.

Finn and Luther followed the truck to the garage and after some diagnosing and phone calls, they were told that the car would be ready the day after tomorrow. "Now what?" Luther sighed as they stood outside the garage. Bardo squirmed anxiously in Luther's arms.

"Well," Finn observed. "Bardo doesn't look too happy, so I guess we'd better look for a motel close to this garage."

"What fun! Stuck in a motel room with you for two days."

"Try drinking and then you won't care." Luther just glared at him. "Look, you might as well give sightseeing a try. We're pretty damn close to the Grand Canyon. We could see if there's a bus or something."

Luther perked up. "That's better than sitting around."

"Then let's find a motel and do some research."

They asked at the garage if they knew of a motel nearby and wound up at one a few blocks away. After picking up a fast food lunch, they spent the afternoon figuring out how to get to the Grand Canyon by bus, where to have dinner within walking distance of the motel, and taking naps. It actually turned out to be a relaxing few hours and they felt recharged when it was time for dinner. They decided on Mexican, even though it wasn't one of Finn's favorites. "When in Rome . . ." Finn said as they looked at the menu.

"Yeah, yeah, yeah. Do as the Romans do. Who said it anyway?" Luther asked.

"Look it up."

"Once a teacher, always a teacher." Luther smiled, as he looked it up on his phone. "Saint Ambrose said it in the fourth century AD."

Finn nodded. "Now you know." The waitress arrived to take their order. "Should we have margaritas to go with the Mexican theme?" "Sure," Luther replied and turned to the waitress. "Two margaritas and I'll have shrimp tacos on the dinner combo."

"I'll have a beef burrito," Finn said.

"Still staying away from fried food?"

"You'll get there soon enough, Luther. Your stomach can only take so much rich, fried food."

"But you can drink to your heart's content."

"Of course I can. I'm Irish."

Luther chuckled. "I'm actually looking forward to our excursion tomorrow. I guess we'll have to leave Bardo in the motel room."

"Can't bring her unless you want to put her in your pocket. I don't think she'd like that." The waitress brought the drinks and Finn downed his immediately and ordered another before the waitress left. "I needed some hard liquor, even if it is Tequila."

"This is pretty good."

"You going to join me in another one?"

"Might as well. I don't have to drive tomorrow."

"That's probably why you're looking forward to going to the Grand Canyon. 'Go Greyhound and leave the driving to us.' That's another saying you wouldn't know. It was a famous advertising slogan in my day."

"Was that AD or BC?"

"You make me proud, Luther. You've learned how to be cynical."

"Thanks, Finn. You can't imagine how great that makes me feel." They laughed, ordered more drinks, ate their food and discussed what they would see the next day.

"The bus leaves from the Amtrak station at 7:45 and gets to the park at 9:30. Then there's a shuttle bus to get around the park."

"What time does the bus leave to come home?"

"6:15."

"That'll be plenty of time, right?"

"Unless you wanted to ride a burro into the canyon. Might not be enough time for that."

"That would be kind of cool, but somehow I can't see you on a burro."

"Hah! Got that right!"

They walked back to the motel with full stomachs and satisfied smiles. They had brought some shrimp out of Luther's taco for Bardo, so she also felt content.

Chapter 32

THE NEXT MORNING A TAXI DROPPED THEM OFF AT THE AMTRAK STATION WHERE THEY FOUND THE BUS TO THE GRAND CANYON IDLING. They boarded and waited for more passengers, but they failed to materialize. It would be a quiet trip, and Luther hoped the park would not be crowded either. He gazed at the snow-covered mountains and bright blue sky. It was crisp outside, but not particularly cold. "I think we need this break," he said aloud.

Finn scoffed. "I'm not exactly outdoorsy."

"It'll be good for you."

"Hah! You sound like my daughter. She always pushed me to go to the beach when we lived together."

"Did you go?"

"Yeah. Every day, but I stayed on the boardwalk."

Luther grinned. "Well, there's all the historic buildings if nature doesn't do it for you."

Finn eyed him. "Well, thank you. I might just forget that we skipped Gettysburg."

Luther took a deep breath and turned to his window to study the passing scenery. The pines were getting more stunted and farther apart, interspersed with rocky outcroppings. Patches of snow lay in the shadows.

They got to the Maswik Lodge and immediately boarded the shuttle for the tour of the South Rim. "This would be a cool job," Luther said between comments about the majestic views.

"Yeah?"

"Yeah. Driving a bus and being a guide, telling people all about the park."

Finn smiled and leaned over to look out the window. "Hmm."

"Or taking care of the trails and plants."

"Sounds like a park ranger," Finn commented. "You probably have to go to school for that."

"Okay," Luther replied. Finn nodded with a sly grin. "What's that for?"

"What?" Finn pretended to be surprised.

"That weird smile."

"Nothing. I think it's a great idea."

"Which? Being a park ranger or going to school?"

"Both. Or either."

Luther listened attentively to the guide's presentation and when they got off the bus to stand at the rim of the canyon, he went over to talk to a uniformed person milling around. "Are you a park ranger?" he asked.

"Oh no. Just a volunteer."

"You can do this as a volunteer?"

"There are lots of volunteer opportunities here."

"And you don't need any special training?"

"Well, you do for some of the jobs. But there are plenty you can do without it."

"Is that true for all the national parks?"

"Far as I know."

"Thanks." Luther went back to where Finn was standing and told him what he'd found out. "Maybe I could do this in the Redwoods near Garberville. Volunteer, I mean. I don't need the money."

"Well, not for a while, at least," Finn suggested. "Better to invest in old age. Benefits come in handy."

"I guess."

"Take it from someone who knows. Is there a national park near the farm?"

"Yeah. Oh wait. Maybe it's a state park. But they must have similar volunteer opportunities."

"You seem motivated, Luther."

"I am. I think I'd like this."

"One never knows, do one."

Luther laughed. "Where'd you dig that up, Mister English Professor?"

"Fats Waller said it. It was his signature phrase. You know who Fats Waller was, don't you?"

"Buster has mentioned him a bit. Maybe my mother too. An old jazz singer, right?"

Finn nodded. "It's coming together."

"What is?"

Finn shrugged with a mischievous grin. "Oh I don't know . . . your life? Your future?"

"You mean I'm getting through this liminal state?" Luther grinned back.

"Something like that." They turned their attention back to the guide, and Luther was all ears. Finn sat back and enjoyed Luther's newfound enthusiasm.

When they got back on the bus to Flagstaff, Luther was on his phone Googling national and state parks for volunteering opportunities. "Is Sequoia and Kings Canyon National Park on our way to Los Angeles?"

"I don't know. Why?"

"It says it's in central California and there might be some volunteer opportunities."

Finn looked at the map on his phone. "It's not exactly on the way, but we could stop there if you want. It's not like we're on some kind of timetable."

"All the other ones in southern California look like desert or just some kind of monument. Sequoia/Kings looks like more of what I'm looking for."

Finn grinned again. "I like the sound of that: 'what you're looking for'."

"Oh come on, Finn," Luther smiled in spite of himself. "Not another lecture."

Finn was quiet, studying Luther and his fresh flash of arrogance. He finally spoke. "I'm not interested in being your teacher or mentor. I'm your friend, trying to help. That's it."

Luther closed his eyes and took a breath. "I know you don't want me to say this, but I'm sorry."

"Apology accepted. Now. Let's figure out how to get to Sequoia/Kings Canyon National Park."

They arrived in Flagstaff after eight and looked around for a place to eat dinner. "Hey, how about there?" Luther said, pointing to a place called Collins Irish Pub and Grill. "Just because we're in Arizona doesn't mean we can't honor your heritage. Anyway, who knows when we might have a chance to eat corned beef and cabbage again?"

Finn put a hand over his heart. "Bless you, young man."

Finn ordered his Jameson's neat while Luther opted for a Dublin Donkey: Jameson's with ginger beer and lime. "This is very good," Luther enthused. "Better than straight, as far as I'm concerned."

"You're such a lightweight. You gonna eat light too?"

Luther looked through the menu. "In honor of you, I'll have the bangers and mash. Sausage, sauerkraut and spicy mustard sounds good to me."

"Well, I'm going with shepherd's pie. My stomach could use a break from all the fried, spicy stuff."

They enjoyed the meal and the discussion of their visit to Grand Canyon National Park. "It's such a relief to feel like I have a direction," Luther sighed.

Finn smiled. "Just one of those transformative experiences they talk about in philosophy."

"Now I wish we had visited some other national parks along the way."

"Never look back and regret. Just look forward. What's past is prologue."

"It's like what we talked about when we first met––about learning from the past but not dwelling in it."

"That's right. And 'what's past is prologue' is from Shakespeare, lest you wish to enlighten someone else."

"I'll stick to myself for now," Luther chuckled. "And the title of your Jonestown book––who came up with that saying?"

"George Santayana."

"Maybe I should be writing all this down."

"Oh, searching through your journal in the middle of a conversation is so disruptive. Better to file it mentally."

Luther laughed. "Yeah. That way I'll always remember you."

"Unforgettable," Finn crooned like Nat King Cole. "That's what I am . . ."

Luther buried his head. "Shhh! You're embarrassing me."

"It's what I do best," grinned Finn. "Unforgettable . . . though near or far . . ."

Luther peeked out at a few diners looking their way. "C'mon. Let's go. Bardo's been alone all day."

Finn gave him a withering look. "She's a cat. What does she care? Hotel room or car? All she does is sleep anyway."

"You're such an old fart!"

"That's lovable curmudgeon to you, young man," Finn winked. "Okay, I'll get the check. See if the hostess can call us a cab."

"What about your phone?"

"Don't bother me," Finn replied as he sifted through his wallet.

Luther sighed and went up to the hostess. Her response wasn't much better. "Don't you have an Uber or Lyft app?"

"Uh, no. Just an old guy from New York City."

Luther could tell that she wasn't sure if she was talking about himself or someone else. "Just a minute," she sighed and then disappeared. Soon she returned with a middle-aged man who showed her the slim phone book under the lectern, where the number was, and what to say. As she spoke hesitantly into the phone, he said to Luther, "Kids. Can't run a restaurant with 'em, can't run one without 'em."

"I've got a few things to learn, too," Luther admitted.

The man smiled. "Thanks for understanding. Truth is, we only call a cab for drunks these days, and I usually deal with that."

"The dark side," Luther murmured.

"Yeah, fortunately few and far between."

Luther retold the situation to Finn as they stood waiting for the cab. "I guess we could have just walked back to the train station and gotten a cab," Finn mused.

"It's not Grand Central with a train coming in every twenty minutes. A cab isn't going to waste time there."

"Well, haven't you grown worldly." Finn watched a beat-up pick up rattle by. "Yep. This is not New York City."

The taxi arrived and the trip to the motel was quick. Luther consulted his phone as they walked down the hall to their room. "The garage never called to say they were done or even if they had gotten the part," he said as Finn opened the door and flopped onto the nearest available bed.

"We'll call in the morning," Finn muttered.

Bardo came over and rubbed against Luther's leg. "Okay, I'll take you out for a quickie." He left with the cat under his coat.

Chapter 33

THE MECHANIC CALLED THE NEXT MORNING, SAYING THE NEW ALTERNATOR WAS IN AND THE CHRYSLER WOULD BE READY IN ABOUT AN HOUR. They were soon on Interstate 40, heading down through a rapidly fading forest.

"It's mostly desert today," Finn announced as he slid his finger over the screen on his phone. "Nothing I can do about it."

"I'll survive, as long as the car does. Did you call Kate with our change of plans?"

"No. Haven't had time until now. Guess I'll text. Less questions to deal with."

Luther was silent as Finn slowly tapped out his message and sent it. Then he asked, "How far is it from Sequoia to Los Angeles?"

"Let me see." Finn put the destinations into his map app. "Not bad. Three and a half hours."

"Good," Luther sighed. "If we leave the park early enough, we'll avoid the worst of the traffic in L.A."

They were quiet for a while, Luther watching for reactions as cars passed them by. The Chrysler was looking a bit shabby with thousands of miles of grime deposited on it, but as the scenery grew bleak, it again became an object of attention. Occasionally someone would wave or give a thumbs up and Luther would respond in kind. "You really like being the center of attention," Finn finally commented.

"Can you think of anything better to do right now?"

"Sleep."

"Probably not the best advice while I'm driving." Finn did not reply as Luther finally offered, "It keeps my mind from overthinking about . . . things. Like Juniper."

"Haven't heard from her, eh?" Luther did not respond, so Finn dug deeper. "Maybe it's a woman's intuition. Maybe she senses you're not coming back. It's easier to let go by not having any contact at all."

Luther looked straight ahead. "Who says I'm not going back?"

"For good?"

Luther frowned at the force of Finn's question. "I wonder how Homer is doing."

"There's little to report during a slow, steady decline," sighed Finn. "Call Dutch if you must know."

"I don't want to put him in the middle."

Finn couldn't help but laugh. "He *is* in the middle. The middle of his own kingdom. If you don't want to deal with him, let it go."

"I don't see anything funny about it," Luther said coldly. He reached for the radio to end the conversation.

"Someday you will," Finn insisted. "You already admitted that the farm was comforting, yet confining. Suddenly you have big new ideas. You're waving at cars——"

"I've waved at cars during this whole trip!" Luther barked back as the radio hissed and spat garble.

"I mean you've found a way to interact with people," Finn snapped back. "You like an audience. Embrace your newfound love. Don't go running back to isolation."

Luther punched the AM button and the radio scanned an arrogant voice, some tinny Country song, Rancheria oom-pah, and settled on an LA traffic report, booming and fading far across the desert.

"Listen to how we focus on the blockages," Finn commented. "What's the alternative?"

"Move away," Luther grumbled.

Finn just grinned knowingly and gazed at the horizon ahead. The signal faded for the last time into the atmosphere, leaving them with the thrum of tires on asphalt. The sun behind them picked out peaks against the dull blue sky. Creosote bloomed along the shoulders of the interstate, then struggled off into the desert landscape, dull and seemingly lifeless. Finn closed his eyes and fell asleep.

"You missed Needles," Luther announced.

Finn blinked his eyes open and looked around. "Everything I need to know about Needles I learned in "The Grapes of Wrath.""

"The grapes of what?"

"Wrath."

"Grapes——that are angry?"

"No, it's a book by John Steinbeck——'oh, never mind," Finn yawned. "You woke me up for that?"

"Well, I was starting to think about lunch. Thought you could start——wait a minute. What does that flashing sign say ahead?" Luther squinted. "Interstate closed at Fenner due to truck collision. Use alternate route."

Finn sat up. "For God's sake, pull over. We don't want to be sitting out on the desert."

"What?" But Luther did as he was told. Cars and trucks flashed by as the Chrysler came to a stop. "No one else is stopping. Maybe we should just follow them to the alternate route."

"Like lambs to slaughter," Finn muttered as he jabbed at his phone. "There's already several miles of stopped traffic at Fenner. No one is going anywhere from there except back to US 95 through a place called Goffs. And . . ." He swiped diagonally. "Phew! We haven't passed US 95 yet. Turn off there."

"Maybe that's what everyone is doing now, like I said."

"Nope," Finn replied confidently, zooming in on the interchange. "Green, free flowing. The road itself——well, some spots of yellow, so maybe a bit heavier than usual."

"Then what?"

Finn tapped the screen. "I'm getting an alternate route via Searchlight, Nipton, and Mountain Pass. Won't save any time by any measure, but better than just sitting there, waiting. Better gas up in Searchlight. Go on, gotta stay ahead of the returning traffic."

Luther watched the mirror, waiting for an opening to merge into. "What about lunch?"

"Mmm," Finn studied his phone. "Casino Coffee Shop––no time for that. McDonald's. He's an uncle of Little Debbie, isn't he?"

Luther laughed as he gave the accelerator an unaccustomed punch. "Yeah, in your world, Little Debbie and McDonald's are related."

"Whoa!" Finn laughed as the Chrysler got off its haunches. "I can hear Damon yelling from here!"

"Better than getting flattened by a semi." Finn held onto the armrest and dashboard until the car dropped out of passing gear and the truck roared past them. Luther swung the Chrysler onto US 95 and weaved through a seeming maze of rock. It was nice to be off the four-lane, and having the desert just beyond the fenders was a bit more engaging. Eventually the road straightened out and drivers became impatient, darting around RVs and trucks.

At Searchlight, Luther gassed up and Finn went in to use the restroom. He returned with coffees and a big bag of Fritos. "Here, these ought to hold you over."

They then went west over a much less traveled road, through Joshua tree forests and a boulder-strewn landscape. "This isn't so bad," Luther murmured.

"Good enough for the 'It' girl," Finn replied, looking at his phone again. "Says here that the Walking Box Ranch we just passed by was hers."

"It?"

"Sex."

"A whorehouse, out here?"

Finn snorted. "I can imagine Clara Bow being very amused by that idea, but no––it was her and husband's escape from Hollywood. She was one of the biggest stars of the 1920s, and her charisma––which centered on sex appeal–– was dubbed 'It' by a self-proclaimed authority on the subject."

Luther looked over a Finn. "Wasn't there sex appeal before the 1920s?"

"Don't look at me like I was there––but well what an intriguing idea." He looked down at his phone. "And now I've lost the signal so I have nothing to back me up. But in my male, yet somewhat educated mind, I'd say women started taking proprietary rights on sex appeal around that time. Sex became less dirty and female sexual desire less of a threat––unlike the silly movie vamp of the decade before."

"I didn't know you were into old movies."

Finn shrugged. "Not especially. Some forty years ago I had a friend who would drag me to silent movies if he was between boyfriends or it was based on literature.

He wanted my expertise, he said, to discuss the adaptation afterwards. Interesting in that way. Silents aren't all pie in your face." Luther was quite sure he had never seen a movie that was silent, but the visual of a cream pie smashing into an overly made up face sounded familiar. He said nothing, however, and concentrated on the easy curves after they crested a range and started down a rocky canyon. The road straightened out and came into a grove of trees at a railroad crossing. This was Nipton, which was for sale. "There you go, you can buy a whole little oasis," Finn chuckled.

"Hm. The café is closed."

"You didn't get your fill on Fritos?"

"I was trying not to."

"Well, there ought to be a signal again now that we're close to Interstate 15," Finn replied. "Yes . . . how about the Mad Greeks?"

"Greek food in the desert?"

"Greece isn't exactly lush. Besides, judging by the photos, the emphasis is on 'mad'."

"What is Greek food exactly?"

"Dolmas, hummus, falafel, gyros, souvlaki."

"Never heard of any of them."

"The Greeks like lamb and chickpeas."

"Don't know that I've ever had either."

"You never ate a lamb chop or leg of lamb?"

Luther shook his head. "I don't think so."

"Dolmas are grape leaves stuffed with lamb and rice. Hummus is a dip made with chickpeas and tahini.

Falafel is some kind of deep fried chickpeas thing. Gyros are Greek sandwiches and souvlaki is shish kabob."

"You know I'm game to try new things. Let's go."

"Okay," Finn replied. "It's about forty miles ahead in Baker."

Luther merged onto Interstate 15 which was heavy with traffic leaving Las Vegas. "Why are all these people out here in the middle of nowhere?"

Finn tapped on his phone. "Apparently Vegas to LA traffic is notorious. You should read some of these horror stories."

"Not if it involves a lack of restrooms."

"Well, then," Finn mused. "Let's just say we should be happy that we're at least moving along."

Luther jockeyed around slow semis while trying to stay out of others' way. He nervously looked at the temperature gauge as he passed a derelict car or two as the long climb continued, but the Chrysler stayed cool. They reached the summit and started a leisurely descent. "Phew!" Luther breathed. "Glad that's over. And look, date shakes ahead."

"I'd rather have a Guinness shake," Finn sniffed.

"That sounds disgusting."

"Don't knock it until you've tried it. It's just a glorified chocolate malt."

The Chrysler climbed another shorter grade and then there was a long, steep descent into a dusty valley. Baker lay there, with a giant thermometer sticking out of it like something sick. As they drew near, the thermometer was registering an innocuous sixty-seven degrees. "For once I'm glad it's not July," murmured Luther as he exited the Interstate.

"There it is, on the right," Finn pointed.

Luther pulled into the parking lot and laughed. "Look at this place!"

There were large statues, columns, and ornate planters surrounding what was obviously once a typical fast food restaurant. They walked inside and were met with an equally gaudy interior, filled to the brim with Greek-style sconces and hanging plants. "What do you think, Luther? Looks like Zsa Zsa Gabor had a hand in this."

"Who?"

"Never mind."

They ordered a variety of things, as usual, so Luther could taste them all. "Looks like the food was a hit with you," Finn said as he watched Luther clean off all the plates.

"It was really good, but I was also very hungry."

"I think you're feeling settled . . . mentally . . . you're not on edge. I can see it in your demeanor."

"I guess I am. It feels good to have some direction. I haven't had much in my life and certainly not in prison. I loved living on the farm a lot, but deep down I think I knew it was temporary. It was a perfect landing spot for me when I had nowhere to go . . . no one to go to. Jed and Monica were my life savers in getting me there."

"They do that a lot."

"You helped me too, I guess." Luther grinned at Finn. "Even if it did take me a while to get used to you."

"Glad to be of service."

They paid the bill and got back on the road. "How far to Sequoia?"

Finn looked at his phone. "Four and a half hours."

"Are there motels near the park?"

"There has to be. There's a town called Three Rivers near the entrance. I'm sure they'll have motels."

"You know, Bardo has been amazing on this trip."

"Jed's cat was like that. She went everywhere with him when he was homeless. She rode on his shoulders."

"On his shoulders? Hah. How did he feed her if he had no money?"

"Mother would eat anything: pizza, French fries, whatever Jed found in a garbage can on the boardwalk. I bought cat food for her sometimes and took care of her sometimes too."

"You're a good friend, Finn."

Finn waved his hand dismissively. "I don't need your kudos."

Luther just smiled. He had learned when to leave things alone with Finn. "After all this food maybe we should just stop on the way and get some snacks for dinner."

"Don't forget a liquor store," Finn added with a wink.

"Of course. Wouldn't want you to go without your whiskey."

After about three hours of driving, they stopped at a Food 4 Less in Porterville, where they found the whiskey under lock and key, and arrived in Three Rivers about seven. Being midweek, and near the end of the slow season, they were able to find a room. Soon Luther and Finn were sprawled out in their room, drinking and snacking. They searched through the Sequoia/Kings Canyon pamphlets they found in the motel office. Bardo made herself comfortable by lying squarely in the middle of it all. "May I make a suggestion?"

"Sure," Luther replied.

"You should talk to someone in the park office about what you'd like to do, and not just as a volunteer."

"Yes, of course," mused Luther. "Let's just drive around when we first get there, so I can get the lay of the land, so to speak. And maybe find a real park ranger to talk to." Luther sighed. "Do you think that maybe I can't be a ranger if I've been in prison?"

Finn shrugged. "Aren't you exonerated?"

"Gordon told me that the felony is off my record, but people can still see that I was in prison."

"You'll just have to think about how you want to present yourself if asked. Maybe even write it out for yourself, but it seems to me that exoneration and your pleasant personality show that you're resilient."

Luther nodded. "Yeah. That makes sense. Hey, shouldn't you call your daughter and tell her we'll be there tomorrow?"

"She knows we're coming. I think we might want to leave it open until we see what tomorrow brings."

"How about Jed? Shouldn't we call him?"

"Go ahead," Finn said.

Luther called and talked excitedly with Jed about his newfound idea of becoming a park ranger. Finn listened in amusement tinged with a bit of pride. Luther was similar to Jed in his magnetism and likability and Finn thought he'd make a great park ranger. As Luther closed the conversation with Jed, Finn found himself hoping that Luther would be given the chance.

Chapter 34

BREAKFAST WAS DECENT AT THE MOTEL, FOR A CHANGE. As they ate, Finn checked road conditions and found a dusting of snow was falling at higher elevations. "Damn," Luther sighed. "I don't want to drive in snow and ice."

"It's April. It's not going to stick to the pavement."

"Still, they might not let us in without chains. We don't have any."

"You mean we're going to have to perform bondage at Sequoia?"

Luther glared at him. "No. Don't they use chains back East?"

"How the hell should I know?" Finn replied. "Stop worrying about it and start worrying about your sneakers getting soggy up there."

"That's not very encouraging."

"Take a look at the road you'll be driving," Finn chuckled and flashed his phone at Luther. "Looks like varicose veins." Luther groaned. "C'mon, let's get going before something stops us from visiting your future."

Luther tried to be nonchalant as he headed east on 198, but he was nervous as he approached the entrance. The ranger didn't ask him if he was carrying chains, however, and only warned him to drive carefully because sections of the road could be icy or slushy. Soon they were climbing in earnest, negotiating the tight curves and switchbacks. It started snowing heavily. "I hope this is only a squall," Luther muttered as he gripped the steering wheel.

"You're doing great," Finn chirped. "Should I sing 'Sleigh Ride'?"

"No." Luther was quiet as he negotiated another fifteen-mile-an-hour curve. "At least this ol' Chrysler handles well. I've fishtailed on slick roads in that old truck back on the farm." He glanced over the gauges and saw FRONT WHEEL DRIVE emblazoned below. "Must be that front wheel drive."

"What other kind is there?"

"Rear wheel, I guess. At least that's what the truck feels like when it loses traction."

"I better text Damon," Finn grinned. "He'll be impressed."

"Shut up."

Fortunately the squall let up as they climbed higher, and soon the road was clear. Eventually the road flattened a bit and the curves became more gradual. "How are you doing?" Finn finally asked.

"Okay. Feeling more relaxed now. We should be almost there."

"I'm feeling a bit . . . nauseous."

"Oh!" Luther looked over and found Finn looking rather pale. "Do you want me to pull over?"

"No. I'll let you know before I puke."

"Gee, thanks." And as if on cue, there was a sudden, loud burp from the back seat. "Bardo! Oh, don't tell Miriam that she barfed on the leather seat!"

Finn slowly turned around. "It's okay," he reported. "She just puked on the blanket."

Another curve brought them in the midst of enormous trees. "Oh my God!" gasped Luther as he craned his neck to look up through the windshield. "These sequoias put the redwoods to shame." He continued to bang on the steering wheel as he drove, gazing above until Finn grabbed the wheel.

"Better to get out than meet them head on," Finn murmured.

"Yeah. Look. There's the sign to the visitor's center."

"Just what the doctor ordered," sighed Finn. "Ooh!"

Luther looked over at Finn clutching his side and parked the car. Finn made a beeline for the restroom while Luther let Bardo out and threw the blanket in a trashcan. He watched her roll around in the snow and leap onto the drifts, but after a few minutes and a growing audience, he put her back in the car and moseyed into the visitor center at Grant Grove Village. He looked around for Finn in the restroom, but didn't see him so he returned to the car. Finn wasn't at the car either, so he returned to the visitor center to check out the gift shop and walked through the exhibits. He found himself in front of the theater and made a mental note when the next 15-minute movie would start. He checked the clock periodically and realized that a good twenty minutes had passed. Now he was getting a little worried. He went to the information desk. "Excuse me?" he said.

"Yes? Can I help you?" the woman at the desk replied.

"I, um, wondered if you saw an elderly man. He's kind of a little guy with a lot of white hair."

"No, I'm sorry. Would you like me to page him?"

"Oh no. That's okay. Just if you see him, please ask him to wait here for me here. His name is Finn."

"And your name?"

"Luther. Thanks." He walked back to the restroom and this time he looked under the doors of all the stalls. There was Finn, sitting on the floor of one, next to the toilet. "Finn! Are you okay?"

"Yeah," he replied weakly. "Just relaxing on a public restroom floor."

Finn struggled to reach the lock on the door and was able to open it. "Jesus, Luther, I thought you'd never come. I've got a pain to beat all pains right here." Finn held on to the side of his stomach.

"Oh man. What should I do?"

"I don't know. I'm hoping it will subside."

"Can you get up?"

"Not really."

"Let me help you to a couch or someplace you can lie down."

"No! I need to be near the toilet."

"Can this be from that curvy road?"

"I don't know. Maybe also the high elevation."

"I need to get help, Finn."

"Just let me be for a while longer and see if it gets better."

"What if it's serious? We shouldn't wait."

Finn grimaced. "Okay. Get help." Luther ran back to the information desk and told the woman what was going on. The bathroom was soon abuzz with uniformed people trying to help. The lead park ranger announced that they were going to call a helicopter and get him to a hospital in Selma. "Helicopter?" Finn asked disgustedly. "Just get an ambulance to drive me there."

"It's a good ninety minute drive and it would take as long for the ambulance to get here."

"I don't want to ride in any damn helicopter!"

"Finn. Let them help you. This could be life threatening and there's no time to waste. I'll drive there and meet you."

Finn finally acquiesced when it became clear that the pain was not going away. The helicopter arrived and the EMTs loaded Finn onto a stretcher. "Hey Luther!" Finn said as they started to cart him away. "Maybe you should call Kate."

"Give me your phone and I'll look up her number while we walk to the helicopter." Finn handed him the phone and Luther put the number into his own phone. "I'll see you in about an hour and a half. Oh wait, what's the name of the hospital?"

"Adventist in Selma," one of the EMTs replied.

Luther watched them put Finn inside the helicopter and walked back to the car. He took out his phone and realized how much he had relied on Finn to look up directions on the map app. He played around for a few minutes and found Selma and made a mental note to take a left on Kings Canyon Road after driving quite a distance back on 180. He figured he'd pull over after he got onto Kings Canyon Road and memorize the rest of the directions. He was nervous and frightened for many reasons. Not only was he alone in an area he knew nothing about, but also he was once again facing the possible death of someone close to him.

Chapter 35

LUTHER HAD DRIVEN QUITE A WAYS BEFORE
REMEMBERING THAT HE HAD NOT CALLED FINN'S
DAUGHTER KATE. He expected cell service to be poor
to nonexistent, but after a mile or two, he found a wide
turnout with a dim view of the San Joaquin Valley
below and indeed his phone was picking up a fair signal.
Luther dialed, but as he expected, Kate did not pick up.
He hesitated as the call switched to voice mail, not
knowing quite what to say without frightening her. "Hi
Kate. This is Luther, the guy your father is traveling
with. Um, we are in Sequoia/Kings Canyon and, uh, Finn
had a bad stomach pain. He's gone to the hospital –
Adventist in Selma." He stopped to try and get his
thoughts straight on what to say. He decided not to
mention the helicopter in the message. "The EMT's
took him to the hospital and I'm driving there. I should
be there in an hour or so. I'll call you from there." He
hung up feeling pretty satisfied that he had told her the
truth, more or less.

The remainder of the drive to the hospital was
uneventful, although he watched Bardo carefully since

he had no other towel to cover the leather seat with. 180 was far less curvy, though, so Bardo just napped most of the time. Luther found the hospital, parked, and went into the emergency entrance to get information. He was told that only family was allowed with the patient in the examination room. "Can you at least tell me how he is? I was traveling with him and I need to give his daughter some information."

"I'll see what I can find out."

"Thanks." His phone rang just as he went to the waiting room to sit. "Hello?"

"Luther? This is Kate."

"Oh hi."

"How is he?"

"I just got to the hospital, so I'm trying to find out. They won't let me see him because I'm not family."

"Okay. Lawrence and I are leaving here in about half an hour and should be there in three or four hours, depending on traffic."

"Okay."

"I'll text you when we get to the hospital and you can tell me where you are."

Luther hung up and thought of other people he should notify, but hesitated. He really had nothing definitive to share, but he felt contacting Jed would be a reassuring connection, so he texted him the basics. He continued to play with his phone until he realized half an hour had passed. He went back to the window and asked, "Did you find out anything about Finn McGee?"

"Oh yes, sorry. It got so busy. They are doing lab work and a CT scan. That's all I know."

"Thanks." He glanced at the clock. It would be three hours until Kate got here. He might as well take Bardo for a walk. He took the cat out of the car and put her onto his shoulders. "What do you think, Bardo? Do you like this way of traveling?" He smiled, thinking of Jed and Mother. "I'll bet Finn will like that you're riding on my shoulders."

He looked up and down the parking lot, trying to decide which direction to walk in. All he noticed were medical-related businesses and doctors' offices. After a few blocks, however, he saw a park and put Bardo down to do her thing. He walked a few more blocks and saw some restaurants and stores, but realized he probably couldn't take Bardo inside and wasn't comfortable leaving her outside by herself. His phone rang and it was Jed. "Hey man," Luther answered.

"How is he?"

"I don't know much. He's in the hospital in Selma."

"Selma? Where's that?" Jed asked.

"I dunno, really," Luther admitted. "We were at Sequoia/Kings Canyon National Park and——"

"Oh, so you're near Fresno."

"Yeah, I guess. Anyway, he started experiencing pain and nausea, so they flew him to the nearest hospital. Kate's on her way."

"Well, let me know as soon as you know something."

"I will. Did Finn tell you we got a cat named Bardo?"

"No. Cool."

"He told me about Mother and how you took her around on your shoulders. I tried it and Bardo likes it too."

Silence told Luther he had hit on something sensitive. Finally Jed spoke. "All we had was each other. Such bittersweet memories."

"Sorry, I didn't mean——"

"It's okay, man. Just telling you the truth. And I'm glad the cat trusts you like that."

"Yeah. Give Monica a hug for me."

"Do I get one, too?"

"Yeah, yeah——sure!" Luther laughed with embarrassment.

"Good!" Jed boomed. "Remember to call me when you get any further info."

Luther walked back to the hospital slowly. He had plenty of time until Kate arrived, and he didn't have any hope that he would be able to learn anything without her being there. He put Bardo back in the car and entered the waiting room. As expected when he questioned the clerk, she had no more information. "Could you at least tell me if he's still in the emergency room or if he's in a regular hospital room?"

"No sir. I don't know."

"There's no one you can ask?"

She glared at him. "Do you see all those people in the waiting room? They're waiting to be admitted. They're my priority right now."

Luther grimaced and stepped back, deciding to take the high road instead of getting into an altercation with her. He glanced at the clock and figured Kate would be here in a short while. He could wait. He looked at his phone, debating about calling Juniper again. But he didn't want to bother her if she was, in fact, trying to distance herself from him. And he didn't want to hear any bad news about Homer. One sick old man that he cared about was enough to deal with right now. He put the phone back in his pocket and closed his eyes. He didn't really want to sleep, but he found himself nodding off anyway. He woke up when a pretty White lady with a pixie blonde haircut, standing next to a handsome Black man with graying sideburns, said, "Luther, I presume?"

Luther stood up abruptly. "You must be Kate."

"Yes," she smiled. "And this is my husband Lawrence." The men shook hands.

"They won't tell me anything other than he's getting a CT scan and lab tests," Luther said.

Kate stalked over to the clerk and asked in a sharp voice, "I am Finn McGee's daughter. What room is he in?"

"I will have to find out," the clerk stammered.

"Never mind. We'll find him."

"I-I have to get someone to escort you. Hospital policy."

"That's fine. But now, please!"

Luther turned to Lawrence, smiling. "Does she always get her way?"

"Most of the time." Lawrence smiled back. "Takes after her father, I guess."

"I dunno," Luther mused. "She seems nicer than him."

Lawrence laughed. "Most of the time she is. She has her soft, caring side anyway. Finn––well, you just gotta embrace the crank."

"Yeah," Luther chuckled. "But he has been good to me."

"Glad to hear it." Lawrence watched Kate disappear through the swinging doors to the exam rooms. "But we'd better catch up with Kate or we'll hear about it later!"

Kate approached another reception desk, and naturally got what she wanted. She turned back to report to the men. "They've moved him to a room. They think it's a kidney stone."

"Ow!" Lawrence exclaimed.

"Yeah," Luther said. "Painful enough to have him sitting on the floor of the bathroom stall at the visitor's center."

"Come on, you two," Kate called to them as she hustled down the hall.

"We have our marching orders," Lawrence grinned as he led Luther by the elbow.

They got to Finn's room and found him in bed, berating a nurse. "There is no way under the sun that

I'm going to use that bedpan so you can just put it away."

"We've given you a lot of fluids so you'll pass that stone," the nurse replied in equal measure. "I'm sure you'll agree a bedpan is better than surgery."

"I'm not so sure," Finn snapped back. "I'm awake when I'm on the bedpan." He finally noticed Kate. "Oh. Kate! I didn't expect you to come."

"And leave you alone to torment the nurses? Do as she says, Dad, because I sure as hell don't want the job."

Finn looked over at Lawrence. "Ah, there's the calm in the middle of the storm," he piped. "I don't know how you do it."

"It's simple. I just do what she says."

Finn groaned. "Maybe some whiskey to numb my sensibilities."

"Like that ever worked," Kate sighed. She looked over to the nurse. "How long do we wait to see if the stone passes by itself?"

"It's only been a few hours, so we still have a couple of options. We're reporting to the doctor and she'll make a final decision––"

"She?" sputtered Finn. "I'm not letting a woman loose on my––"

"Dad," Kate warned. "You're a terrible liar." She turned back to the nurse. "Have you ever had a worse patient?"

The nurse tried not to smile. "It's been awhile . . ."

Kate turned back to Finn. "Do as she says. All this talk has me ready for the restroom, but I'll be back." She then turned to her husband and Luther. "Why don't you two get something to eat in the cafeteria——and please bring me back a salad."

"Sounds good to me," Lawrence answered. "How about you, Luther?"

"I guess I am hungry. You sure you two don't want to go? I can wait here with Finn."

"No, go ahead," Kate replied. She turned back to the nurse with a questioning look, and the nurse pointed down the hall. "That way, ma'am."

Lawrence and Luther finally found the cafeteria after wandering around a maze of halls and stairways. They bought a couple of sandwiches and sat down at a table. "Finn hasn't said much about you except that you're a retired professor."

"Yeah. English. At UCLA."

"Wow. Impressive. Are you a writer too, like Finn?"

"Just in the academic field, nothing remotely best-selling."

"Maybe being respected in your field is a bigger honor."

Lawrence smiled broadly. "I like your style. Now, what's your story?" Luther drew in a breath and held his reticence on the subject. Maybe Finn had told his story to Kate, but then why would Lawrence ask? "Oh," Lawrence surmised. "Maybe it's none of my business."

"I was in San Quentin for twenty years," Luther blurted out. I was accused of a murder I didn't commit. The Innocence Project got me out."

"Now that's a best-selling story," Lawrence murmured, pausing to take a sip of coffee.

Lawrence's words had a strange effect on Luther. He suddenly felt like crying. He blinked hard and looked down. "No one ever thanked me for telling the truth," he finally whispered.

Lawrence reached out and tipped Luther's chin up. "I hear you brother." Luther held his head up and managed a small, quavering smile while Lawrence reached for his coffee again. "They just gave you some money, right?"

"Yeah," Luther sighed. "But I am thankful for it. At least it pays my way until I figure out what to do with the rest of my life."

"So, have you figured it out?"

"I think so––I want to be a park ranger."

"Like Shelton Johnson," Lawrence smiled, looking off into space.

"Who?"

"He's a Black ranger at Yosemite who gives talks all over the country about the Buffalo Soldiers. He also tries to get more Blacks to visit national parks. Did you ever go to one when you were a child or before you went to prison?"

"No. I don't think it ever crossed my mother's mind as a place to visit, even if we had the money to do it." Luther then paused. "What's a Buffalo Soldier?"

"It's a nickname given to the Colored Cavalry by Native Americans. Among other things they helped keep the peace in the West and were among the first to patrol the Sierra Nevadas against poachers and other illegal activities. Essentially, they were some of the first park rangers." Lawrence then leaned forward. "You see, it's important for America to understand that we're part of the natural landscape."

"Wow," Luther murmured.

"Never heard of any of this before, have you?"

Luther shook his head. "I need to meet Shelton Johnson."

"Get yourself up to Yosemite. It's only a couple of hours from here."

"Yes––but what about Finn?"

"Don't worry about him," Lawrence replied with a wave of his hand. "He's our problem now. It's one of the perks of being retired."

"Then I think I'll never retire."

Lawrence laughed heartily. "Oh, there's a Black woman ranger who retired at a hundred, but that's another story. We better get a salad to Kate so she can continue battling with her father."

They bought the salad for Kate and returned to Finn's room. "Thanks," Kate said, taking the salad from

Lawrence. "I'm famished." She put the salad down in her lap and took his hand.

He smiled down at her. "Any news?"

"Yeah," snorted Finn. "No stone passed. Just frostbite on my ass."

Kate dropped Lawrence's hand. "To match your heart," she retorted.

"You'll be fine once it passes, right?" Luther interjected. "I mean it isn't like a heart attack or something."

"Luther's right," Kate agreed heartily. "You could have even had a stroke."

"That's my girl," Finn sniffed. "Always coming up with the worst case scenario."

"Dad . . ."

"Hey Finn," Luther asked brightly. "Have you ever heard of a ranger named Shelton Johnson in Yosemite?"

Finn scowled. "Is he the guy that was on that Ken Burns series about national parks?"

"Why didn't you tell me about that?"

"Because I'm old and forgot about him until now," Finn admitted. "But I will tell you now that you need to go to Yosemite."

"That's what I was thinking."

"Glad to hear you're thinking."

"Ah, shut up!" they replied in unison.

Finn chuckled and then winced in pain.

"I think I'm going to Yosemite to check in with that Shelton Johnson guy. I'm leaving you with Kate and Lawrence. Okay, Finn?"

"You asking my permission?"

"No," Luther scowled.

"Good. Now go."

Chapter 36

LUTHER LEFT FINN'S HOSPITAL ROOM WITH A NEW BOUNCE IN HIS STEP. He hadn't felt so relaxed since––well, he couldn't remember. He unlocked the Chrysler and got in, patting the front bench seat to encourage Bardo to now ride shotgun with him. The cat complied, sniffing around and giving Luther a look, before curling up on the leather where Finn once sat. Luther put the key in the ignition and was rewarded with the characteristic rusty rooster sound of the starter. EVA reminded him to put on his seat belt and that 'all systems are operating normally'. "You're telling me!" Luther laughed back.

He headed towards Highway 99 to find a cheap place to eat and sleep. It was late and there was no reason to drive an hour or so and spend more money near Yosemite. After picking up a hamburger and fries, he found an okay place to stay and soon was sneaking Bardo into the room. The cat gnawed on a French fry as Luther's hamburger ran down his arm. He watched YouTubes of Shelton Johnson giving speeches while he ate. Lawrence had told Luther an outline of the Buffalo

Soldiers, but he was mesmerized by Johnson's skillful storytelling. He wondered if he could be that good with an audience someday.

Luther then called Jed to give him an update on Finn's condition. He also hoped someone had contacted Jed about Homer's condition, as his interest in inter-acting with Juniper was slipping further as each day passed. Jed didn't answer, so he left a long message and took distinct pleasure in switching off his phone. He would sleep soundly.

The next morning Luther went to the motel lobby for coffee and soggy, sweet pastry. He heard Finn grumble in his head about Little Debbie, and he grinned and stuffed the rest of the mess in his mouth. He then went back to his room, rounded up Bardo and stuffed her in his jacket. Soon the Chrysler was heading up 41 to Oakhurst as Luther rehearsed conversations in his head. After paying the entrance fee, he drove straight to Yosemite Village and found the visitor's center and a cheerful young ranger behind the counter. "I'm looking for Shelton Johnson."

"You're not the only one," the woman smiled. "His presentations are very popular. I believe there's one at––"

"No, I mean I'd like to talk to him personally."

"Oh," she replied. "Are you a friend of his?"

"No-o," Luther admitted, suddenly feeling embar-rassed.

"That's okay," she said, trying to smooth over the situation. "I can't locate him directly or speak to him myself anyway. You'll have to talk with dispatch. See that door over there?" she said as she pointed. "Go in there and ask if they can help you. Good Luck!"

Luther felt her 'good luck' was a bit forced and he was tempted to flee. Then he heard the cussing Finn would give him for giving up so easily. Grimly he walked over and opened the door. A middle-aged man looked up from his desk and registered surprise at the civilian standing there. Luther just started talking, his voice all wobbly. He felt sweat dripping as he continued telling this stranger everything he wanted to do, where he had been. Everything. In turn, the man's bright blue eyes registered humor and confusion as he tried to follow along, but as Luther wound down, his gaze became steady and sympathetic. When Luther ran out of words, he took a deep breath and started backing towards the door.

"Hold on," the man smiled gently. "That's quite a story. I probably should send you right to recruitment, but––well, darn it, you should meet your inspiration. He usually gets a lot of attention after a program, so telling you to hold out for that might not work, either." He drummed his fingers on his desk. "Let me talk to the boss lady." He paused, lost in his thoughts. "I have to ask if it's okay to call him in." He forced himself out of his chair, tapped on the door behind him, and waited to enter.

He was gone for quite awhile, but the door finally opened and a petite, uniformed woman with gray streaked hair piled on her head appeared. The man stood behind her, a grin on his face. The woman studied Luther, smiling politely, and finally spoke. "Hobbs here has told me your story, Mr. Banks. I trust you won't put Hobbs––or me––in a compromising position with your intentions."

"No, ma'am," Luther gulped.

She nodded. "It's highly irregular, really, but it happens that Mr. Johnson is coming in to file a report in about an hour. Please don't waste his time. You may wait for him in the visitor's center."

"Thank you, ma'am," Luther replied, bowing his head slightly. She nodded as Hobbs gave a thumbs up behind her. As she turned, Hobbs put his hands behind his back and she gave him a significant look before shutting the door behind her.

Luther put out his hand. "Thank you so much." Hobbs shook his hand and half pushed him out the door at the same time.

Luther sank into the nearest chair in the visitor's center and let the tension ooze out of him. He felt exhausted and ready to leave, but after a few minutes he started feeling excited again. He rehearsed in his head what he was going to say over and over, editing himself, making it more and more concise. He was deep in thought when a voice behind him asked, "Luther?"

Luther twisted around and saw Shelton Johnson standing there and scrambled up. "Yeah. Thanks for taking the time to meet with me, Mr. Johnson."

"Just part of the business. Besides, they tell me you have a great story. And it's Shelton."

Luther nodded. "Okay . . . Shelton. I'll keep it as short as possible."

"I appreciate that, but don't dull it down too much."

Luther started talking a little too fast, but soon noticed how Shelton kept eye contact and nodded as if to pace him. Soon Luther's speech pattern fell into something normal, with the usual pauses for emphasis or a break for the listener. Shelton made no comments until Luther was finished about five minutes later. "So," Shelton smiled coolly. "You're the one with the kitten in the Chrysler Town & Country from New York."

"Uh, yeah . . ."

"Well, one of us left a citation under your wiper for leaving a pet in a car. I'll have to amend that to a warning." He cocked his head aside. "That's a lot of the job around here. Policing. However, if you work hard and give your time, you make a lot more of it. And lord knows we need a lot more representation in the parks."

"You're doing so much to make that happen," Luther said.

"It's a long leap between inspiration and installation," Shelton sighed. He then straightened up. "I really have to go, man, but I do have a late lunch break. We could talk a little more then if you like."

"I'd like that and I'll buy you lunch," Luther grinned.

"Then it's a deal," Shelton smiled, offering his hand again. "Meet me here at two. Meanwhile, your assignment is to enjoy Yosemite."

"Thanks. I will!" Luther steeped out into the crisp sunshine and took a deep breath. Granite rose above the treetops all around him. Below, the crowd was rather sparse. And rather White. But he felt comfortable, relaxed—ready to be inspired in real time. He decided a long walk to Bridal Veil Falls was in order and started off. Along the way he made a point of making eye contact with passersby, smiling if they acknowledged him. A blonde man with a heavy accent stopped and asked him for directions, and soon they were laughing over their pamphlets, trying to decipher the maps. Once he approached the falls he stayed back from the flying mist, to thank the veils that April day.

As two p.m. approached, Luther found himself trotting the last few hundred feet back to the Visitor's Center. Johnson was waiting for him, and they went through the cafeteria line together and found a table. "So you want to become a ranger?" Shelton asked.

"I think so."

"Have you spent much time in the national parks?"

"Uh, not really. Actually, other than Grand Canyon and a very short stop at Sequoia, I'd never been to one."

Shelton nodded. "Yes. That's what I've been trying to change in the African-American community."

"I thought I might volunteer while I was working on whatever I'd need to do to become a ranger."

"You got a trust fund or something?" Shelton grinned. "I mean if you volunteer, you'd still need to pay for a place to live and to eat."

"I was awarded a compensation for false imprisonment, thanks to the Innocence Project, so I'll be okay for awhile." Luther paused and was inspired to say, "And I like the idea of using it, at least indirectly, to sorta improve society."

"Hmm," Shelton replied. "You'll go far on that statement alone. Hone it for your future interviews. But it'll take quite some time to become a ranger. You need a college degree for starters."

"I've got nothing but time."

"Where do you want to volunteer? Which park?"

"I don't know. I just like being in nature. I loved living on the farm, but I don't know if or when I can return."

"You know, when you volunteer and you don't have experience or a particular skill, you pretty much do as you're told. It might be working inside a building or doing grunt work to start."

Luther shrugged. "That's okay. I did stuff I didn't particularly like to do on the farm. I was just grateful to have a place to live and work."

"Speaking for farms," Shelton mused between bites of his sandwich. "Have you ever heard of John Boyd?"

Luther shook his head. "No."

"He's a civil rights advocate. He started the National Black Farmer's Association."

"I didn't know there was such a thing."

Shelton nodded. "There's a lawsuit that Black farmers have been discriminated against in getting loans. They finally won billions. Then the White farmers countersued."

"Oh man!"

"You ought to look it up, I mean the Association and John Boyd. It might be of interest considering what you went through."

"Yeah. I will."

Shelton finished his sandwich and started putting the wrappers and such back on his tray. "Ask at the information desk for pamphlets on becoming a volunteer. I think you should spend some time at a park before embarking on the ranger path. There are pamphlets on becoming a ranger too."

"Thanks so much. Can I contact you if I have questions?"

"Sure." He reached in his pocket and took out a card and gave it to Luther. "Let me know where you end up and how things are going. And thank you for lunch."

"Thank *you*," Luther smiled broadly, shaking his hand. Luther went back to talk to the woman at the information desk. He got his pamphlets, asked her a few questions about her volunteering experience. He then pulled out his phone and saw a message from Kate, so he hastily called her. "Oh I'm so sorry. I've been talking to all sorts of people and––"

"That's quite alright," Kate cut in. "I know you had important business today and Finn is doing well now. He passed the stone late last night and we can take him home later today."

"I can be at the hospital in a couple of hours."

"No need. You could meet us in Los Angeles at our house."

"Oh." Luther suddenly felt nervous about driving into Los Angeles without Finn navigating. "Um, okay."

"Do you still want to come?" Kate asked.

"Sure. I mean––I don't know. I hadn't thought about being in Los Angeles other than taking Finn to your house." Now Luther was starting to feel uneasy again. Having a vague idea of wanting to work in a national park wasn't going to happen immediately. He still needed to be somewhere until things fell into place. He had to apply for the position. And what park? Where did he want to be? "I need to think about it. I'll call you back shortly."

"No pressure," Kate replied lightly. "You're always welcome. And thank you for looking after Dad."

"I think it may have been the other way around," Luther chuckled.

"You're too kind," Kate laughed.

Luther walked back to the Chrysler and pulled the citation from under the wiper. He sighed and wondered what he should do. Shelton hadn't said anything more about it. He pulled the business card from his wallet, hesitated and stuffed it back in. He looked inside the car and Bardo was sleeping on the back seat again. Luther felt absolutely stuck. He started chanting to himself, 'Transition. Liminality. It'll all work out.' He tried to remember other sayings that Finn, Homer, Buster, and even Miriam had said. 'Life is what happens when you're busy making other plans.' 'Without confusion no clarity will emerge.' He smiled, thinking wisdom does come with age. And he was still young, relatively speaking. And there were people who would help him, like Jed--so he called him.

"Hey Luther. How's Finn?"

"He passed the stone last night and is going to Kate's today."

"Good news. And you?"

Luther proceeded to tell him about his conversation with Shelton and what he was struggling with right now. "I guess I still need more time to just be."

"Why don't you call Juniper and find out what's going on at the farm? It is your home."

"You think I can?"

"Can what?"

"Call Juniper. I mean she seemed so distant when I spoke to her last and she hasn't called or texted me. Maybe you could call Dutch and find out what's going on at the farm."

"Okay. I can do that. I'll let you know."

Luther hung up and sighed. He waited several minutes and finally got a text from Jed that said that he left a message for Dutch but hadn't heard back. Luther texted back. "Could I come to your house? I don't know where to go."

"Of course," Jed texted back.

Luther checked the map app and found that it would take three and a half hours to get to San Francisco. He'd rather be at Jed's. At least he knows the city and his host. He texted Kate about his decision and then started the car. "Let's go, Bardo. You can ride shotgun again."

Chapter 37

LUTHER WAS WAITING TO TURN BACK ONTO 152 AFTER GASSING UP IN LOS BANOS WHEN HIS PHONE PINGED. No one was behind him, so he picked up the phone and saw a text from Juniper. A flood of emotions came over him, excitement not one of the biggest. "Please call me," her text read. He took a deep breath, checked the rear view mirror and backed the Chrysler into a parking space. He let his finger linger over the call button. All his plans started shuffling in his head, but he sighed and pressed the button. She answered promptly, "Thanks for calling me."

"Uh, why wouldn't I?"

"Well, I've been ignoring you," Juniper murmured. "Or so it may seem to you."

"Is Homer okay?"

"He's here and holding on." Juniper paused, waiting for a response that did not come. "I wanted to tell you that you can come back if you like. There was a plea bargain yesterday on a Murder Mountain case."

"So?"

"So they also claim responsibility for the body found near the farm. You're--we're off the hook."

Luther sucked his teeth. "That seems like a highly unlikely scenario."

"You're telling me. Let's just take our breaks any way we can. Case closed."

"But why--"

"God knows. Everyone is sick of it, I guess, and they found a willing scapegoat. You know how our judicial system works."

"Okay." Luther didn't know how to proceed.

"Dutch has been hounding me to call you ever since the news came out. And then Jed has been calling Dutch and--well, I need to act like a grown up. I didn't want to hang on to you if you had to stay away, but now you can come back. And live again with--us. If you like."

"Us?"

"Me. Unless there's someone else . . ."

"There's been no one but an old man."

Juniper laughed. "I didn't know that side of you." Luther chuckled. After a long silence she finally said, "Won't you come home?"

"I just made plans with Jed and Monica."

"Oh, they'll understand," Juniper moaned. "Dutch hasn't returned Jed's call yet, so just tell them the news. Tell them we'll come down and visit them later."

"We?"

"Yes, we."

"Okay, but it's like a four or five hour drive to the farm. I'll be exhausted by the time I get there."

"You know how to let yourself in," Juniper said coyly. "Just snuggle up against me and we'll catch up later."

Luther felt a surge go through him. "I guess I can't refuse that."

"Nope. You can't. So hang up and call Jed. Bye for now."

Luther stared at the screen showing the ended call. He felt antsy, but not for all the right reasons. He didn't like breaking the commitment he just made with Jed, and he didn't like being pulled away from his pursuit of becoming a ranger. Still, he would be near the Redwood State Park and being with Juniper was a no brainer. He scrolled and tapped Jed.

"Hi," Jed answered. "What's up? Hope it's not car trouble."

"Nope, the Chrysler's fine. But Juniper just called––"

"Oh!"

"Yeah. There was a plea deal involving the body, so they closed the case."

"You're kidding! Someone came forward?"

"I guess. Juniper wants me to come home . . . today."

Jed burst out laughing. "A man's gotta do what a man's gotta do."

"Well, I'm embarrassed and––"

"Aw, hell. Go enjoy yourselves."

"I wanted to talk to you two about meeting Shelton Johnson––"

"Oh yeah? That's cool."

"––And wanting to become a park ranger."

"Cooler yet. Come down once you settle in again, and we can visit when you're more relaxed."

"Juniper said we'd both come down."

"Alright then," laughed Jed. "That gives us time to buy an air mattress or something. The sofa's not big enough for two."

"You're too good to me."

"You know, Luther, I've never heard you this happy."

Luther paused. "You know what? I think you're right. I keep worrying about making a decision––but they're all happy decisions."

"Right on. Now get a big cup of coffee before you hit the road. Drive carefully. And remember, I'm always here for you."

"Thanks, Jed."

Luther ended the call and looked over at Bardo, who looked back at him with bedroom eyes. "I'm going in to get some coffee, but it wouldn't hurt if you actually co-piloted." Bardo yawned. "Yeah, try to at least look interested."

Armed with coffee and a bag of jerky, Luther was soon heading up Interstate 5. He was dimly aware of the outward rush from the Bay Area, but his timing was good and he stayed ahead of the worst of it. After the tangle of downtown Sacramento he was soon out midst the rice fields and then almond orchards. He topped off the tank at Williams and then headed west through the hills to Clear Lake. The sun had set and the sky was orange above the dark blue water, so he stopped and got out for Bardo and him to stretch for a few minutes while enjoying the view. Luther bought another cup of coffee in Nice and kept driving and driving and driving. Bardo made an attempt at keeping him awake by batting at the keys dangling from the ignition.

Eventually the Chrysler's headlights flashed on the farm's gate. He reached through the window for the keypad, counting out the code aloud as he punched in numbers. Nervousness overcame exhaustion as he drove up to the house. He could hear Gypsy barking as he parked, and he automatically stuffed Bardo into his jacket as he got out and slammed the door. As he reached the kitchen door, it flew open with shouts and laughter. Gypsy broke from Dutch's grip and jumped up on Luther, licking his face. Then he started nudging at the squirming lump under Luther's jacket. Luther let Bardo's head poke out, and the dog started lapping at it like ice cream. Bardo mewed like Gypsy was her giant, long lost mother.

"What's that?" laughed Scarlett, coming forward and holding out a glass of sparkling wine for Luther. Cheese and fruit and crackers were spread about, and it was obvious that they were already deep into a celebration.

"My cat, Bardo," Luther grinned, taking the glass and allowing Bardo to drop to the floor. Gypsy kept licking its newfound friend, who now was flattened and blissed out on the floor.

"Bardo?" Tasha asked incredulously.

"Bardo!" exclaimed Dutch. "The state of existence intermediate between two lives on earth."

"You know?" laughed Luther as he took a sip of wine and reached for some grapes.

"Hell, they'd take away my hippie credentials if I forgot!"

Everyone laughed as Luther looked around. "Where's Juniper?"

"In bed," announced Scarlett. "But don't get any ideas. She's fast asleep. She takes her two to five a.m. Homer watch very seriously."

"Wow," Luther murmured. "She wasn't joking, then."

"About?" Scarlett grinned.

"Nothing," Luther replied, stuffing some grapes in his mouth to hide his embarrassment. Finally he was able to mumble, "How's Homer?"

"Asleep, too. I just took some snacks to Buster, who's on watch right now. Buster's always strumming and sometimes Homer says something out of the blue and Buster just goes with it. He's making some great music."

Dutch moved over and put his arm around Luther's shoulder, pulling him close to his side. "Homer's going home, Luther. It couldn't be more beautiful. Life and death and music."

Luther looked down. "I guess I've missed a lot."

"Hell no," Dutch growled. "You've been living your own life, and now you're here. We're just glad you can be part of this family again . . . and part of Homer's journey." He gently shook Luther out of his guilt. "Now tell us something. Tell us––oh, something that just happened in the last few days, before Juniper finally called you."

Luther rolled his head shyly and said, "I met Shelton Johnson and I want to become a park ranger."

"Shelton Johnson!" cried Tasha. "Awesome!" She then started explaining Johnson's career to the others before covering her mouth. "Sorry! It's your story."

"You're doing just fine," Luther laughed, and then yawned in spite of himself. "Oh, and Johnson told me about John Boyd, a Black farmer fighting to get Black farmers the same financial aid White farmers do. I guess farming would be a totally different pursuit, though . . ."

Dutch tipped his head. "I dunno. There's education and social justice in both."

"But I'm finding I really like working with the public. Well, the idea of it, anyway."

Dutch nodded. "So add a program to farming for inner city kids to get the outdoor growing things experience."

"Hmm," Luther replied. Theo immediately came to mind. He yawned.

"Off to bed you go," Scarlett commanded, reaching out to pull Luther by the sleeve. "We will catch up tomorrow morning." She reached down and picked up a soggy, content Bardo. "And here's your cat. She's already had her bath. Say goodnight, John Boy."

Luther waved a hand. "Goodnight, John Boy." Everyone laughed and Tasha blew him a kiss. Luther stumbled down the hall and opened the door to Juniper's room. He could hear her breathing as he stripped down to his shorts in the dark. He crawled carefully into bed and lay there, feeling both excited and practically dead.

"You've been drinking wine and eating cheese," murmured Juniper.

"Sorry."

"No need. You'll need the energy later." She reached out and fumbled for his arm. "Cuddle up and go to sleep. You sound exhausted."

"I am."

Juniper pulled his forearm over her. "I'm glad you're home."

"Me too."

Chapter 38

TASHA AND SCARLETT WERE SITTING AT THE KITCHEN TABLE DRINKING COFFEE WHEN JUNIPER AND LUTHER WANDERED IN HAND IN HAND WELL PAST NINE O'CLOCK THE NEXT MORNING. "Well, if it isn't the lovebirds," Scarlett grinned.

"Thank you for not applauding," Juniper murmured as she let go of Luther's hand and reached for the coffee pot. Luther handed her a couple of mugs.

"You're welcome." Scarlett winked at Tasha while Juniper rolled her eyes,

"How was Homer last night?" Tasha asked.

"Oh, fine." Juniper replied. "Sometimes it seems he's super conscious of what's going on. It's like he knows stuff we don't talk about in front of him. He asked if Luther was finally getting some rest and we hadn't ever mentioned that Luther was coming home."

Luther shifted uncomfortably. "Maybe I should go see if he's awake." He got up, brushed the back of his hand across Juniper's cheek, picked up his coffee, and left. The women gazed at where he exited, lost in their thoughts.

"He's getting used to the idea of being back," Juniper finally said.

"Yes," replied Scarlett. "But are you?"

"You don't think I have it in me?"

"Well, I wasn't sure. I've only seen you express love by fierce devotion."

"Is there something wrong with that?"

"No––"

"We're all damaged goods," Tasha murmured. She looked over at Scarlett. "Afraid of opening our hearts."

"I'm not fond of the term 'damaged goods' but I'll agree that it has made me stronger," Juniper replied. "Fierce, if you like. I just knew I needed to take control." Juniper was quiet for a moment. "That's why I removed myself when he couldn't stay."

"You just have to face the source squarely. You keep the past on a shelf, in plain sight, but it's the past. You acknowledge it from time to time as a couple, especially when you hit a rough spot."

Juniper smiled softly. "Your strength is in your gentleness."

"So is Luther's," Scarlett said. "You could really elevate one another." Juniper turned away. "Are you blushing?" Scarlett teased.

"No," Juniper replied, turning back.

Luther found Dutch in Homer's room, holding a little bowl of broth that he was patiently spooning into Homer's mouth. When Homer saw Luther, his eyes lit up and his arm waved wildly. "Hey-y. It's––the man," he said slowly. "Did that––wild wo-man let you––sleep last––night?"

Luther came up to Homer's bed and took his hand. His grip was surprisingly strong, and he held tight. "Yep, thanks to you," Luther laughed.

"Juni-per. She––sits here. Doesn't talk. Just thinks––of you." Homer took a deep breath. "She's makin'––plans. We all––are."

"Homer," Dutch warned. "You talk too much."

Homer craned his neck and looked up at Dutch. "Well. It's––true."

"You got that right," laughed Dutch. " But you still talk too much."

"Hell---no," gasped Homer. "I––can––bare-ly string––two words––to-geth-er."

Dutch put the bowl down and rubbed back the few wild hairs on Homer's head. "Alright, old man."

"I wan-na see," Homer gulped, "his re-act-ion. I could––kick––the––buck-et––to-day."

Dutch made a face like an indulgent father and took a deep breath. "You know, Luther, Buster is making music with Homer here. Buster and I have big ideas to work it into an album." Dutch paused and put his hand on Luther's shoulder. "I'm not growing pot anymore, so I don't need all this. I want to give you eighty acres to pursue this farm education idea. I'm not sure of the details of how to do that yet. Maybe a no cost lease and you inherit when I die."

Luther stared at Dutch. "I--I--"

"You could build a house and whatever facilities you'd need. You have Tasha on hand with her plant genetics. You have Juniper and her managing skills. You have that inner light to inspire."

"I--" and then Luther burst into tears.

"Hey, hey, buddy," Dutch said, reaching out and taking Luther into a bear hug. "I know it's a lot to think about. The offer will stand until you're ready to make a decision."

Luther wiped his eyes and looked over Dutch's shoulder to see Homer with tears running down his furrowed cheeks, a beatific look on his face. A strange glow seemed to emanate from him. "You've been planning this?" sniffed Luther.

"Well, it's been on my mind," admitted Dutch. "You mentioning John Boyd last night brought it to a head. But I haven't said anything except to these old farts I'm hanging out with all the time now," he chuckled. "Oh, but I did ask Tasha this morning if she would be interested in taking part. I didn't want to put her on the spot. It's safe to say Juniper can speak for herself."

Homer managed to snicker. Dutch looked over at him. "Old man, you look like a Renaissance painting."

"Only," Homer took a deep breath, "older."

Buster suddenly appeared in the doorway. "What's goin' on? Why is everyone crying? Why didn't you call me?!"

"Everything's fine," Dutch said, pulling him into the room. "Take a look for yourself. The star is performing as usual."

Buster peered at Homer, who was somehow expressing laughter without making a sound. Buster then looked around. "Then why is everyone crying?"

"Be-because Dutch is-is giving me the-the farm," Luther stammered.

"Oh please say yes!" Buster cried, grabbing Luther's arm. "I'm sick of being the only Black dude around here." Luther smiled and Buster started laughing, slapping him on the back. "No pressure, no pressure!"

They all fell quiet, thinking of the big changes ahead. From down the hall they heard the *tick tick tick* of Gypsy's claws coming towards them. She entered, followed by Bardo, for whom, by all appearances, Gypsy was giving a tour. She licked Homer's hand and then flopped onto the floor under his hospital bed. Bardo jumped up and started kneading Homer's chest.

"No re––sus––i––tation," Homer wheezed. "Please." He lifted a wavering hand over Bardo, who stretched to give his hand a head bump.

"Did we miss the party?" Juniper now stood in the doorway, with Scarlett and Tasha crowding in behind her. "It's suddenly awfully quiet in here."

Dutch looked over at Luther. "Go on. Tell her."

Juniper gave Luther an inquiring look. "What's up?"

"Um." Suddenly Luther was aware of Juniper's long history on the farm and was doubly embarrassed. "Uh." He looked down. "Dutch has offered me eighty acres to start an educational farm for underprivileged kids."

"With genetic research for sustainable agriculture," Tasha piped in cheerfully. "We'll teach them perma- culture."

Dutch cleared his throat. "I thought your mana- gerial skills would come in real handy, Juniper." Juni- per's head had been swiveling around from one speaker to another, and now her gaze settled squarely on him.

"Well," Juniper replied slowly, seeming to shake off some sort of visceral response. "It seems like a square deal. We all get a job we're good at---and I can tell Scarlett here that her job is to help Luther with the kids because I'm sure as hell not going to."

"But," Luther still hung his head, but he was eyeing Juniper, "you've been here so long."

"Meaning I deserve eighty acres?" No one said anything, and she relaxed. "I've had a rare combination of freedom, shelter and purpose here for a long time." Juniper sighed and slowly reached out for Luther. "I wouldn't be ready for this---for you---without that long apprenticeship." Luther grabbed her, sniffed and held her tight.

"Aw, hell," Buster mumbled, wiping his eye. "I need my guitar."

Buster shuffled out of the room, bringing Homer back into view. Again Homer seemed to glow, a tear sliding down the side of his face. His eyes were closed, and his hand lay over Bardo, who was now stretched out over him. Juniper released herself and came to his side, taking his other hand. His lids barely moved, but there was still strength in his grasp. "I'm--" he breathed so softly, "ready."

"I know," Juniper murmured. She paused and then shyly leaned down to kiss him on the forehead.

"Go," he breathed into the deep silence of the room.

Juniper turned away, her eyes bright. "Come on, Luther. Let's go ride Zorba."

"But--"

"Homer and I discussed this a long time ago," Juniper quietly explained. "The others are here. You can stay, of course, if you want. I'll bring Zorba around and you can decide then."

Juniper started past Luther, paused and turned to kiss him tenderly on the mouth. Tasha and Scarlett parted in the doorway to let her through and then Scarlett stepped forward and picked up the cold bowl of broth. "I'll get a glass of ice water," Tasha murmured as she turned away. "And a straw."

Dutch put his hand at the small of Luther's back and gently pushed him forward. "Just go hold his hand again," he whispered. Luther reached for Homer's hand as Dutch pulled a chair over for Luther to sit down.

Homer's grasp was weaker, but still present. Bardo's purring somehow harmonized with the rattle in Homer's chest.

Tasha returned. "Homer always likes his ice water," she said. She paused and stared at the glass in her hand. "I guess it's a little silly now."

"It's an offering," Dutch said. "Just the sound of the ice against the glass will refresh him."

"That's beautiful, Dutch," she nodded. She handed Dutch the glass and he gently tipped it back and forth so the cool sound was clear. He then placed it on the table next to Homer's head and grinned up at her. "Just like makin' music."

Scarlett came in, holding Buster's hand while his other carried his guitar. He said nothing and went over to the easy chair in the corner of the room—the one everyone rested in as they took turns watching over Homer. He sat and started strumming, then humming—slowly picking out an earthy dirge. Sometimes he'd softly moan out some wordless sound that said everything. Luther sat there, holding Homer's hand, which barely gripped and loosened in cadence with the cords. Luther suddenly thought of the father he had hardly known, his mother dying without his knowledge. His whole body seemed to vibrate for a few seconds. He focused on the hand in his so he wouldn't gasp aloud in surprise, and then there was a flash of a younger, darker hand. His mother's hand. There and gone. Now he couldn't help but gasp, and Dutch looked over at him. "Did you feel that?" Luther whispered.

"I felt something," Dutch replied, lifting his hand slightly off of Homer's head, "but, man, you look like you've seen a ghost."

Luther nodded slowly. "The best kind."

"I'm ready." Everyone turned to see Juniper standing in the doorway. "Zorba is at the back porch steps, if you want to come."

Homer's hand gripped tighter than it had all morning. Luther turned and looked at him, but his face was expressionless. His grip loosened and Luther let go. He turned back to Juniper. "Okay," he said, getting up slowly. He felt real light on his feet, and both Scarlett and Tasha smiled and brushed their hands over his back as he passed by. He followed Juniper down the hall and out on the porch. Zorba was standing there, head down to sniff at Minnie who was pacing around her hoofs. Luther reached down and scratched Minnie's head and then looked back up at Juniper.

"I really want you to ride with me, but please stay if you need to," Juniper said. "It's just a weird pact Homer and I made."

"I don't think anything is weird anymore," Luther replied. "I——I was holding his hand and it turned into my mother's."

Juniper's lower lip fell open and her eyes started brimming as she searched his face. Then she quickly turned and made a graceful mount on Zorba's bare back. "Come," she said, turning back to him. Luther scrambled on and slid down into her. "Hold me," she said, grabbing his hands and putting them around her waist.

"I love you, Juniper," Luther said, squeezing her.

"I have no idea how to give it back," Juniper whispered.

"That's all I need to know," Luther replied softly. "Where your heart is."

"It's right here," Juniper sniffed, pressing her thumb into the palm of his hand. She sniffed again, clicked her tongue, and Zorba moved off into the dappled morning sunlight.

Acknowledgments:

I have written all my books at the Tin Roof Café in Chico, California. The camaraderie of the baristas and the other regular customers with their words of encouragement and suggestions, and my endless cups of Earl Grey tea, are what keep me going. My husband, David Gallo, and my son, Chris Saur, have provided more than just encouragement and suggestions in their critiques and ideas. They give me the confidence and support that authors need during the writing process.

Most of all I must thank my incredibly talented editor, Daniel Nauman. I can't imagine publishing any of my books without his keen imagination, his way with words, his artistic and creative perception, and his honest critical sense.